SCRAPIRON
BLUES

SCRAPIRON
BLUES

DAMBUDZO
MARECHERA

Compiled and edited by
Flora Veit-Wild

Africa World Press, Inc.

P.O. Box 1892
Trenton, NJ 08607

P.O. Box 48
Asmara, ERITREA

Africa World Press, Inc.

P.O. Box 1892
Trenton, NJ 08607

P.O. Box 48
Asmara, ERITREA

Copyright © 1992 The Dambudzo Marechera Trust

First Africa World Press, Inc. edition 1999

Cover design: Jonathan Gullery
Cover photograph of Dambudzo Marechera courtesy of Ernst Schade.

Library of Congress Cataloging -in-Publication Data

Marechera, Dambudzo
    Scrapiron blues / by Dambudzo Marechera ; compiled and edited by
Flora Veit-Wild. -- 1st Africa World Press, Inc. ed.
      p.   cm.
   In English; 1 story in Shona with a parallel English translation.
   ISBN 0-86543-730-0 (hc). – ISBN 0-86543-731-9) (pbk.)
   1. Zimbabwe--Social Life and customs Fiction. 3. City and town life-
   (England)--Social life and customs Fiction. 3. City and town life-
   -England--London Fiction. 4. Africans--England--London Fiction.
   I. Veit-Wild, Flora, 1947- II. Title.
   PR9390.9.M3S37 1999
    823--dc21   99-15296
                                               CIP

Contents

Glossary vii

Acknowledgments viii

Introduction ix

TONY FIGHTS TONIGHT—PUB STORIES 1

    Smith in Dead Skin 2

    Dreams Wash Walls 5

    The Power 8

    The Shining 11

    Babel 13

    What Available Reality 16

    Snakes in Tracksuits 18

    Riddled with Opium 20

    A Description of the Universe 22

    The Pinpocketing Roadside Preacher 27

    Decline and Fall 28

SCRAPIRON BLUES—CITY PLAYS 31

    The Alley 32

    The Breakdown Scrapiron Blues 48

    The Servants' Ball 61

    The Servants' Ball (English translation) 73

    Alien to the People 85

    Killwatch 96

First Street Tumult—More City Stories 107

    First Street Tumult 108

    The Skin of Loneliness 112

    Black Damascus Road 123

    Evening Star over 28 Highlands Avenue 125

    Fragments 127

When Rainwords Spit Fire—A Township Novella 131

The Concentration Camp 157

Fuzzy Goo's Stories for Children 211

    Tony and the Rasta 213

    The Magic Cat 217

    Baboons of the Rainbow 225

    Fuzzy Goo's Guide to the Earth 239

Thoughts of a Rusty Nail 249

Glossary of words used in the text

bandiet— convict (orig. Afrikaans).

biltong—sun-dried lean meat.

Castle—locally brewed conventional beer, popular with all ethnic groups.

Chibuku—commercially brewed beer produced mainly for low-income urban blacks.

Chikurubi—prison in Harare.

Chimurenga—the War of Liberation.

dzakutsaku—literally many or multitude. Used by UANC supporters, in a prophetic sense: "the party for everyone".

ganga—mbanje; marijuana.

Jobs—nightclub in Harare.

kachasu—very potent home-brewed alcohol.

Lacto—a nutritious milk product.

maheu—food drink made from maize- and sorghum meal.

Mazoe—orange crush.

Mbare—a high-density suburb of Harare.

mbira—hand piano.

mbamba—beer.

mopane—the dark reddish-brown wood of the mopane tree.

msasa/musasa—a common, medium to large Zimbabwean tree.

Mwari—God, the Supreme Being (in Shona belief).

Pfumo Revanhu—Spear of the Nation, which was an armed wing of Bishop Muzorewa's party, the United African National Congress.

povo: the proletariat.

sadza: stiff porridge (prepared from maize meal), the staple diet of the indigenous population of Zimbabwe.

smanjemanje—South African music of the sixties.

SWAPO—South West Africa Peoples' Organisation—the indigenous party which led Namibia to Independence.

Target—word puzzle in *The Herald,* Zimbabwe's leading daily newspaper.

tsotsi—hooligan; a member of a criminal gang.

Vhigoroni—in the song, a woman's name/nickname (after *Vigoron,* a medicine) with connotations of physical strength and plumpness.

ZANLA—Zimbabwe African National Liberation Army.

ZIANA—Zimbabwe International African News Agency.

Acknowledgments

I WISH to thank Leonard Maveneka and Richard Mhonyera for the translation into English of "The Servants' Ball."

Scrapiron Blues is the last volume in the series of posthumously published works by Dambudzo Marechera. It has been preceded by The Black Insider (Baobab Books, Harare, 1990 and Lawrence and Wishart, London, 1992) and Cemetery of Mind (Baobab Books, Harare, 1992). Research work on these posthumous works was made possible by funding from the Federal Republic of Germany.

Introduction

AT a lecture in Harare in 1986, Dambudzo Marechera said: "My whole life has been an attempt to make myself the skeleton in my own cupboard."[1] When he died less than a year later, he left behind a large number of unpublished literary skeletons. Since then, on behalf of the Dambudzo Marechera Trust, I have tried to assemble as many of them as possible and so ensure that the contents of his cupboard can, as he wrote in a 1985 book review, "send a mad look to the end of time."[2]

Scrapiron Blues[3] is the third and last volume in a series of posthumously published Marechera works. It follows *The Black Insider* (1990) and *Cemetery of Mind* (1992). Marechera's complete literary estate with all unpublished manuscripts and other primary and secondary sources has been deposited at the National Archives of Zimbabwe where it is accessible to the public. It includes the unedited versions of the pieces published in this volume.

This volume brings together pieces of various literary genres written by Marechera during the last years of his life when he was living in Harare, from February 1982 until August 1987. With one exception they have not been published before.

The common theme of this selection from Marechera's last phase of literary creation (his poetry of that period was published in *Cemetery of Mind*) is urban life. He draws multicoloured sketches of the cityscapes of Harare and captures the vibes and psyche of a big urban centre in 20th century Africa. Thus he contributes to the body of literature of urbanisation which plays an important role in the development of postcolonial literature.

Yet, the style of Marechera's writings towards the end of his life also reflects some of the loneliness and mental depression in which he found himself progressively enclosed.

For two years after his return to Zimbabwe in 1982 he was very much a public figure.[4] In his public appearances as well as in his last book *Mindblast* (1984) he challenged the political and cultural authorities of the newly independent state but earned the admiration of younger Zimbabweans: students and aspiring writers.

In mid-1984, after two years of homelessness, he rented a small flat in the "avenues" of Harare, near the city centre. Tired and worn out from his rough lifestyle, he was relieved finally to have a quiet place of his own. He divided his days between reading and writing at his flat and drinking in the hotel bars and shebeens of the city centre.

Marechera's major anxiety in the last three years of his life concerned his role and vocation as a writer: he seemed unable to produce work that publishers considered worth publishing. In 1983, he submitted "Killwatch or Tony Fights Tonight" to Longman who rejected it because they were anxious "about our ability to market non-educational books which is what we are best at".[5] In 1985, his novel "Depth of Diamonds" was rejected by College Press in Harare and Heinemann in the United Kingdom. Selections of poetry that he submitted to Zimbabwean publishers were poorly received. This situation depressed him deeply and was compounded by his deteriorating health. He never completed the other manuscripts which he began between 1986-87 and did not try to submit any to publishers.[6]

Psychologically, Marechera was isolated, with few contacts apart from drinking companions and some expatriate friends. Though he tried to obtain new books from abroad, his intellectual horizon had receded. Yet he tried to investigate new areas: to break out of himself by doing research for his writing, interviewing people and recording life around him. Many Harareans remember the image of him, always carrying a pile of books and a notebook around with him, quietly scribbling notes amidst all the noise and commotion of public bars.

This method gave a new quality to his work. The pieces compiled in *Scrapiron Blues* have more narrative distance than is usual in previous writing. Though his unique, witty style and unconventional perceptions of reality are still evident, these late pieces have lost some of the brutal force of earlier writing. Before, the literary persona seemed almost identical with the author's own self. Marechera seemed all the time to fictionalise his own biography; in *Scrapiron Blues* autobiographical elements still appear occasionally but now rather as allusions to his former life than the raw experience they used to embody. Hence, while most of his previous prose works were written in the first person, we now find the third person narrator mediating between author and reader.

Does this narrative distance reflect a greater maturity, as some contemporaries observed? Greenwell Matsika was Marechera's fellow-student at the University of Rhodesia in 1972/73; more than ten years later he frequently drank with him in Harare bars. Matsika noted that Marechera "was no longer the rebel, the iconoclast of former times. He was more mature, less violent. I don't remember him calling anybody names during the times I drank with him at the Norfolk or having an outburst. He was really controlled. People would gather around him just to listen to his views."[7]

Or does Marechera's more subdued style reflect a mellowing: was he "cracking up", as he sometimes fearfully asked himself in the last years of his life? "Since I came back I seem to be gradually compromising with the harsh reality about practical problems, whereas most of my work before has been based on total protest against society . . .I no longer have the initial anger I had when I was writing *The House of Hunger* and *Black Sunlight*. I seem to have come to the stage where I think I am ready to sell out my profession. . .It's that loneliness which is increasingly driving me to all this. . .The isolation is terrible. I'm like a rat in a corner, I can only continue respecting myself as a writer by living in my head, and that can be dangerous sometimes, especially if one has also experienced paranoia. The only true reality is the new novel or the new collection of poems you are reading."[8]

While *Scrapiron Blues* might indeed be toned down, sometimes to the point of detachment, this writing shows new subtlety and a gentle, descriptive lucidity. It offers complex perceptive insights into Harare life in the 1980s; light-hearted or serious, they are underlined by traumatic reminiscences of his country's past and are coloured with the author's typical idiosyncrasies.

* * *

"Tony Fights Tonight—Pub Stories" is a sequence of stories taken from the manuscript "Killwatch or Tony Fights Tonight". This manuscript was Marechera's own compilation—similar to *Mindblast*—of quite diverse pieces written at different times, which he then labled a "novel". The "Tony Fights Tonight" sequence was apparently written shortly after his return in 1982; the rest was completed around October 1983 when he submitted the manuscript to Longman. I have included some parts of this in *Scrapiron Blues* but rearranged them in various sections: the "Tony Fights Tonight" stories (some of them shortened), the play "Killwatch," and the beginning of the children's story "Tony and the Rasta" which formed the first part of Marechera's compilation. I left out other parts which mainly served as connecting links.

In "Tony Fights Tonight" Marechera recorded some of the modern "urban legends",[9] the new oral literature of contemporary African cities. Profane and mostly sexual, these stories are told among drinking companions in the bars and shebeens. In a light-hearted way they satirise typical themes of cunning, adultery and the like; they resound with modern urban slang. Marechera interweaves these mundane stories with the very different narrative strand of Tony and Jane, who are enclosed in their own dreams and nightmares. Ironically, the narrator is engaged in an ongoing dispute with his characters about the story which is to be written. Thus Marechera subverts the concept of the invisible and infallible literary creator and shows how the literary process reflects the writer's multiple selves. When the narrator eventually sleeps with his character, Jane, Marechera is back to the question raised in his earlier writings, such as *Black Sunlight* and *The Black Insider,* of the borderline between fiction and reality: "Who was the reality? Fred and Jill? Or Tony and Jane? Was I myself a character in someone's head? I resolved to get sickeningly drunk." (p.17)

The next section comprises five short plays written at different times. All of them focus on the "seamy-side" of city life, in ghettos, alleys and servants' quarters. With strong influences from the theatre of the absurd—especially in "The Alley" and "Killwatch"—they mix realism with grotesque and surreal elements. "The Servants' Ball" is the only known piece by Marechera in Shona; he originally submitted it as part of the *Mindblast* manuscript, intending it to come after "The Toilet", but the publisher omitted it. It is reproduced here in the original and in English translation. The last part of "Killwatch" has been cut; the other plays are reproduced without any major editorial changes.

The third section comprises short stories and fragments written separately. "First Street Tumult" was published in *The Sunday Mail* of 29 May 1983, under the title of "The Lonely and Lovely Tumult". "Black Damascus Road" and "Evening Star Over 28 Highlands Avenue" were written at the end of 1983. The other stories are fragments, found after Marechera's death and partly edited here. In all of them we encounter ordinary city people haunted by the nightmares of history.

At the end of 1983 Marechera wrote some children's stories, together with six-year-old Max Wild who illustrated "The Magic Cat" and "Baboons of the Rainbow". Shortly before he died, in July 1987, Marechera started "Fuzzy Goo's Guide to the Earth" as a contribution to the International Book Fair in Harare which focused on "Children and Books". It was never completed. The stories—compiled in this book—reflect Marechera's close relationship with children. Refusing to grow up himself, he identified with their uninhibited imagination and rebellious spirit: "Paranoid means seeing all the things which big human beings have been taught not to see", explains Fuzzy Goo in his "Guide to the Earth", which the author wrote from right to left, starting from the last page of his note-book.[10] But Marechera's children are also wise, knowing the "ugly facts" of life, the "stealing, killing, fighting, fucking, the incest and rapes" ("Tony and the Rasta") in the shanty towns. Publishers found the stories "unsuitable" because of the disparity between the child-like narrator and the sarcastic, older voice which permeates the writing. Thus "The Magic Cat" and "Baboons of the Rainbow" were rejected by Zimbabwe Publishing House and Longman.[11]

"When Rainwords Spit Fire" is a prose narrative, or novella, written in 1984. The title—which Marechera added later—is a line from "The Concentration Camp" written in 1986. The tightly structured novella describes "one day in the life of Rutendo Township". Here the changes in Marechera's style and attitude are particularly noticeable. While in earlier writings he was mostly obsessed with his own self, he is now trying to get into other people's minds. Returning to the theme of his childhood experiences in the township, he describes the anxieties of first love but also portrays emphatically everyday life of adult men and women. Where The *House of Hunger* is full of despair, narrative fragmentation and violent images, here the same township life is described by a distant third-person narrator in a composed, calm and simple language. Though the children are poor, they seem cheerful: untouched by their predicament. It is only the sudden attack of some unpredictable madness which smacks of Marechera. Yet, while in his earlier writings such paranoia emanated directly from the social circumstances, life and madness now appear to be unconnected.

In "The Concentration Camp", an unfinished novel-like piece consisting of prose, drama and poetry, Marechera again employs the children's perspective, this time to express his horror of the Zimbabwean war of liberation. He describes life in the "protected villages", the "keeps", in which parts of the rural population were kept by the Rhodesian army during some of the wartime, and parallels them with concentration camps. He shows how their inmates were subjected to traumatising acts of brutality: beatings, torture, helicopter attacks. Alternating with the scenes in the camp are those in the "The City of Anarchists" where Marechera projects his own anarchist inclination onto a small group of bomb-throwing city fighters. In his interview with the Dutch Journalist Alle Lansu of February 1986 he talked about his method and ideas while writing "The Concentration Camp":[12]

"I have never written a book like that before for which I have to interview people. I have been going around Harare interviewing some of the people here in Harare who were former inmates, prisoners in these protected villages. They told me all these horrifying stories of what had happened to them and to their families. I also had the opportunity to interview some of the black guards of the camps, who served under a white officer.

"The format of the book is—I am following the experiences of two fictional families. The problem I am having is the technique, because I don't want it to come out as a documentary and so I am using a kind of expressionist technique and here and there certain surrealist techniques and here and there straight narrative. The chapters alternate between the concentration camp, the life here in the city centre and in the suburbs, the ghettos, and life at the university, for instance. I am looking at the level of revolt or submission in the concentration camps as well as in the intellectual camp and in the ghettos; especially at those people who used the situation of the Struggle for criminal ends, to make money; the informers, the petty criminals, and how they linked with the black and white intellectuals who had dropped out of university because they no longer wanted to be part of the system. One of the characters is a university dropout who has a totally anarchistic world view and gets money or guns clandestinely from those agents interested in destroying the system. So I am not just exploring the concentration camps, I am trying to bring out the psyche, the psychological personality of that particular period, especially from 1978 to the end of 1979, to Independence. Because the most dangerous time for those in the concentration camps was when the Ian Smith soldiers knew that they were losing the war. Of course the models for this are books about Auschwitz or some other concentration camps.

"My plan is not to end the manuscript with Independence. The second section will be from 1980 to 1982 or 1983; it will be about the survivors: what happened afterwards to all those people of the first section in the concentration camps or the guards or the soldiers."

Marechera often denied that there was any historical element in his work because, he said, he mistrusted writing which used history as a platform for political propaganda. But, interestingly, the "Concentration Camp" places him among those writers whose work does offer an historical perspective of the Zimbabwean experience, albeit one that subverts and challenges a one-dimensional view of history.

It is therefore fitting to end *Scrapiron Blues* with his fine and previously unpublished poem "Thoughts of a Rusty Nail" which includes a typical Marechera image:

"History on three feet crawls toward the dungheap, the rubbish pit of all my yesterday's names."

And the poem ends, as does this collection, with a haunting evocation of his literary cupboard:

"Fear is the flesh, the gorgeous dress my skeleton wears."

Flora Veit-Wild,
Berlin, May, 1994.

NOTES TO INTRODUCTION

[1] "The African Writer's Experience of European Literature", in Flora Veit-Wild, *Dambudzo Marechera: A Source Book on his Life and Work,* Hans Zell Publishers, London, 1992, University of Zimbabwe Publications, Harare, 1993, p.362.

[2] "Demented Voice in the Wilderness, ibid., p.353.

[3] Marechera's spelling in "The Breakdown Scrapiron Blues."

[4] For details of Marechera's life in Harare in those years see chapter 8 in Veit-Wild, *Dambudzo Marechera.*

[5] Letter from Marilyn Poole, Longman Zimbabwe, to Marechera, 16 November 1983.

[6] "The Concentration Camp", "Confessions of a Rusty Dread (Hammered Yet Again into a Nail)" and "Prince Street". For details on all unpublished manuscripts mentioned here and rejections through publishers, see Veit-Wild, *Dambudzo Marechera,* pp. 340-352.

[7] Quoted from Veit-Wild, *Dambudzo Marechera,* p.320.

[8] Quoted from interview with Alle Lansu of 1986, in Veit-Wild, *Dambudzo Marechera,* pp. 35-36. See also ibidem, p. 319.

[9] Arthur Goldstuck collected such legends in South Africa in his book *The Rabbit in the Thorn Tree: Modern Myths and Urban Legends of South Africa* (Penguin, London, 1990).

[10] The beginning of the story is reproduced in Marechera's handwriting in *Dambudzo Marechera* 1952-87, edited by Flora Veit-Wild and Ernst Schade (Harare, Baobab Books, 1988), pp. 22-23.

[11] See Veit-Wild, *Dambudzo Marechera,* pp. 341-343.

[12] This part of the original interview has not been included in the edited version published in Veit-Wild, *Dambudzo Marechera,* pp. 5-48.

Dreams Wash Walls

ALWAYS perched on a barstool. His dry, wiry, biltong skin. The shrunk-in mouth. Grey hair dyed black. That was Fred. Perched on his barstool promptly at opening time. Trying to tell me his life story. Like he had tried hundreds of times since he had learnt that I was some sort of writer. It was not his fault. I get broke many times. When I do I get copies of my book in lieu of royalties from my publisher and roam the bars trying to sell them. That's when all the other drunks know that this drunk—me—is some sort of writer. After the initial surprise, incredulity and suspicion, the stories come pouring out. Like pub stories everywhere, they are sexual, profane. Only now and then do I hear anything otherwise.

I try not to listen. I try hard not to. Because I am trying to pounce on my own story too. I am trying to grasp the kind of story that will take in the swimming-pool skin of the Harare skies, the slightly mocking darkness that underlines sunset's briefly glowing coals, before the black hand of anxiety clenches its darkness around the city. In the mind the roof rattles. The plaster comes down. And millions of tiny red ants slowly but inexorably creep through the egg-cracks into the sleeper's dream.

Tony is trying to wash all the blood from the inside walls of his flat in Montague. He uses a stiff brush, soap and a bucket of water. Tony is a short plump guy who wears wire spectacles with very thick lenses. The lenses make his eyes look as bulgy as the full

5

moon on a bitterly clear winter night. He is still trying to wash the gore from his walls. He wears tracksuits everywhere he goes. Bright blue ones. With bright red Bata plimsolls. He coughs a lot, trying to get rid of the tiny red ants he thinks have made their nest in his fragile chest. The ants hurt a lot. They hurt him the way it hurt him when Jane, his girlfriend, confessed that "there was another man" in her life. He did not ask Jane to leave. She did not want to leave him. She said it was perfectly natural to love several individuals at one and the same time.

He is trying to wash the walls. It is hard work trying to wash invisible blood from perfectly clean walls, Jane thinks.

She is sitting at the desk marking her pupils' exercise books. She is a teacher at the school nearby. There are all kinds of colours among the pupils. There are black ones. There are white ones. There are brown ones. There are yellow ones. And then there are the ones whose colour you could never put a name to. She is marking their exercise books. Tony is washing the walls.

Jane likes to "go native" whenever she is in the flat. So, as she is marking the exercise books of the black ones, the white ones, the brown ones, the yellow ones and the strange-colour ones, Jane is wearing nothing but a very brief loincloth that leaves her buttocks and thighs exposed. Tony, scrubbing loyally away at the blood and gore of history, is covered from neck to foot by his blue tracksuit. Today he is wearing a bright yellow golfing cap.

This is a quiet flat. It is so quiet none of the people in the other flats are sure anyone lives there. In fact, the old-age pensioner in the flat below thinks Tony and Jane are ghosts; she thinks Tony and Jane are the ghosts of two of her own children whom she aborted in her own very distant wild-oats past. And Tony is still scrubbing and washing the blood from the dead skin of time. And Jane, while idly marking the exercise books, is far away in quite another dream.

Jane loves dreams. They are more real than reality, she says. Dreams are the fulcrum, she says. Dreams are the only reality, she says. The other day she had a fight with a dream that refused to come. The dream was critically injured and when Jane took it to hospital she could not understand why the doctor and all the nurses could not see the severe injuries and gave her a sedative and phoned Tony to come and take her home.

But Tony said he was too busy washing the blood from the walls to be able to come and the doctor drove her home instead. Was there a one-plus-one somewhere?

And there was the other dream that had an accident and she had to phone the garage for the breakdown truck. The breakdown truck driver arrived within five minutes. Jane was delighted.

"You're very prompt," she said brightly.

The truck driver wildly looked round. He croaked: "But ma'am, where. . .?"

Jane pointed. The driver turned. There was nothing but the brittle bitterly cold winter night. Hairs standing on end, the driver leapt back into his truck and with a scream of gears and shriek of tires backed away and was soon a glow-worm speck screeching down the road. Jane shook her head in disgust, puzzled.

Nothing ever puzzled Tony though. He bought a bottle of white wine and a hunk of cheese. He was waiting for her. She came in and he thought she looked a bit teary. He coaxed the story of the insane breakdown truck driver out of her. They put their arms around each other and cried a little. They looked at the walls he'd washed the whole day but which were still covered with the gore of misunderstanding. They cried a little more. It was a beautiful world. It was a rhapsody; a magic dance. Then why, O God, why? He dried her tears with a silk handkerchief. She kissed his tears and swallowed every single glittering drop. She filled their two glasses.

He cut the cheese. The velvet curtains were drawn. There was a hush. But sometime later the old-age pensioner downstairs woke out of a deep sleep, startled to hear the whiff of a long-ago melody remarkably like the glory of Vienna, which had so enraptured her youth before the grumbling thunder of the early century whipcracked into the terrible lightning of the First World War.

The Power

FRED looked morose. He was talking to Jill, his chocolate-cream girlfriend. Jill looked outraged. Actually they are not boyfriend and girlfriend. It's a long story. Part of it he wants to tell me so I can write it "like it is". The hair on my head keeps crawling around like I have got millions of tiny red ants creeping deep within it. But I guess it's last night's drink doing it. Or maybe it's because Tony and Jane have got away from me again. I don't like it when the story I'm trying to write evades me. I've been to several bars looking for *it*—the Masasa, the Long Bar, the Sportsman, the Oasis, even Magaba—but I still have not found Tony and Jane. Their story is mocking me. Now here I am back in the Jacaranda and what do I find? Fred and Jill in a jolly mood. They are going to tell me their story. I can feel it. I am too tired to try to escape. At least they are still arguing. I buy myself another drink.

I have a lot of time to kill. And I don't want to kill it. I want to drag it all into full consciousness. *Make it live.* Maybe that's what makes me, forces me to write. Can't just sit around listening to the little sounds of my hair going grey. Can't just sit still feeling more of my skin dying, wrinkling, having to peel off the dead flecks of skin. There's a Smith in dead skin. I sat around in Harare Gardens daring the flowers and strange bushes for once to look beautifully significant. They did not. I turned to my newspaper—I used to be wryly amused by the sight of old-age pensioners giving up everything but their

8

Babel

JANE was still smiling when the full glistening sunlight smacked her eyes. Her tooth-
paste advert teeth reflected the brilliance of it all back into the laughing street. But
her smile was gradually losing its power. The gleam was slowly going out of her eyes. She
did not really know why this should happen each day she left the flat. Perhaps it was the
bad dreams that lived in the streets. Those overalled dreams bowed down by pick and
shovel. Those snotty-nosed urchin dreams that were reluctantly creeping out of the
alleyways to face another day of cold and hunger. Those pot-bellied limp-shouldered
dreams already casting their pessimistic but appraising eye on those passing by who
would want a quick one against some crumbling wall. Or were they the wrinkled white
dreams that sulked past you as though you were personally responsible for the downfall
of their racial and political supremacy?

There were so many queer dreams that attacked Jane from all sides. It was somehow unfair. These were not *her* dreams. These were other people's dreams. When she
stopped to buy a paper, the white newsvendor's dream hit her squarely on the jaw. She
reeled, about to faint. But she steadied herself and rearranged the pile of exercise books
under her arm so they would not fall. Very high above her head, as she walked to the
school, the brilliant blue morning burred softly with the dream of a Boeing 747 which
was also carrying the dreams of the minds and passions inside it.

It was right, was it not, to live only your dream and no one else's? It saved time, terror and trouble. There had been a time when everyone tried to live everyone else's dream. The history textbooks called it the Struggle. Called it Chimurenga. It was death, living someone else's dream. She had seen the pictures. The massacres. The atrocities. The dying sons and slogans. The vivid hatreds. Minds exchanging nightmares of blood and mutilation.

The streets always forced her to remember weird things like that. There was something terrible and tangible about such a past. It lurked in wait. It set its wire snares. It lay in ambush. In the hotels. In the lush and green park. In the shops. It bared its teeth whenever one dream encountered another. It would take only the sound of a needle dropping for the nightmares to crunch with real teeth and real bullets the fragile bone and flesh Jane was. This sense of permanent danger made the dreams very real to her. More precious than anything ever.

Hell is other people.

Other people's dreams. Like the axe-killer. Like the Highfield man who threw a chopped-off human head into his girlfriend's bedroom. What was he trying to *wake* her into? Jane shuddered. And then there were the dreams that came in the shape of relatives and friends. Sulky, yet sharp-eyed, trying to get something out of her—hinting that if she did not give it, the spirits and ancêstors would. . .

Talk of pouring beer over graves to appease obscure long-dead drunks. And they would try to get something out of Tony but he was so much in his own dream they could never really get at him. Their method was to try and convince Tony that, because he had been part of the thing called the Struggle, he was under a curse. They said they wanted to take him "home" and engineer him with the spirits. But at that point Tony would look enigmatically at them and suggest that they needed a wash like the walls did.

Tony, when he could, stuck to the flat. He did not like the Outside. It's the inside that's the only important thing in the whole world, he thought. He admired Jane's courage: she went out every day, to return intact, unsullied, still holding fast to her own. He earned his wages from inside the flat. She earned hers from the outside though basically she was also an inside person. Maybe that was the enigma of woman. And he was. . .

She hungered for the time when the spill of blood and the crump of bombs would have been wiped off the face of the countryside and the streets. She hungered for the brutally pellucid technicolour dream which others called a vision of God, and others called Truth and yet others called Beauty. Some, she knew, would merely call it Ecstasy. Others, the Opium of the People. But each to his dream, each to his destined climax.

You looked the past in the face at your own risk, Jane said to herself. You thought of the future with the self-inflicted risk of unhinging your mind. The future is controlled by people who inflict *their* dreams on other people. Even the present is controlled in the same way. And the people who do it have guns with bullets in them. With real bullets in them, not flowers. There are prisons out there. Detention centres. The only little safety left is your own small dream. Entomb yourself alive in your modest dream—it is the only realisable individuality left. Jane turned into the street in which her school stood, already hearing the crying, laughing Babel of the black ones, the white ones, the brown ones, the yellow ones and the strange-colour ones. Such vulnerable unsuspecting dreams. . .

What Available Reality?

MY first pint of the day too! I could not keep it down. I spewed it all out in the toilet bowl. The second one went down well. I would be all right for the rest of the day. It was Tony's fault. He had angrily entered my last night's dream, slamming the door behind him. He had stood there shaking, almost in tears, his smooth plump face working itself like the bones underneath were trying to come out and judge me.

"Well, Tony, what is it? I'm rather busy," my voice was stern. I do not like my characters to act out their tantrums in my dreams.

"You're making it out like I am an idiot. An imbecile armed with stiff brush, soap and a bucket of water." His stutter had come out. I had not noticed before. That was interesting. It would perhaps bring in a Freudian significance.

"What's wrong with washing walls, Tony?"

"There's no point to it!"

"Three points, in fact. Clarity, cleanliness, conscience," I pointed out.

He clenched his pitiful feminine fists. "The point is *you* know that I am a serious writer. A poet. And in this book in which you have imprisoned me you cast me as a *fool* and in a tracksuit too."

I pricked up my ears. So Tony thought he was a writer.

"What are you writing, Tony?" I had to keep the excitement from my voice.

16

"I'm not a writer. I've never written anything except letters and filling in forms. So I wondered if you'd be interested if we sort of collaborated on this novel, based on the diary?"

I thought a bit.

"Have you your father's permission to use it?" He plucked the question from my brain before I could articulate it. "Actually, no. I was sort of going through his things looking for something he'd asked me to take home when I found the diary. He's very old now. I know he would not object."

"I can't work on something like this without the writer's—your father's—permission. But you say you have read it? What makes you think anyone would be interested in it?"

"There's all this mind-blowing stuff, like when he describes some of the cases he had to deal with."

"But he was collaborating in the oppression of our people." My voice was without expression. I was interested in these diary entries of the small-time informer his father had been.

"It's so long ago, man. But it shows us how the enemy was operating, shows us through the eyes of a—"

"*Traitor.*"

He looked down, controlling himself.

"Look," I said softly, "this really interests me. But it's your show. I don't and have never helped anyone write a book. I have a difficult enough time trying to write my own. Incidentally, do you know a guy called Tony?"

"Tony? I can't say. Well, there's a Tony I know who's just come out of jail. There he is, at the bar. The one with the racing coupons."

In a flash I was at Tony's side, grinning. "You don't know me, Tony, but may I get you a drink?" My voice was pulsing with excitement.

A brick face, blackening with anger, swung round, the eyes tiny luminous stars. Tony? The voice, harsh and like a brute's, rasped: "I done my time. Why don't you Special Branch guys just leave me alone? I'm sick of your hounding!"

I crept back to my chair. Tony left soon afterwards, glaring at me over his shoulder. I felt sick of diaries and everything.

No, not sick. There is this shallowness to everything. This elaborate hollowness. Sometimes I think it's just that I miss the intense literary intrigues of the London journals and circles, the nightlong heated arguments about what constitutes art, the times when it was easy to believe that there was more than "something" in living a life totally devoted to literature. Here in Harare all that seems frivolous, trivial, nothing to do with "real" living. The few other writers in the city also seem paralysed by the ungainly atmosphere; we eye each other with the oblique glance of mistrust, competitiveness, and when we are not busy pontificating to tired reporters, we casually stab each other in the back. It all seems hopeless. Meanwhile, all and sundry are talking loudly about the need to invigorate the national culture. Which seems to mean a lot of fat women dressed in the Leader's colours and a crowd of half-naked traditional dancers leaping in clouds of dust. Those who talk about our national literature usually turn out ignorant of even the titles of the novels they praise or disparage. At the same time they seem to think there is a future, that is, there is money in "writing." Money, the way it comes and goes, at once terrifying and pitifully elusive.

Tony and Jane are in the lounge of Meikles Hotel. He is drinking tomato juice with Worcester sauce. Jane is teasing her gin and tonic. They are somewhat pleased with themselves. It is a quiet pastel green atmosphere, filled with the hushed polite conversation from the depths of the muted armchairs and couches. Jane is wondering about the dream in the heads of the waiters who are dressed in starched white uniforms and inscrutable black masks that are quite ready to break into equally inscrutable smiles. Tony, in his best pinstripe, looks like a minor diplomat; one who has triumphed over a Graham Greene-ish "other man." He glances again at *The Herald* and smirks over the story of an ex-Rhodesian Front MP in London charged with theft. In mitigation, the MP pleaded that he was homeless, penniless.

Tony and Jane are now far from homeless. Tony has bought a house in Brightwood, a quiet suburb on the outskirts of Harare. He has also bought a car. Gone are the days of the tracksuit, the golfing cap and the tragic washing of the walls. Tony is now something in the Ministry of Information. He still doesn't know exactly what but he has an office, a telephone, a secretary and several big ideas.

The Pinpocketing Roadside Preacher

FRED used to say:
There's no time like now;
No place like here and now
To scream praises to the Lord of the Day.

(Fred is wearing his sheepskin waistcoat and his leather pants and mocassins. He and his flock are gathered under the wild syringa tree with its cream-white drooping tassels. I remember how it makes good charcoal. And the bark is a very dainty fish poison. Ah you, wild syringa, host of the unforgettable delicious caterpillar! Fred has given the sermon. He has blessed his flock. Fred is passing the hat round. The coins clink. The erstwhile congregation departs. Fred hurries to the bar where Jill is waiting impatiently. He gives her half the money. They drink. Strange thoughts are whispering at Fred's door: I could have made a damn good preacher, if only. . . Had it in for me, he had. After all, what's wrong with a bit on the side when your real work is going okay? Fucking missionaries. Ruined my life. I'm just a pinpocketing roadside preacher.)

Fred used to say:
Ha'penny bread and soup, sir,
Is meat an' drink for heaven's military coup;
A starving belly doesn't listen to explanations.

27

Decline and Fall

I CAME out of prison today. I had been inside for twelve months. I still don't know whether it was a stupid or a necessary thing. My crime, I mean. My hotel manager had become quite impossible. I was unable to assure him of my future solvency. He became insulting. The servants openly laughed at me whenever I came down for break-fast. In a situation like that I become so sensitive to the atmosphere that I become afraid of losing my mind. Was the hostility of the manager a figment of my imagination? Were the servants really laughing and jeering at me? With each mind-wrenching day I could not tell illusion from reality. More than ever I sought out Fred and Jill night and day and, with them, I roamed the town in search of stories and drunken oblivion. There is some-thing about this city that is wrong, all wrong, for a writer, the way London was not wrong.

I should feel wonderful, free, to be out again. But what have I come out to?

The horror and hollowness of my coming out into yet another prison hit me on the forehead with the force of blood rushing into the bitter day. This city, like all small cities, is a prison. It imprisons the mind, the imagination, the soul, even the body in petty significancies, petty prejudices, petty and seemingly atavistic histories.

Fred is gone forever. Another drunk down the drain. I'm free. What does that matter? Another convict free to get another conviction. Maybe if I find Tonyjane they'll help me. In the cramped fetid cell, for the whole twelve months, I just couldn't find Tonyjane. I looked at the walls, willing them with all my strength, to wash Tonyjane into

Scrapizon Blues—
City Plays

The Alley

Characters:
ROBIN, a white tramp
RHODES, a black tramp

Place: An Alley in Harare, Zimbabwe

Time: Right now

about. . .well, sounds kind of silly, but what I think of most is the impossibility of love. Something more than just the feeling.

ROBIN [*surprised*]: You sick or something, Rhodes?

RHODES [*grins*]: Guess it must seem like that to you. It's the feeling of having been cast on the rubbish heap and you don't have the strength to pick yourself up. Like you'd missed the train when everybody else had got on it and anyway there wasn't room for you. Like you've got all these great feelings bursting inside you but there is nothing and no one out there to give them to. See what I mean?

ROBIN [*laughs harshly*]: Stop dreaming, Rhodes my boy. You and your dreams of the great People's Lawyer—that's what got us into this fucking shit.

RHODES [*detached*]: Sometimes, I think heaven is just the bright neon-lit street and all those shop windows stocked full of excellent things. And hell is an Alley like this where souls like us have to hide themselves day and night. The ones in purgatory are those who are still afraid of the Alley and they sit in front of the great big shops with hymns in their heads and rusty begging bowls in their hands. [*Smiles*] A sort of Catholic analysis of Harare's souls.

ROBIN: Here, grab a swallow of that. You sound like you're ready for the lunatic asylum.

RHODES: You get bed and board there.

ROBIN: Like prison. But know what's wrong with that scene?

RHODES: Yes. [*Bitterly*] There's no booze. And there are plenty of nightmares. I was only joking , Robin.

ROBIN: I know. But jokes like that are not lucky. They have a way of fulfilling themselves. . . Guess you and I were born with a ghost twin brother. The one who is an explosive charge of bad luck. Always going off, detonating, when you think everything is going well. Know his name?

RHODES: Yeah. His name was Salisbury but he's changed it to Harare. Wonder what he'll change it to next time, just to keep clinging to our backs. [*Drinks, looks up thoughtfully.*]

ROBIN [*startled*]: Hey—what's that? [*Points fearfully at the wall.*]

ROBIN [*peering intently*]: It's gone. But I could have sworn.

RHODES: Just, nerves, Robin. Nerves. [*Pause*] I get nervous too sometimes. When I have to slink out into the street and heaven's people stare right through me as if I wasn't there. All those hundreds of people staring right through me. And I begin to question my own existence, like maybe I'd faded away during my sleep. I mean if they can all look right through me, who am I to insist that I'm still there—something solid in their direct line of vision? Don't they say only a lunatic insists on his sanity when everyone else has confirmed he's bonkers, conked out, round the bend, mentally kaput, ironed out of his thoughts, greased out of his imagination? [ROBIN *is still staring at the wall*] Oh, quit it, Robin, there's nothing there. Just a wall.

ROBIN [*abstractedly*]: Yes. . .a wall. I'm trying to remember when I last saw it. [*Thinks*] Know what's behind that wall? It's something that wants me. Something that has always wanted me from the very beginning of human life. It's there and it's not there. [*Hoarsely*] Sometimes I mistook it for my own desires, my own needs.

RHODES: Damn, it's just a brick wall. And behind it there's maybe a shop, an office, a warehouse. Anything.

ROBIN [*significantly*]: Ahah, there you have it. You said it yourself. It can be anything behind that wall. [*Slowly*] Do you think it's a crematorium? Or one of those secret offices where germicidal decisions are made? A conspirator's den, perhaps? [*Sniffs*] There is a funny smell—can't make it out. [*Continues sniffing.*]

RHODES: I can't smell anything funny, only this garbage. [*Cocks his head*] What's that sound? [*Looks up. A heap of garbage falls on him, covering him. Choking sounds.*]

ROBIN [*looking round, seeing only the pile of rubbish*]: I say, Rhodes, where are you? [*Calling*] Rhodes! I knew he was a ghost. [*Drinks, wipes mouth*] Maybe I better get out of here. Still smells funny. *[He begins to inspect the garbage]* Could have sworn in the highest court of law this rubbish wasn't here a moment ago. Maybe there's something useful in there. [*He pokes at the rubbish, finds a book*] Ah, reading material. Nothing like a nice book to pass the time. [*Fumbles for his cracked spectacles, opens the book*] Shit, a fucking Bible. The prophet Hosea. What would he not have prophesied here in Harare? [*Reads aloud for a while and as he does so, a hand clutching a wine bottle emerges out of the pile of rubbish, slowly followed by the emergence of a horrible monstrous shape. ROBIN looks up, sees,*] *screams in total silence, begins to babble*] I thought it was a good idea at the time. It was meant to be good fun. She was in the bathroom, naked, combing her hair and a force urged me forward. The money—what money, your Lordship? In conclusion the prosecution has produced not a shred of concrete evidence, only a heap of circumstantial slander on my honourable client. I ask, indeed I expect it, that my client be acquitted. [*Whining*] I wasn't doing anything to the boy. His trousers—[R ODES *has wiped off some of the muck and is drinking*] Rhodes! It's you. [*Hurls the bible at* R ODES] You all the time.

R ODES [*echoing* ROBIN]: Me all the time.

ROBIN: You all the time. [*Winces*] You're the one behind the wall.

R ODES: The one behind the wall.

ROBIN [*hysterically*]: I've seen you in my dreams. You've been the shadow all the time.

R ODES: Been the shadow.

ROBIN: You spied on me. You told them. You black bastards are all the same. [*Picks up rubbish, throws it at* R ODES *who does not duck.*]

R ODES: Black bastards are all the same.

ROBIN [*picking up an iron bar*]: I'm going to kill you once and for all. [*Advances on* R ODES *who does not move an inch*] You and the fucking Jews—you did it to me. I'm going to kill you.

R ODES: You want to know what's behind the wall? [ROBIN *pauses, uncertain*] I'm not behind that wall. Black bastards are not behind the wall. Harare is not behind the wall. The only way is for you to strike that wall. Go on. Strike it! [*With anguish*] Strike it, Robin, and the nightmares will end. Go on.

[ROBIN *moves forward, hesitates, then savagely strikes the wall. A girl screams.*]

ROBIN'S DAUGHTER [*offstage*]: Daddy, no! no! No! DADDY!

ROBIN'S VOICE [*offstage*]: You do it with all those boyfriends—so why not with me, you slut. I'll rip them off you if you don't take them off nice and slowly.

ROBIN'S DAUGHTER [*Offstage*]: Please don't make me, daddy. . .

ROBIN [*a savage whisper*]: Turn it off! Turn it off!

R ODES: It turns off if you hit it.

ROBIN: Hit it—I can't.

RHODES [*calm*]: Go on. . . It's just a brick wall. Hit it.

ROBIN: She was a fucking bitch anyway—they all are. Sluts. Can't get enough of it.

> [*In agony, as though wounding himself, strikes the wall. The sounds cease; he collapses on all fours, striking the ground with his fists.*]

BLACKOUT

SCENE TWO

The light, filtered reddish, slowly comes on to reveal, in the same Alley: a desk, a hard chair, a mattress. ROBIN in army camouflage uniform sits behind the desk. A map of Rhodesia is stuck to the wall behind him. Smudges of mud and blood are in evidence. A pistol lies on the desk

ROBIN [*shouts*]: Next!

> [RHODES *dressed as a woman enters as though pushed violently from behind.*]

ROBIN [*toying with the pistol, not looking up*]: Name?

RHODES: Cecilia Rhodes.

ROBIN: Rhodes? [*Scrutinises her. Laughs. Pause*] Now Cecilia, I am your friend. You know that, don't you?

RHODES: No.

ROBIN: You're thinking of your brother.

RHODES: You killed him.

ROBIN: There is a war going on, Cecilia. A war means people get killed. There is nothing new in that. You people were always killing each other before we came to teach you better.

RHODES: I can see that.

ROBIN [*sharply*]: Don't you get uppity with me. [*Points gun at her head*] Now. I have no time to waste. All the others who have come into this office and refused to talk are out there being shot. Can you hear the firing?

RHODES: Yes. [*Indeed gunshots can be heard outside.*]

ROBIN: My platoon knows how to do a job well. They take it slow and easy. Like this. [*He shoots at her ankle, deliberately missing by about an inch*] See? And then maybe it's the kneecap or the elbow. All done slowly and correctly. Of course killing is a matter of taste. Can't say I approve of some of my men's methods. But why make a fuss when the job is still well done in the end. One of my guys likes to prime a grenade in your cunt. Another would rather stuff it with a bayonet. They are regular psychopaths, my men. There's this guy who throws babies in the air and as they fall catches them on his bayonet. He once stuck three in the same expert motion. Like a grisly sort of juggler. Can't blame them—he'd seen some of your comrades' handiwork. You wouldn't like that happening to you, would you, Cecilia?

[*Silence. Odd sounds from* RHODES *who suddenly doubles up, retching.* ROBIN *strides to her, and with deliberate precision hits her full in the face. She collapses, still retching.*]

ROBIN: You and your fucking communist Jews think you can rule this country, eh? [*Kicks her in the ribs, her dress writhing upwards. His face changes as he stares at her thighs; his voice has become hoarse*] Know what's that between your legs? [*Dramatically points at the map of Rhodesia*] That's what's between your legs. Know what I'm going to do? I'm going to fuck it out of your mind. [*He gestures at his crotch*] Know what I have here. A rocket-propelled grenade that's going to fuck the soul out of your identity. We don't need blacks with identity crises in their heads. We want zombies who know how to say "Yes, baas", No, baas". [*Pause*] GET UP, SLUT. It's all one with me whether you want it or not—you're still going to get it, and get it good—you'll never forget me even after you are dead. That's what we want to do to the whole country. We'll screw the ancestors out of you; screw Mwari out of you, and your God will be the Big White Cock! [*RHODES gets up, cupping the spilling blood with her hands.*]

ROBIN [*sits*]: Come sit on my lap. [*She hesitates*] I said sit on my lap. [*She does so*] Right, now, daddy will sing you a song. You want daddy to sing you to sleep? A nice sweet little song that won't hurt and will be a sweet little secret between us. You mustn't ever tell Judy. And when I touch you here and there you must also touch me here and there with your sweet little fingers and your sweet Cupid bow lips. You want to hear it, that sweet little song that daddy sings only to you, my very own beautiful creation? Huh?

RHODES [*coyly*]: Yes, daddy. And afterwards you must kiss me goodnight. You forgot to kiss me goodnight last night.

ROBIN: Then tonight daddy will kiss you a thousand, a million little kisses even after you've fallen asleep and are in that wonderful dreamland we discovered together. [*Sings*]:

> Little Jack Horner
> Sat in a corner
> Eating a Christmas pie
> He put in his thumb
> And pulled out a plum
> And said "What a good boy am I".

[*Exclaims*] Shit! You're bleeding on me, you black bitch. [*Pause*] Never mind. A little blood always stimulates the loins—that's the only good thing about war. Now [*he turns her face to his, licks the blood from her face. He holds her face between his palms*] Open your eyes. Full. That's right. Now sing "God bless Africa" because he is about to bless you. [*He begins to caress her slowly, becoming more and more agitated as she sings. At the climax of the song, sung at first in a tragically beautiful voice, and as it progresses in a defiant tumultuous barrage from her and from behind the wall,* RHODES *has got hold of the pistol.* ROBIN *is nuzzling her, ripping at her clothes; she shoots him point blank in the head. The song rises in crescendo as though the wall would burst. For a few seconds she looks at the dead man, then at the map of Rhodesia. She aims straight at the head of the nightmarish creation and guns it down from the wall. As she is firing the last shots, a soldier bursts in, swivelling his FN rifle, firing at her. As she falls she shoots him right between the eyes. Other soldiers are rushing in firing burst after burst into her body as* BLACKOUT.

SPOTLIGHT

42

THE ALLEY

ROBIN'S DAUGHTER [*screaming in long surrendering anguish*]: Oh daddy, no, no, no, NO!

ROBIN [*savagely attacking the wall with the iron bar, but his daughter's muffled screams cannot be silenced. In utter self-knowledge he hurls the iron bar to the ground*]: BITCH. BITCH! [*A broken sound issues from deep within his chest—a daemonic discord—he throws himself to the ground, crouches on all fours and like a severely wounded animal, in its death throes, prances around the Alley smashing everything in his path*].

CURTAIN

SCENE THREE

The Alley at noon. ROBIN *the tramp is asleep on the mattress. He seems to be having nightmares, muttering about someone called Judy or Cecilia. He snarls and kicks, and punches. His fist hits the wall and he abruptly wakes up in pain.*

ROBIN: What the hell is going on around here?

RHODES [*the tramp, entering, carrying bottles of cheap wine, and a loaf of bread*]: Nothing is going on. It's all in your mind.

ROBIN [*laying out a newspaper and setting the bread and margarine on it*]: If nothing's going on, then what the hell is going on in my mind. I've just had the most frightful nightmare. [*Pause*] It wasn't like that. We weren't such barbarians.

RHODES [*noncommittally*]: The war, you mean?

ROBIN [*startled*]: What war? I'm not talking about any war.

RHODES: Of course not. [*Opens bottle, passes it on*] Nobody talks about the war. It's indecent to remind ourselves of all that. Bayoneting children, ramming primed grenades into vaginas, bombing cattle and herdboys, shooting schoolboys in so-called crossfire, murdering missionaries and blaming it on the boys.

ROBIN [*staring*]: I said I wasn't talking about the war.

RHODES: I'm not talking about the war. I said it's indecent to remind ourselves of genocide at Chimoio, the unbelievable massacres at Nyadzonya, the callous mass executions at Rusape—incidentally, I was born at Rusape—Vengere Township—and you guys reduced my home to acres of mass graves. But I quite agree: it's indecent to remind ourselves of all that.

ROBIN [*chewing*]: Good fresh bread this. I didn't know you had any money.

RHODES [*drinking, chewing*]: No I didn't—looked up one of my last few friends, a chap who makes films for ZTV. He gives me a handout now and then.

ROBIN: He must be a nice guy.

RHODES: He isn't. He's going to lose his job. He's a fool in my mould—a stubborn, selfish, independent mind. So he quarrels with the big shots about budgets and the need for committed investigative documentaries—not the usual claptrap they always want him to make. We grew up together in Rusape, but he was lucky to get a scholarship to the U.K. That's where he studied film-making. My judgment is the guy's a genius. [*Drinking*] But doing your job well and being a genius doesn't go down too well these days. So I think he's going to get the sack. Remember the Sleeping Minister's newsreel? [ROBIN *nods*] He did it. I've told him he's welcome in the Alley any time he gets the boot on the seat of his pants. The Alley is Dante's First Circle for those whose minds really do a job well.

ROBIN: Did you hear the story about the guy who arrived in hell and the devil was showing him all the several kinds of punishment, and asking the newcomer to choose the one kind for himself eternally? This guy sees all these frightful disgusting sections, and the devil is getting impatient when he sees all these naked men standing in a pool of effluent up to their waist, and he chooses it. But as he is getting into the shit pool, the devil angel rasps: "Right. Your five minutes teatime is over. Back on your heads!"

RHODES: Sounds like what happened to the Zimbabwe Rhodesia guys.

ROBIN [*warily*]: Rhodes, let's not be political. Let's just enjoy the bread and the wine.

RHODES: Yeah, like the Alley is a regular Upper Room. The bread is my flesh. This wine is my blood.

ROBIN: It doesn't do to discuss politics, religion or sex when dining.

RHODES: Who says?

ROBIN: Oxford. If you do you get sconced, they make you stand on the bench and drink a big jug of common beer in full view of everyone.

RHODES: I like beer.

ROBIN: It's not that. It's the social disgrace.

RHODES: The Alley people don't give a fuck about social disgrace. [*Pause*] What's got into you?

ROBIN: Do you think Salvation, Redemption, really is there? That nightmare I had. It's making me review my life. I mean is this all there is to it? Do we just die like the beasts whose flesh we eat?

RHODES [*quietly*]: Thousands died like animals to the slaughter during the war. You've seen those photographs of hundreds of skulls and ribs dug up from those mass graves. [*Pause*] Did you use them for target shooting? [*Drinks*] Do you want to hear them? They are right there behind the wall. [*Slowly*] You just strike the wall like last time and you'll hear if they'll talk about reconciliation. Want to try? [ROBIN, *frightened, stares at the wall*] Do you want to hear my sister talking to you like that last time?

ROBIN: I didn't even know you had a sister.

RHODES: Of course, you did. She was in your nightmare. You even know her name, don't you?

ROBIN: What are you driving at? The war is over, dead and forgotten.

RHODES: She's dead but not forgotten. [*Softly*] She's right here with you, and you're right there behind the wall with her.

ROBIN: What are you trying to do to my mind?

RHODES: I'm not trying. *You* are doing it by yourself.

> [*Silence.*]

RHODES: Your daughter, Judy, is right there with her. I can see them. They are kissing.

ROBIN: My daughter kissing who? Be careful what you say. She was a pure, innocent, beautiful young thing until your comrades did things to her and slit her throat.

RHODES: She's kissing Cecilia. They are very much in love with each other. What you did to both of them left them with nothing but sheer disgust for men. For this world. [*Pause. Looks away*] I used to suffer from world weariness, but the wall said that too was nothing. I cannot get away from you, though that's the only thing I want from life, from the whole last ounce of the universe. You also want to get away but, like me, you can't, and for the same reason. I am your wall, and you are my wall. And the game we tried during the war of mounting each other like dogs in severe heat has not yet been settled. Maybe that is the matter of what is going on in your mind. But, come, you are not drinking.

ROBIN [*sulkily*]: You said it's indecent to remind ourselves of these things.

RHODES: Indecent, ye-e-s. But the war created a necessity. Necessity brooks neither decency nor indecency. [*He picks up the iron bar and savagely attacks the wall. A very prolonged thin mournful wail, like a fierce wind drawing nearer and nearer, bowls as though from a tomb*] Listen, that's the song that will forever blow like an unsettled spirit from the Zambezi—through Harare, Bulawayo, Mutare, Gweru, down the Limpopo and back again to the Zambezi—from which it will again turn restlessly back searching for you and for me so that again and again we can retell their story, which is not our story. Listen to it. How sad, how profound, and yet so heartbreakingly pitiful. [*Laughs, as if possessed*] Was it all then a mere breath of wind? A susurrating nothingness? All that butchery which left so many human carcasses strewn all over the hills and the valleys, all those shrieks and cries for mercy. Shit. [*Opens another bottle, breaks off a piece of bread*] I never told you what I did, did I? [ROBIN *shakes his head*] I was a medic in ZANLA. When you and your platoon had finished executing—if that is the word for such a ghastly ghoulish business you did—I and my medic cadres cleaned up after you. That's how I found my sister. And that's how I found out about you. We had a rather good intelligence system. That's why I have stuck by you all these years.

ROBIN: You murdered our people too. Including Judy, my daughter. . .[*Uneasily*] What are you raking all this up for? And why now? [*The bowling wind falters then gathers momentum.* RHODES *and* ROBIN *slowly rise to their feet, vicious looks in their faces.*]

ROBIN: Know what's wrong with you? You talk too much for your own good. [*He grabs the iron bar. Advances. Makes a perfect swing, catching* RHODES *on the shoulder.* RHODES *goes down. He raises the bar like an axe to finish the job but sees something in* RHODES' *face and throws away the bar. He helps him to his feet*] Know what's wrong? It's the Alley itself. Never knew any other country with such an ability to run men into beasts. Rhodes, let's drink. Let's eat. I know one day we'll try to kill each other again but I call it quits for today. I'm just going to get drunk.

RHODES: Don't mind me.

CURTAIN

The Breakdown Scrapiron Blues

Characters:
DRAKE
BETSY, his wife
NOMA, their daughter
RINGO, Betsy's lover
VERA, Ringo's wife

THE BREAKDOWN SCRAPIRON BLUES

SCENE ONE

Sitting-room. BETSY *and her daughter* NOMA. BETSY's *arm is in a sling.*

BETSY: Don't worry. He's coming soon.

NOMA: But I want to worry. I love you both.

BETSY: Don't touch there—it hurts.

NOMA: Sorry.

BETSY: I'm sorry too.

NOMA: But who's the one in your bedroom?

BETSY: That's my. . .

NOMA: Your boyfriend.

    [*Enter* RINGO, *hurriedly putting on a jacket.*]

BETSY: When will I see you again?

RINGO: I don't know. As soon as I can get away Vera is getting suspicious.

BETSY: That woman!

NOMA: Don't come back. I'll tell my father.

BETSY [*slapping her*]: Shut your face.

RINGO [*at the door*]: I'll phone.

NOMA: I don't like him.

    [*Exit* RINGO.]

BETSY: You're not to say what you think.

NOMA: I think it all the same.

BETSY: But don't say it.

NOMA: You hit me in front of him.

BETSY: You were rude.

NOMA: But I don't like pretending.

BETSY: It's not pretending. It's growing up—you're just a child.

NOMA: I'm fourteen.

BETSY [*with scorn*]: Of course.

NOMA: And I have a boyfriend.

49

BETSY: Well, don't get pregnant. Daddy will thrash you.

NOMA: He won't—because he's the one. . . He's my boyfriend because you treat him so bad.

BETSY: I don't.

NOMA: Yes you do. Ringo is always sneaking in when father is not here.

BETSY: Shut up.

NOMA [*curiously*]: Do you love him?

BETSY: Who?

NOMA [*disappointed*]: Oh, that's how it is.

[*Enter* DRAKE. *His head is bandaged. He is drunk.*]

DRAKE: Ah, Lady Macbeth. How are you? [BETSY *turns her back on him*] And you, my sweet Noma? [*He chucks her chin.*]

NOMA [*hugs him*]: She hit me in front of him.

DRAKE [*stiffens*]: Oh, I see. Betsy? [*He is waiting. He mixes himself a drink*] You will have some wine, Noma?

NOMA: Yes, please. [*They sit together on the couch*] Take me away from her, Daddy.

DRAKE: There's time enough.

NOMA: You don't have another girlfriend, do you?

DRAKE: As a matter of fact, yes.

NOMA: And Mama doesn't know?

DRAKE: She knows.

NOMA: But do you know about Ringo?

DRAKE: Uhuh.

NOMA: And you don't care?

DRAKE: No. It's not worth it.

NOMA: I thought I was your only girlfriend.

DRAKE: Of course you are. You're my daughter.

NOMA: But I *love* you.

DRAKE: I'm your father. They'd throw me in jail if I loved you like that.

NOMA: I know. But I don't see why it's not permitted.

DRAKE [*mixes himself another drink*]: Betsy, will you have one?

BETSY: After listening to both of you I feel like a stiff one.

DRAKE [*giving it to her*]: That's right—let's all put on a brave face.

BETSY: I wish you'd tell your daughter that.

DRAKE: She's *our* daughter.

BETSY: Sometimes I wonder.

NOMA: I'm not a third person singular.

BETSY: You—not singular!

DRAKE: Take a break, Betsy.

BETSY: Sometimes I don't know why you married me.

DRAKE: I didn't. You married me.

NOMA: What did I do?

BETSY: You arrived without an invitation.

DRAKE: Give us a kiss, Noma. [*She does, impulsively, then winks at* BETSY *over his shoulder.*]

BETSY: You do love me a little, don't you Drake?

DRAKE [*kissing her on the forehead*]: My darling!

[BETSY *makes a rude gesture at* NOMA *behind* DRAKE's *back.*]

NOMA [*springs up*]: I hate it. I hate it all. [*Smashes her glass.*]

BETSY: Come, come, Noma—what do you hate?

NOMA: Everything!

DRAKE: That's all right then. We all hate everything. Don't we Betsy?

BETSY: It's nice to hate everything and enjoy the details.

BLACKOUT

SCENE TWO

Sitting-room. DRAKE *in long night shirt.* NOMA *in her pyjamas. He has just finished reading poetry to her. He puts the book down—mixes himself a drink.*

DRAKE: I don't think Betsy is coming home tonight.

51

NOMA: She's with Ringo.

> [*The phone rings.* DRAKE *answers it.*]

DRAKE: Is that you, Vera? How are you? [*Listens*] Oh, Ringo isn't home? Well, he's not here. . . I see. Betsy isn't here either. Come and spend the night here. Sure, why not?. . . I'll expect you soon. Ciao.

NOMA: Who's Vera?

DRAKE: One of my friends.

NOMA: But she's Ringo's wife.

DRAKE: Yes.

NOMA: I don't understand it.

DRAKE: It's obscene, isn't it?

NOMA: What's wrong with me, Daddy? What's wrong?

DRAKE: It's called adolescence. I've a book about it. [*Searches the bookshelves and tosses her a book*] There's another book also about King Oedipus. He married his mother. [*He finds it, gives it to her. She flicks through the book. He helps himself to another drink.*]

NOMA: So there's nothing. . .strange about me?

DRAKE: No.

NOMA: So there's nothing wrong with me—it's you and mother who are wrong.

DRAKE: Wrong? That's an understatement.

NOMA: This guy really married his mother?

DRAKE: Uhuh.

NOMA: So I can marry you.

DRAKE: You'd have to kill Betsy.

NOMA [*curiously*]: If I really killed her would you. . .?

DRAKE [*grimly*]: No.

NOMA: I love you like I could kill you a million million times.

DRAKE: It's madness my sweet, a burning paradise.

> [*Some overwhelming force drives them into each other's arms. Loud knocking. Pause.* NOMA *runs out, sobbing.* DRAKE, *about to throw his glass at the audience checks himself, forces himself to relax and goes to open the*

door. He returns with VERA.]

VERA: I don't know what you'll think.

DRAKE: There are no thoughts here.

VERA: I just couldn't bear that big empty house.

DRAKE: You've come to an even emptier one.

VERA: Your daughter is here, isn't she?

DRAKE: No, not my daughter. She is not here.

VERA: Of course she is. Only yesterday you told me. . .

DRAKE: Yesterday she was my daughter. Today it's another matter.

VERA: What's she done?

DRAKE: Been herself.

VERA: You're talking so strangely.

DRAKE [*controlling himself visibly*]: It's the drink. Of course she's here.

VERA [*he mixes her a drink*]: A wonderful girl.

DRAKE: I didn't know how much I loved her until today.

VERA: And you should too.

DRAKE: Do you mean that?

VERA: Of course you should love her. It's only natural.

RINGO [*echoing her*]: Natural.

[*Pause.*]

VERA: I don't understand about Ringo. He's never. . .

DRAKE: Don't worry. He's with my wife somewhere.

VERA: What!

DRAKE: Oh, it's been going on for quite a while.

VERA: Ringo and Betsy?

DRAKE: I've been wearing the horns for exactly eighteen months now.

VERA: But don't you. . .?

DRAKE [*calmly*]: No.

VERA: You don't care?

DRAKE: Give me one good reason why I should care?

VERA: But it's not natural. [*Pause*] Not natural. [*Pause*] You could at least

53

have told me.

DRAKE [*simply*]: You didn't ask.

VERA: But I'm your friend.

DRAKE: When sex rears its head everything explodes inside out.

VERA: Does your daughter know?

DRAKE: Oh, she's started to hit her in front of him.

VERA: Betsy?

DRAKE: Uhuh.

> [*Silence.*]

VERA [*hugging him, kissing him*]: Love me a little. [DRAKE *sees* NOMA *watching them from the doorway.*]

DRAKE: Come in Noma. This is Vera. Noma, my daughter.

NOMA: How do you do?

VERA: I've heard a lot about you Noma. Your father always talks about you.

NOMA [*to* DRAKE]: Do you?

DRAKE: Go to bed, Noma.

NOMA: I can't sleep. [*Pause*] Are you going to sleep with her?

DRAKE: Yes.

NOMA [*slaps him hard*]: You brute! [*She rushes out.*]

DRAKE [*taking off his night shirt*]: We may as well do it here, Vera.

VERA [*taking off her underpants*]: Yes, my Sweet.

BLACKOUT

SCENE THREE

Sitting-room. DRAKE *comes in. He is wearing a business suit. Drops hat and briefcase. Mixes himself a drink. Pacing up and down, drinking, argues with himself.*

DRAKE 1: What can I do for you?

DRAKE 2: Get lost!

DRAKE 1: Come, come, my dear fellow.

DRAKE 2: The sin of Onan.

DRAKE 1: You will have your little joke. But a little rationality goes a long way in these matters.

DRAKE 2: You sneaky little runt. One: I resign. Find another negotiator. Two: I've already issued a press statement. Three: I'm not going to kill myself.

DRAKE 1 [*takes out a revolver*]: There is no way out. [*Places the gun on the table*] You are a man of honour—in spite of everything.

DRAKE 2 [*staring at the gun*]: No.

[*Silence.*]

DRAKE 1 [*mimics gesture of shooting himself through the mouth*]: I repeat: there is no way out of this.

DRAKE 2 [*screams*]: Betsy! [*Silence. Screams*] Noma!!

[*Silence.*]

[DRAKE 2 *picks up the gun, places the barrel in his mouth, and is about to press the trigger when* NOMA *rushes in.*]

NOMA: What—why—Daddy?

DRAKE [*replaces the gun on the table*]: A nice little toy, isn't it Noma?

NOMA: You were about to kill yourself.

DRAKE [*laughs bitterly*]: Give me one good reason why I should or why I shouldn't?

NOMA [*at a loss, but she brightens up*]: I love you, Daddy.

DRAKE [*with an affectionate cry*]: Sweet Noma!

[*She watches him anxiously as he mixes himself another drink. She wants to say something about it but is suddenly tongue-tied. He senses it.*]

DRAKE: My drinking worries you?

NOMA: Yes. But it's all right if that's what you want.

DRAKE: It's not at all what I want. [*Laughs harshly*] If it was I'd resent it.

NOMA: Is it because of Mama?

DRAKE: It's because of nothing. [*Pause*] I don't know what to do with myself and I don't even know whether it's necessary to do anything at all. [*Pause*] There was this guy, Oblomov, who was dying of boredom. . . There was another guy, Bazarov I think, who discovered the importance of nothingness and actually died of it. . .

NOMA [*stopping her ears*]: Please Daddy don't. I hate to see you like this.

DRAKE 1: Get lost.

DRAKE 2: Don't you dare talk like that to my daughter, Sir. I will not be responsible for my actions.

DRAKE 1 [*laughs*]: The sin of Onan.

NOMA: Stop it Daddy!

DRAKE 2: You heard the lady, Mister. Beat it.

DRAKE 1 [*picks up the gun, levels it at* NOMA]: There's no way out of this one.

NOMA: It's all right. You can shoot me, Daddy.

DRAKE: What? [*He looks at the gun, drops it. It goes off*] The thing actually works. [*Enter* BETSY, *laughing, and* RINGO, *smiling*] You're just in time to join me in a little celebration, folks. The bar is open. Help yourselves.

BETSY: Drake, my husband. Ringo.

DRAKE: Is she good in bed?

RINGO [*at the bar*]: Marvellous.

DRAKE: Vera is not at all bad.

BETSY [*picks up gun*]: What's this doing here?

DRAKE: I wanted to shoot Noma.

RINGO: Why didn't you?

DRAKE: She loves me. I can't screw a person who loves me. It's indecent. [*Pause. He takes the gun and puts it inside his coat*] But—yes, the celebration. We mustn't forget that.

BETSY: In aid of what?

DRAKE: Two things in fact. One: our wedding anniversary. Two: I've just been promoted I'm now the head of my department in the Ministry. May I propose a toast to myself and to you, Betsy. [*They toast*] May I also propose an extra toast to Ringo for solving my sexual problem.

BETSY [*angry*]: What sexual problem?

DRAKE: We may hate everything but the details are best left unsaid, my dear.

BETSY: Well! [*To* RINGO] Are you going to just stand there while he insults me?

RINGO [*at a loss*]: Well, eh. I mean, my good fellow I. . .

DRAKE: Get lost! [*Laughs*] Let's all get drunk. Noma—where's Noma?

NOMA: Right here.

DRAKE: Treat yourself to two glasses of wine. [*She does. He continues, reasonably*] You two, I want you to know that I don't mind at all. Though of course I wish I could believe that. I mean if I believe that the earth is round why should I not believe in anything my wife chooses to. . . Of course it's another matter if it turns out that the earth is not round. . . I mean running a department is like revolving round the sun with all of you ants crawling on my green and blue surface. I don't believe a word of what I'm saying.

BETSY: Did you have a nice day at the office?

DRAKE: I fired three guys five minutes after my promotion. [*Turns to* RINGO] One of them was your brother. I enjoyed that.

RINGO: But why?

DRAKE: You're fucking my wife.

BETSY: That's crazy!

RINGO: You can't do that—it's obscene.

DRAKE: Why must I not do crazy obscene things if I feel like it?

NOMA: Yes, why not, if he feels like it?

DRAKE: It's not at all the way you put it Noma.

NOMA: But you said. . .

RINGO: Who are the other two you fired?

DRAKE: Friends of your brother. [*Reasonably*] They can get their jobs back the minute you get out of my wife's life. So, you see, it's up to you. [*Surprised*] But your glass is empty, Ringo. Fill up. Fill her up. Let's impregnate ourselves with Noah's discovery—the only good thing to come out of the Flood. It's in Apocrypha, you know. Grapes the size of Betsy's breasts. And Noah squeezing, squeezing, sucking the juice to the last glittering drop. [*Pause*] Milk comes from bottles, right Noma?

NOMA [*tipsy*]: Yes Daddy.

DRAKE: Good girl. Give us a kiss. [*She does—but he suddenly kisses her full on the mouth.*

Betsy *and* Ringo *are aghast*] Oh, my sweet, sweetest Noma.

Noma: Do it again.

Drake: Have some more wine, my dear.

Betsy: Well...!

[Ringo *starts to whistle between his teeth.*]

Curtain

SCENE FOUR

The sitting-room. Drake *is dressed in a clown's outfit. He mimes what he feels are the details of his life. He tires of the game. He instinctively goes to the bar, but, with a sob, checks himself. He is trying to give up drinking. He aims for the bar again, looking round and peering over his shoulder. A jazz tune or a snatch of ragtime music accompanies the miming. Finally he can't stand it. He hastily, spillingly, helps himself to a drink.* Noma *comes in.*

Noma: Oh no, Daddy, you promised.

Drake: In foreign affairs there is no promise that cannot be broken. It's called statesmanship. Why, when I was in Dakar and you were two years old I promised the devil I would never lie. Goes to show, doesn't it?

Noma: You can't talk your way out of this, Daddy. [*Pause*] I thought my love for you would help you stop drinking.

Drake [*harshly*]: Stop dreaming. You cannot reform an old cynic like me. Have you ever seen a clown crying? No? Then watch this. [*He tenses*] Just watch this. Watch me turn the tears on, my sweet Noma. [*He tenses even harder. The tears do not come.*]

Noma [*uncertain, giggles but stops short as he suddenly bursts into tears*]: Oh Daddy. No, no, no. It's all right.

Drake: Don't touch me, you bitch!

58

NOMA: Wha. . .?

DRAKE: Yes, you filthy little slut. I've schooled you on books. Nothing but books. And it's going to destroy you. . .

NOMA: Don't, please. You'll hate yourself.

DRAKE: I like to hate myself.

NOMA: No, you don't. You're just deliberately trying to make me hate you. [*Laughs bitterly*] I wish it was that easy. . . No, Daddy, you're wrong. So wrong. . .

DRAKE [grinning]: Do you know what wrong means? No. I'll act it out for you. Watch this. [*He acts out "wrongness". The music accompanies his miming.*]

NOMA (*bursts out laughing shouting*): Stop! Stop! [*He relentlessly goes on. Enter* BETSY *carrying shopping parcels.*]

BETSY: What on earth is going on here?

DRAKE: Nothing. Only sparks of happiness, darling.

BETSY [*kissing him*]: Thanks for everything.

DRAKE: What did I do?

BETSY: Everything. It's been wonderful. [*She notices the drink*] Oh Drake, you promised. I know it's hard but do try. You've been wonderful. Noma, take these to the kitchen. [*As* NOMA *takes the parcels*] Oh, I bought you a pair of lovely earrings. [*She takes them out of her handbag.*]

NOMA: Oh Mama. Thanks, thanks very much. [*Exits.*]

BETSY: I'm tired. [*Mixes herself a drink and sprawls on the couch*] You do look funny. And cheeky, my dear.

DRAKE: Out of this world. It's ages since we danced together. May I have the pleasure? [*The music starts again. They dance.*]

BETSY: Darling?

DRAKE: HHmm.

BETSY: I've been thinking. . . I mean, let's have another child.

DRAKE: But Reagan is going to press the button. What kind of a world is it to drag a child into?

BETSY: I'm serious

DRAKE: So am I.

BETSY: Please.

DRAKE: Okay, we'll have another child. But—don't you think you should consult it first?

BETSY: Oh, come on. Let's. Right now. Come on. We haven't been together for so long.

DRAKE: Okay. But I'd better get this paint off me first.

BETSY: No, no. I want you just as you are right now.

DRAKE: But then it won't be mine. It will be a clown's child.

BETSY [*laughs*]: Right!

CURTAIN

The Servants' Ball [*]

Characters:
Norman Drake
Thomas
Sarah
Mupangani
Majazi
Mbuya Beri
Bonzo
Alfie
Dick
Raven

Place: The servants' quarters at NORMAN DRAKE'S residence in Harare,
   Zimbabwe.

Time: Any time between twilight and midnight.

---

[*] This play is a sequel to "The Toilet" published in *Mindblast*. Norman Drake, Alfie, Dick and Raven are characters from
that play. Dick is Drake's nephew (white), Raven is the niece of Mrs Nzuzu, the minister's wife (black).

The stage is the whitewashed half interior and entrance way of the servants' quarters at NORMAN DRAKE*'s residence. A log serves as a bench for the guests. A wheel-less bicycle leans against the wall, rusting.* BONZO,*the servant from next door, is sitting on the log drinking kachasu from a Mazoe bottle. He is playing a mbira and occasionally singing:*

> Hii - iiiye - iiye vakomana imi
>
> Varungu vafa tatora nyika
>
> Hii - iiye -iiye nyika yaenda
>
> Ngatiende kuhondo.

[*On the bench also are* THOMAS, MUPANGANI, SARAH, MAJAZI—*they are drinking Chibuku from packets. Inside the room, sits* MBUYA BERI,*the shebeen queen, hunched over her sewing machine and selling kachasu and Chibuku. A dog barks. Other dogs from every quarter bark in reply. As they do so,* NORMAN DRAKE*'s voice is heard calling out to* THOMAS, *the cook-houseboy*]: THOMAS! THOMAS! HEY THOMAS!

THOMAS [*cursing*]: Can't a man have a rest? I've been working the whole fucking day; and now I can't even sit for five minutes without that slave-driver howling for me. [*Loudly, to* DRAKE]: YES BAAS! [*Hastily gets to his feet.*]

DRAKE'S voice: WHERE THE HELL ARE YOU, THOMAS?

THOMAS: YES BAAS! HERE BAAS!

DRAKE'S voice: TELL YOUR FRIENDS NOT TO MAKE TOO MUCH NOISE!

THOMAS: YE—EES, BAAS! [*Resuming his seat*]: Basa ibasa zvaro but sometimes it's too much, man. This one ariright zvake but maparty ake anyanya. Izvozvi tomorrow mumba imomo there'll be hundreds of dirty or broken glasses, hundreds ye maempties, thousands of cigarette stubs nemaashtray akazara kwekuzara. Mukitchen there will be millions of greasy dishes, burned pots and all kinds of stains on the walls. Iwo varungu awa nemashef kufara vanofara but they should think about who cleans up after them. [*Drinking*]: ME!

MAJAZI: Mbuya Beri, tiisireiwo record iya inonzi Tiyi Hobvu. [*To* BONZO] Iwewe chimbonyarara nekanhu kako ako.

BONZO: Ndiani arikutaura mazwi andisikunzwa? Ngekuti ndikaanzwa dzakutsaku ririkutaura

62

izvozvo richandiziwa zvakanaka.

MAJAZI: Tibvireipo. Kachasu kamurikumwa kanokunyeperai, m'dhara.

MBUYA BERI: Majazi, geza kumeso usatiwataura. Bonzo anemakore ekuti ndibaba wababa vako. Haunyari? [*Pause*] Vanawemazuwaano madhodhi arimunzira yesuvanhu vakuru. Hapana pakanaka pekutsika.

THOMAS: Apo mataura nekushure, ambuya. Mazu'a ano it's youth isusu who are the future of Zimbabwe.

BONZO: Future ipi? Minimum wage ine future here?

MAJAZI: But iwewe m'dhara unogaya here kuti kare kare kusatikwaita independence waitambira four dollars pamwedzi chete. Mazuaano urikugrafta fifty dollars. And hauna mukadzi kanavana. Pekugara nezvekudya mavet ako anokupa. And kachasu urikuimwa, so urikutaura-chii zvekuti hauna future?

BONZO: Ndisiye so, mufana. Zvangu ndezvangu. [*He plays the mbira*] Sarah, simuka utiimbire nzwiyo.

> [SARAH *stands, beams at everyone, begins to sway. She does not so much sing as recite the following words*]:

> Mapureti ndageza
> Murungu avhaya.
> Imba ndatswaira
> Missis adhakwa

[CHORUS]:
> Ndipeyi minimum yangu!
> Kumba muchemo ndaoma nenzara
> Ndipeyi minimum yangu
> Imba yachena nyika yafamba
> Ndipeyi minimum yangu
> Ndati ndipeyi minimum yangu
> Hamunzwi here, ndati
> Ndipeyi minimum yangu
> Ndipeyi! Minimum yangu!

BONZO:
> Wirrrrrrr Hande hande!

SARAH:
> Ndipeyi!

ALL: Minimum yangu!

SARAH: Ndati ndipeyi!

ALL: Minimum yangu!

SARAH: Toireti ndageza

           Bathroom nda porisha

           Imbwa ndaifidha nyama

           Mapreti ebreakfast ndabvisa

           Imi hamunzwi here

           Ndati ndipeyi!

ALL: Minimum yangu!

SARAH: Ndipeyi!

ALL: Minimum yangu.

[AMBUYA BERI *is nodding to the rhythm over her sewing machine; she is humming, stitching away.* BONZO *is playing his mbira as if he is in a hypnotic trance.* THOMAS *is dancing, the rest joining in, humming, ululating, exploding epithets of glee. As the song ends,* BONZO *starts another on his mbira and* SARAH *automatically improvises the words.*]

SARAH: Imwayi doro imba yatswa

           Imwayi paraffin gore rapera

           Imwayi maheu nzira yapera

[CHORUS:] Mazuwaano kupondana

           Kudanana nezvibhakera

           Kwazisa zvaunoziva

           Tsvoda pfumvu masikati

           Manheru ndokuona mugumbezi

ALL: Mazuwaano kupondana

           Kudanana nezvibhakera

BONZO [*as if possessed, erupts in grunts, deep bass grunts*]:

           H0-00 WoWo Ho-oo W0 W0.

SARAH: Kuhura hakuroi

           Mwoyo wakanaka

64

Kufa hakurwadzi

Vaendakumusha

Ndaona Vhigoroni

Apakwa musango

Missis arara

Magetsi ndadzima

[CHORUS:] Ndarota Satani

Aisa whaitewash padoor

Ndaisa mubhuku

Ziso rakafunda

[CHORUS:] Ndarota Satani

Aisa whitewash padoor

Svosve radonha mumukaka

Smith arikugeza muKariba

[CHORUS:] Ndarota Satani

Aisa whitewash padoor

Mvura yaramba kunaya

Isai maoko nemakumbo pamwechete

Ndipei coffee ndanenyota

MAJAZI: Ko, Iwe Bonzo, varungu vako ipwere, here? Kana kuti vanopenga?

BONZO: Wakamboona murungu asingapengi iwe?

MAJAZI: Vangu havapengi. Vanongodya mazai ekitsi.

THOMAS: These vets it doesn't matter kuti anoitasei as long as achikupeya mariyako.

BONZO: Awondisingadi mashef echiboy anokuseenzesa fanike uri ngombe mumunda.

MBUYA BERI: Ndevekuto ngwarira wayawaya. Unopedza mwedzi mitatu usativapeyiwa. Futi vanounza hamadzavo dziyadziya dzisingaziwe kushandisa toilet.

THOMAS: That type makes your life one long misery. Vanokumutsa nafive o'clock mumangwanani and basa unozopedza after midnight. Me—I'll never work for a black person. Mamisers. And vanokudzvinyirira zvekudzvinyirira chaizvo chaizvo. Ko mufero uyawuy-a, Mupangani, arikupi?

MUPANGANI: Dziripano.

THOMAS: Ndiwe unosevenzera mabenzi matema. Titaurireka.

MUPANGANI: Ndimimunotyora nyika. Munhu munhu whether arimuvet kanapovo. Mazuvaano taanemitemo inorongazvose zvebasa. Muimploya akakubata zvisingaitwi unomumhan'arira kuministri yeLabour.

THOMAS: Asi iwewe uri sell-out, ngekuti mafero aya unovasevenzera fifteen hours mazuwa ese. Havakupi Off futi. Zvino izvi handiti vatotizaka kuti umbo zorora zvako. And utsinye hwavo ndewekuti vanongokupeya minimum chaiyo chaiyo, pasina kana penny rekukwidzira kwekunyepera.

MAJAZI: Asi iwe Thomas murungu wako akaita seyi?

THOMAS: Wangu ndiComrade chaiye. Tinotukana. Tinofarirana. Tinobhowana. Tinocracker majoke. Anondipeya ninety pamwedzi. AND anondi bvumidza kuita sheeben yangu pano. Bvunza Mbuya Beri.

MBUYA BERI: Comrade Drake? Ndiye munhu chaiye chaiye. Haatinetse. Haanei nesu kana tichiita zvedu. Haana hanya. Handiti mese murikufara henyu? Panechakashata here?

BONZO: Mbuya, ndipeyi imwe Kachasu yethirty-five cents.

MBUYA BERI: Unza kapu yauinayo iyo.

BONZO [gives her the cup]: Nyatsaikusvitsa kururimi rwekapu. Mofunga kuti ndakaberekwa nezuro ini?

MBUYA BERI: Kanawadhakwa wadhakwa, Bonzo. Kutaura hakusikusura. Iwe Majazi, gitari rako ririkupi?

MAJAZI: Riripano.

MBUYA BERI: Tamba-ka. [She gives BONZO his kachasu.]

MAJAZI [starts needlessly tuning his guitar and singing]:

> Vakaenda kuhuni havadzoki
>
> Vakarova guwa inyenyedzi
>
> Vakakohwa zvapfuura ibvaipano
>
> Mauto edu izano remangwana
>
> Imi Mai wa Boy zuwa ranyura
>
> Pindai mugumbeze ndatonhorwa
>
> Mwedzi ngezuwa agarirwa nhaka
>
> Muchenachena anobva paMachipisa

Shiri tsvuku dzinoimba manheru

Mwoyo wakuvadzwa muti wadonha

Huyayi mese kumusangano

Huyayi huyayi huyayi mese

BONZO: HO-OO WoWo Ho-oo WO WO.

MAJAZI: Huyayi! Huyayi! Huyayi!

Huyayi kumusangano

MBUYA BERI [*ululates shrilly.*]

BONZO: Bopoto rabhobhojani

Harifambisi nyika!

THOMAS: Shake - Shake!

MAJAZI: Huyayi Huyayi Huyayai!!!

BONZO: Bopoto rabhobhojani

Pasi naro pamberi neredu. [*In a frenzy over his mbira.*]

DRAKE's Voice: THOMAS!

THOMAS: BAAS!

DRAKE: WHERE IS THAT WOODEN CORKSCREW I BROUGHT FROM EUROPE?

THOMAS: IN THE KITCHEN. THE SECOND DRAWER FROM THE BLUE ONE!

DRAKE: OKAY. [*Pause*] THOMAS!

THOMAS: BAAS!

DRAKE: I'VE GOT A CRATE OF BEER FOR YOU. COME AND GET IT BEFORE I DRINK IT!

THOMAS [*hastily*]: DON'T YOU DARE DRINK IT BAAS! I'M COMING. [*Exits.*]

MBUYA BERI [*smirking*]: Murikuzvionaka? Thomas nemurungu wake wanonzwanana chaizvo. Doro anopihwa. Zvekudya anopihwa. Hapana chaanoshaya. Uyu Comrade Drake ndiComrade chaiye chaiye.

THOMAS [*enters carrying crate of beer. He puts it down by* MBUYA BERI]: Neo-colonialism inodhaka.

MAJAZI: Neo chii?

THOMAS: Doro ratirikupihwa iri. Ndio neo-colonialism.

BONZO: Iwewe Thomas., chirungu chako ichi hachisi chekunyepera ichi?

THOMAS: What do you know, m'dhara?

BONZO: Taura neShona kanawakagara nemaShona. Taura chirungu kana wakagara neVarungu. Izvizvekudada hazvifambi nikisi.

THOMAS: Majerasi chete. Imi hamunakufunda. Isutakafunda tiregereyi tipangidze kufunda kwedu. Unongoteedzera kutaura kunoita murungu wako. Zvekutaura zvisirizvako zvinofamba here, nhai wakomana?

MAJAZI: Apo mataura, m'dhara.

MBUYA BERI: Ah imi! Mwana wangu atadza chii. Handiti ndiye arikukupayi doro nekufara pano?

MAJAZI: Ineo-colonialism yake. Dai angaachitipa mahara zvaiita. But manje arikuita fifty cents chipack cheChibuku. Thirty-five cents kakapu kekachasu. Four cents mudzanga umwechete. Iwe Thomas wakangwara fanike murungu wako. Mari dzese dzatinosevenzera dzinoguma pano padoro raThomas.

MBUYA BERI: Maakutaura chii? Tokudaidzai here? Handiti munouya mega?

MUPANGANI: Koiwe M'dhara Bonzo, uchapedza kusona bhutsu dzangu rini? Wagaranadzo three months. And mariyacho ndakakupa.

BONZO: Huya mangwana udzitore. Unondibvunza zvebasa ndiripadoro unofungakuti ndinosona bhutsu mushabhini inini? Hausati wambosvika pamba pangu kubvira musi wawakandipa zvibhutsu zvako. Murungu wangu akambouya akabvunza kuti bhutsu dzirikunhuisa imba ndedzaani? Ini ndikangonyararawo.

MUPANGANI: Kunhuwa, bhutsu dzangu? Asi urikuda kundiwona fani, m'dhara?

SARAH: Ha-aa iwe Mupangani, nyarara. Hazvitewedzerwi zvamudhara, hauvizivi here. [Pause] M'dhara Bonzo, tambai mbira tifare. Ndodakuimba zvangu ini.

BONZO [chuckling]: Right. [He plays. As usual SARAH improvises the words.]

SARAH [singing]:

Ko, ndadii mudiwa wangu?

Sango remumba ririkutsva

Kondadii mudiwa vangu

Makuhwa anhasi makomo amangwana

Ko, ndadii mudiwa vangu

Gudo radya ndowe kuGlen Norah

Haunyari haunyari here, mudiwa,

Nzara mazino machena mubani
Gara paumba gadzira bhasikoro
Enda kubasa vakafa vanoona
Ko, ndadii mudiwa wangu
Zvibhakera hazvipikiri rudo
Kondadii mudiwa vangu
Wuraya zvako ivhu harifi
[*She stops singing.* BONZO *continues to play.*]

THOMAS [*tipsy*]: Mavheti! I'll show you mavheti. [*Begins parodying* DRAKE] "My dear Comrade Minister. A pleasure. Yes, education with production is a sound maxim of socialist endeavour. And you will agree I think, Dr Gumbeze, so is growth with equity. Ah, excuse me gentlemen, bring the oysters and the Mozambican prawns. Yes, thank you, Thomas. As I was saying, gentlemen, there is no such thing as construction without sound thinking. May I therefore propose a toast to a writer of no mean talent, Zimbabwe-born and bred. Gentleman: To Dambudzo Marechera!" [*He stops. Thunderous applause*] Hey, Mupangani komadam vako Mrs Nzuzu handiti anodai. [*He begins to parody Mrs Nzuzu's manner*] "Oh Comrade Drake, you are just delicious. I could eat you. You are a Turkish Delight. My husband the Comrade Minister actually said you are the cornerstone of our commercial enterprise. And Norman—I may call you Norman, Mr Drake, may I? And Norman my heartiest congratulations for winning the presidency of the Congress of Commerce." [THOMAS *begins to laugh. The others laugh. Suddenly the whole stage is laughing. Enter* ALFIE, *with bandaged bloody palm*] Ah blaz Alfie! Komuriright here!

ALFIE: So so. Zvirikufamba?

THOMAS: Zvirikufamba.

ALFIE: Mbuya, maswera sei?

MBUYA BERI: Ndaswera kana waswera wo.

ALFIE: Ndaswera. Iwe Thomas ndipezvipack sikisi. Ndipe one—the rest ipavanhu varimuno.

[MBUYA BERI *gives him some packs of Chibuku.*]

THOMAS: Nhasi makabata?

ALFIE: IBonus.

THOMAS: Konhasi dzine maplans api?

Alfie: Party ka pemuvheti wako. Uyu Drake. Mukadzi wangu arimo. Asi I think I will try Jobs later on. Handigoni kurara before six a.m.

BONZO [to ALFIE]: Rega ndikupe dhora rako ndisatindakanganwa.

ALFIE: Ha iChristmas box M'dhara. Imwayi. Muchazondimwisawo kana ndabroka.

THOMAS: Ruoko rwaitasei rine ropa?

ALFIE: Woman trouble. [Chuckles. Enter RAVEN and DICK running] The Bush Babies! How is the ear? Better I hope. And you Raven how is that index finger? Still giving trouble?

DICK: I don't have an ear—I mean I have it but not the one you mean.

RAVEN: What's wrong with my index finger?

ALFIE: I'm merely fooling. [Nods] Psychiatric greetings, not unlike the Rorschach Test.

DICK: The pedagogue. What next?

RAVEN: Sherlock Holmes.

DICK: The architect of the Zimbabwe Ruins.

Thomas: Vhigoroni.

DICK: Goncharov's "A Hero of Our Time."

RAVEN: The Statue of Liberty.

THOMAS: The sound of one hand clapping.

ALFIE: Add Allah to whatever is in your thoughts. Wow, I should note that down like a desperate Hamlet after the patriarch's ghostly visit.

RAVEN: A professor of linguistics suffering from sunstroke.

DICK: It isn't Eugene Ionesco.

RAVEN: I'm sick of this game.

ALFIE: Well, the answer is, It Could Not Have Been Einstein. [Groans from RAVEN and DICK] And crème de menthe to you too, Dick.

DICK: Crap!

RAVEN: Eau de Cologne

THOMAS: Sadza nesauti.

ALFIE: Too much of the edible and digestive. More stone.

Dick: Kurt Vonnegut

Raven: Philip K. Dick

Alfie: Raven wins! [*Drunken applause.*]

Majazi [*scornfully*]: Magames enyu aya anorewechii?

Alfie [*laughing*]: Ndeekunyepera chete. Hapana zviripo. Hey, Dick, you're not a drinking man. Get that opaque beer down. You know there are many good beer songs in ancient medieval Latin literature but they never taught us those when we were at school. [*Pause*] Say Tom, let's make up Shona ones, good beer-drinking Shona songs. Hmmmm. [*Sings*]:

> Hwahwa inyenyedzi murwizi
>
> Bvisai bhutsu pindai muKariba
>
> Garwe chidhakwa raruma chironda changu
>
> Yo-wee ndaona chiutsi chemheni!

Thomas: But iweM'dhara Alfie, unopenga here? Rega ndimbokupengesao nhasi. Mbuya Beri, tipeyiwo six Chibuku. Nemidzanga four.

Mbuya Beri: Urikupeya iwewe? Hapana zvemahara pano.

Thomas [*counting up the money*]: Motihandina mari inini? Iyoka. Comrade Drake andipawo bonus futi, mukoma Alfie.

Dick [*in hesitant Shona*]: Mbuya, ndipeyi matatu.

Mbuya Beri: Ah uyu murungu anoziva Shona?

Majazi: Anoitaura zvakaoma.

Mbuya Beri [*in hesitant English*]: You want three Chibuku?

Dick [*nods*]: Eh.

Mbuya Beri [*giving him*]: Ndovarungu vatinodaka. k,asi nyika yafamba. Inonzichii iweThomas?

> [Dick *and* Raven *drink.*]

Thomas: Reconciliation.

Mbuya Beri [*tasting the word as though it was very sweet*]: Re-con-ci-lia-tion. Ndizvozvo?

Thomas: Ndizvo. Ko M'dhara Bonzo pano hapana rufu. Ridzai mbira: mofunga kuti yakagadzirwa kuti ingo gara chete isingaridzwi?

Bonzo [*grumbling*]: Mbira hainzwanani nezita reChirungu.

71

THOMAS: Ibvaipo, M'dhara.

BONZO [*playing and singing*]:

> Rimwe zuwa rematombo nemagetsi
>
> Mbavha dzichakarara dissident ririmujeri
>
> Mukadzi akabika seven days muchikari chemoto.

[CHORUS]: Basa rawanda mumunda

> Huyai doro iri upenyu

ALFIE: Ngatipe makorokoto kunevana awa. [BONZO *is playing softly. To* RAVEN] Muchato wenyu urikutogadzirwa zvinoizvi na Comrade Drake naamai nababa vako. Thomas! Open those packs, man. I don't come here to drink molten coal from Hwange. [*Toasting* DICK *and* RAVEN]: Ngatimwe kadoro aka kune awa vaviri vanodanana nekutsvodana—vaya vanonzi nevakuru venyika. The Future of Zimbabwe!

ALL [*in Shona, English, Ndebele, Nyanja, etc.*]: THE FUTURE OF ZIMBABWE!!

CURTAIN

The Servants' Ball

ENGLISH TRANSLATION*

Characters:
Norman Drake
Thomas
Sarah
Mupangani
Majazi
Mbuya Beri
Bonzo
Alfie
Dick
Raven

Place: The servants' quarters at NORMAN DRAKE's residence in Harare, Zimbabwe.

Time: Any time between twilight and midnight.

---

* For expressions used in Zimbabwe only, see Glossary.

SCRAPIRON BLUES

The stage is the whitewashed half interior and entrance way to the servants' quarters at NORMAN DRAKE'S *residence. A log serves as a bench for the guests. A wheel-less bicycle leans against the wall, rusting.* BONZO *the servant from next door is sitting on the log drinking kachasu from a Mazoe bottle. He is playing a mbira and occasionally singing:*

> Hii-iiye-iiye friends
> The white men have died, we have taken the land
> Hii-iiye-iiye the land has gone
> Let's go to war.

[*On the bench also are* THOMAS, MUPANGANI, SARAH, MAJAZI. *They are drinking Chibuku from packets. In the half interior of the room, sits* GRANNY MBERI, SHEBEEN *queen, hunched over her sewing machine and selling kachasu and Chibuku. A dog barks. Other dogs from every quarter bark in reply. As they do so,* NORMAN DRAKE'S *voice is heard calling out to* THOMAS, *the cook-houseboy*]: THOMAS! THOMAS! HEY THOMAS!

THOMAS [*cursing*]: Can't a man have a rest? I have been working the whole fucking day and now I can't even sit for five minutes without that slave-driver howling for me. [*Loudly to* DRAKE] YES, BAAS! [*Hastily gets to his feet.*]

DRAKE'S voice: WHERE THE HELL ARE YOU, THOMAS?

THOMAS: BAAS! HERE BAAS!

DRAKE'S VOICE: TELL YOUR FRIENDS NOT TO MAKE TOO MUCH NOISE!

THOMAS: YEE-ES, BAAS [*Resuming his seat*] I suppose having this job is something, but sometimes it's too much, man. This boss is all right, but he holds too many parties. Tomorrow there will be hundreds of empties, thousands of cigarette stubs and the ashtrays will be overflowing. In the kitchen there'll be millions of greasy dishes, burned pots and all kinds of stains on the walls. These white people and the chefs really have a good time, but they should think about who cleans up the mess after them. [*Drinking*] Me!

MAJAZI: Granny Mberi, can you please play that record "Thick Tea". [*To* BONZO] Stop playing that lousy thing of yours.

BONZO: Who is mumbling things I can't hear? 'cause if I hear the sell-out who is talking that rubbish I shall fix him.

MAJAZI: Oh, come off it. The kachasu you're drinking is giving you funny ideas, old man.

GRANNY MBERI: Majazi, wash your face before you open your mouth. Are you not ashamed of yourself? Bonzo is old enough to be your father's father. [*Pause.*] You young people of today are just a load of shit thrown in the way of us older people. We can't even walk without fear of treading on your shit.

THOMAS: You are really talking through your arse, old lady. How can you imagine it's us, the youth, who are the future of Zimbabwe?

BONZO: What future are you talking about? Is there any future in the minimum wage?

MAJAZI: But you, old man, can you recall that before Independence you were getting paid only four dollars per month? But you are now being paid fifty dollars a month. And you are not even married. Your white employers are giving you free accommodation and food. You can afford to drink kachasu, so why are you talking about having no future?

BONZO: Leave me alone, young man. I mind my own business. [*He plays the mbira.*] Sarah, stand up and dance for us.

> [SARAH *stands, beams at everyone, begins to sway. She does not so much sing as recite the following words*]:
>
> I have washed up the dishes
> The white man has gone away
> I have swept the house
> The missis is drunk

[CHORUS]:
> Give me my minimum wage
> I have no food at home
> Give me my minimum wage
> The house is clean and things have changed.
> Give me my minimum wage
> I say give me my minimum wage
> Are you deaf, I say
> Give me my minimum wage

75

Give me my minimum wage

I say, give me my minimum wage

BONZO: Wirrrrrrr—Let's go, let's go

SARAH: Give me!

ALL: My minimum wage!

SARAH: I say give me!

ALL: My minimum wage

SARAH: I have cleaned the toilet

I have polished the bathroom

I have fed meat to the dog

I have removed the breakfast plates

Are you deaf, I say!

ALL: My minimum wage

SARAH: Give me

ALL: My minimum wage

[GRANNY MBERI *is nodding to the rhythm over her sewing machine; she is humming stitching away.* BONZO *is playing his mbira as if he is in a hypnotic trance.* THOMAS *is dancing, the rest joining in, humming, ululating, exploding epithets of glee. As the song ends.,* BONZO *starts another on his mbira and* SARAH *automatically improvises the words*]:

SARAH: Drink beer the house is on fire

Drink paraffin, this is the end of the year

Drink maheu this is the end of the road

[CHORUS]: These days killing each other

And showing love for each other

Fighting with our fists

Welcome only what you know

Kiss problems in broad daylight

In the evening I will meet you in bed

[CHORUS]: These days killing each other

And showing love for each other

Fighting with our fists

[BONZO *as if possessed, erupts in grunts, deep bass grunts*]: HO OO WoWo Ho-oo WO WO.

SARAH: Whoring is not witchcraft

A good heart

Death is not painful

They have gone home

I have seen Vhigoroni

Someone has parked into her in the bush

The missis has gone to bed

I have switched off the lights

[CHORUS]:   I dreamt of the devil

He had put whitewash on the door

I have noted in my book

The learned eye

[CHORUS]:   I dreamt of the devil

He had put whitewash on the door

The ant has fallen into the milk

Smith is bathing in Kariba

I dreamt of the devil

He had put whitewash on the door

The rain has refused to fall

Put your hands and your feet together

Give me coffee I am thirsty

MAJAZI: Bonzo, tell me this, are your white employers kids? Or are they mad?

BONZO: Where have you seen a white man who is not insane?

MAJAZI: My white men are not mad; they only eat cat's eggs.

THOMAS: It does not matter how these whites behave as long as they give you your money.

BONZO: What I don't like are the black chefs. They make you work like an ox in the field.

GRANNY BERI: You have to be careful with them. You may not be paid for three months in a row. And they also bring some of those relatives of theirs who do not know how to use a toilet.

THOMAS: That type makes your life one long misery. They will wake you up at five in the morning and you will only finish work after midnight. Me—I'll never work for a black person. They are misers. And they will really oppress you. Where is that fellow Mupangani?

MUPANGANI: He is here.

THOMAS: You work for these mad black people. Tell us about it.

MUPANGANI: You are the people who get the world wrong. Human beings are no different whether they are whites or blacks. These days there are regulations which lay out our conditions of service. If an employer does not treat you right you can report him to the labour ministry.

THOMAS: But you are just a sell-out because you work for those fellows for fifteen hours a day. They do not even give you a day off. I am sure you have run away now in order to take a little rest. And they are so insensitive that they only pay you the bare minimum wage only, and not a cent extra.

MAJAZI: But what sort of employer is your white man, Thomas?

THOMAS: Mine is a real comrade. We shout at each other. We also share jokes. We get angry at each other. We crack jokes. He pays me ninety dollars a month. And he allows me to run my shebeen here. You can ask Granny Beri.

GRANNY BERI: Comrade Drake, he is a really nice person. He does not bother us. He does not interfere if we are doing our own thing. He doesn't bother us. Aren't you enjoying yourselves now? Do you see anything wrong with that?

BONZO: Granny, give me some more kachasu for thirty-five cents.

GRANNY BERI: Give me your cup.

BONZO [gives her the cup]: Fill it right up to the brim. Do you think I was born yesterday?

GRANNY BERI: If you are drunk you are drunk Bonzo. Talking is not the same as farting. You Majazi, where is your guitar?

MAJAZI: Right here.

GRANNY BERI: Play it then. [She gives BONZO his cup of kachasu.]

MAJAZI [starts needlessly tuning his guitar and singing]:

THE SERVANTS' BALL (ENGLISH TRANSLATION)

Those who went to fetch firewood don't come back
Only the stars celebrated the wake
Those who have been successful in the past get away from here
Our troops are our future for tomorrow
You mother of the children the sun has set
Come into the blankets I am cold
The moon has inherited the place of the sun
The white one comes from Machipisa
The red birds sing in the evening
The heart has been hurt and the tree has fallen
Come all of you to the meeting
Come, come, come all of you

BONZO: H0-00 WoWo Ho-oo W0 W0.

MAJAZI: Come, come, come
Come to the meeting
GRANNY BERI [*ululates shrilly.*]

BONZO: The baboon's screams
Do not run the country!

THOMAS: Shake - shake!

MAJAZI: Come come come!

BONZO: The baboon's screams
Down with it and forward with ours. [*In a frenzy over his mbira.*]

DRAKE'S VOICE: THOMAS!

THOMAS: BAAS!

DRAKE: WHERE IS THAT WOODEN CORKSCREW I BROUGHT FROM EUROPE?

THOMAS: IN THE KITCHEN. THE SECOND DRAWER FROM THE BLUE ONE!

DRAKE: OKAY. [*Pause*] THOMAS!

THOMAS: BAAS!

DRAKE: I'VE GOT A CRATE OF BEER FOR YOU. COME AND GET IT BEFORE I DRINK IT!

THOMAS [*hastily*]: DON'T DARE DRINK IT, BAAS! I'M COMING. [*Exit.*]

GRANNY BERI [*smirking*]: You see that. Thomas is such good friends with his white man.

He is given beer. He is given free food. There is nothing he goes without. Comrade Drake is a real comrade.

THOMAS [*enters carrying a crate of beer. He puts it down by* GRANNY BERI.] Neo-colonialism is intoxicating.

MAJAZI: Neo what?

THOMAS: The beer we are getting here is what neo-colonialism is all about.

BONZO: Thomas, tell us, is this real English you are talking or are you just fooling us?

THOMAS: What do you know, old man?

BONZO: Talk in Shona if you are with Shona speakers. Talk in English if you are with English speakers. This showing off does not work at all.

THOMAS: You are just being jealous. None of you are educated. Leave us educated folks to show off our knowledge. Isn't that so, old boy?

BONZO: You are not really educated. All you do is mimic the way your white man talks. Does talking someone else's language really work?

MAJAZI: There you have a point old man.

GRANNY BERI: Get off all of you, what harm has my son done? Isn't he the one who is giving you beer and letting you enjoy yourselves here?

MAJAZI: It's his neo-colonialism. If he was giving it to us for free I would understand. But he is charging us fifty cents for a packet of Chibuku. Thirty-five cents for a small cup of kachasu. Four cents for one cigarette. Thomas, you are just as smart as your boss. All the money we work for ends up here when we pay for your beer.

GRANNY BERI: What are you talking about? Did we invite you? Isn't it that you come here of your own free will?

MUPANGANI: Old man Bonzo, when will you finish mending my shoes? You have had them for three months now. And I have paid you already.

BONZO: Come and get them tomorrow. How can you ask me about my job here. Do you think I mend shoes in a shebeen? Not me! You have not come to my place since the day you left your shoes. My white man has even approached me wanting to know whose shoes were giving off such a bad smell. I just kept quiet about it.

MUPANGANI: My shoes smelling! Are you trying to make fun of me, old man?

SARAH: Oh shut up, Mupangani. Why do you bother with the old man. You must know

him by now. [*Pause*] Old man Bonzo, play your mbira and let us enjoy ourselves.
I want to sing.

Bonzo [*chuckling*]: Right. (*He plays. As usual* Sarah *improvises the words*):

What have I done my love?

Our forest is on fire

What have I done my love

Today's gossip is tomorrow's mountains

What have I done my love

The baboon has eaten cow dung in Glen Norah

Aren't you ashamed, aren't you ashamed my love

Hunger's white teeth on the plain

Stay at home and fix the bicycle

Go to work, the dead have eyes

What have I done my love

Fists are no pledge for love

What have I done my love

You can kill but the soil does not die

[*She stops singing.* Bonzo *continues to play.*]

Thomas [*tipsy*]: White men! I'll show you white men. [*Begins parodying* Drake] "My dear
Comrade Minister. A pleasure. Yes, education with production is a sound maxim
of socialist endeavour. And you will agree, I think, Dr Gumbeze, so is growth with
equity. Ah, excuse me, gentlemen. Thomas, bring the oysters and the Mozambican
prawns. Yes, thank you, Thomas. As I was saying, gentlemen, there is no such
thing as construction without thinking. May I therefore propose a toast to a writer
of no mean talent—Zimbabwean-born and bred. Gentlemen: To Dambudzo
Marechera." [*He stops; thunderous applause*] Hey, Mupangani, your madam Mrs
Nzuzu does this, doesn't she? [*He begins to parody Mrs Nzuzu's manners*] "Comrade Drake, you are just delicious. I could eat you. You are a Turkish Delight. My
husband, the comrade minister, actually said you are the cornerstone of our commercial enterprise. And Norman, my heartiest congratulations for winning the
presidency of the Congress of Commerce." [Thomas *begins to laugh. The others*

laugh. Suddenly the whole stage is laughing. Enter ALFIE *with bandaged bloody palm*] Ah blaz Alfie, come right here.

ALFIE: So, so. How is it?

THOMAS: Okay.

ALFIE: How are you granny?

GRANNY BERI: All right, and you?

ALFIE: I am OK. Thomas, give me six packs. You can give me one and give the rest to the people in this room.

[GRANNY BERI *gives him six packets of Chibuku.*]

THOMAS: I see you are loaded today.

ALFIE: It is the bonus.

THOMAS: What are your plans for the evening?

ALFIE: Your boss Drake's party. My wife is in there. But I think I will try Jobs later on. I can't go to bed before six a.m.

BONZO [*to* ALFIE]: Let me give you the money I owe you before I forget.

ALFIE: Ha, Christmas box, old man. You can drink. You will buy me a drink one day when I am broke.

THOMAS: Why is your hand bleeding?

ALFIE: Woman trouble. [*Chuckles.*]

[*Enter* RAVEN *and* DICK *running.*]

ALFIE: The bush babies. How is the ear? Better, I hope. And you, Raven, how is that index finger? Still giving you trouble?

DICK: I don't have an ear—I mean not the one you mean.

RAVEN: What's wrong with my index finger?

ALFIE: I am merely fooling. [*Nods*] Psychiatric greetings, not unlike the Rorschach Test.

DICK: The pedagogue. What next?

RAVEN: Sherlock Holmes.

DICK: The architect of the Zimbabwe Ruins.

THOMAS: Vhigoroni.

DICK: Goncharov's "A Hero of our Time".

RAVEN: The Statue of Liberty.

THE SERVANTS' BALL (ENGLISH TRANSLATION)

THOMAS: The sound of one hand clapping.

ALFIE: Add Allah to whatever is in your thoughts. Wow, I should note that down like a desperate Hamlet after the patriarch's ghostly visit.

RAVEN: A professor of linguistics suffering from sunstroke.

DICK: It isn't Eugene Ionesco.

RAVEN: I am sick of this game.

ALFIE: Well, the answer is It Could Not Have Been Einstein. [*Groans from* RAVEN *and* DICK] And crème de menthe to you too, Dick.

DICK: Crap!

RAVEN: Eau de Cologne.

THOMAS: Sadza and salt.

ALFIE: Too much of the edible and digestive. More stone.

DICK: Kurt Vonnegut

RAVEN: Phillip K. Dick.

ALFIE: Raven wins! [*Drunken applause.*]

MAJAZI [*scornfully*]: What are your games in aid of?

ALFIE [*laughing*]: They are just for fun, just a pretence. There is nothing to them. Hey Dick, you are not drinking. Get that opaque beer down. You know there are many good beer songs in ancient medieval Latin literature, but they never taught us those when we were at school. [*Pause*] Say Tom, let's make up Shona ones, good beer-drinking Shona songs. Hmmm. [*Sings*]:

> Beer is a star in the river
>
> Remove your shoes and enter Kariba
>
> The crocodile is a drunk and it has bitten my small wound
>
> Oh I have seen the smoke from the lightning!

THOMAS: But Alfie, old man, are you mad? Let me make you crazy today. Granny Beri, give us six packets of Chibuku and four cigarettes.

GRANNY BERI: Are you paying for this? There is nothing for free here.

THOMAS [*counting up the money*]: Do you think I have no money? There you are. Comrade Drake also gave me a bonus today, Alfie.

DICK [*in hesitant Shona*]: Granny, give me three.

GRANNY BERI: Here is a white man who can speak Shona.

MAJAZI: He is very fluent.

GRANNY BERI [*in hesitant English*]: You want three Chibuku?

DICK [*nods*]: Eh.

GRANNY BERI [*giving it to him*]: These are the whites we like. But things have changed. What do you call that, Thomas?

> [DICK *and* RAVEN *drink.*]

THOMAS: Reconciliation.

GRANNY BERI [*tasting the word, as though it was very sweet*]: Re-con-ci-lia-tion. Is that it?

THOMAS: That's it. Old man Bonzo, there is no funeral here. Play your mbira, do you think it was made just to lie there without playing it?

BONZO [*grumbling*]: Mbira is not friends with white names.

THOMAS: Come off it, old man.

BONZO [*playing and singing*]:

> On a day of stones and electricity
>
> When thieves were still asleep and the dissident was in jail
>
> The woman brewed traditional beer in a small clay pot of fire

CHORUS:

> There is a lot of work in the field
>
> Come, this beer is life.

ALFIE: Let us congratulate these kids. [BONZO *is playing softly. To* RAVEN] Your wedding is being arranged right now by Comrade Drake and by your father and mother. Thomas! Open those packs, man. I don't come here to drink molten coal from Hwange. [*Toasting* DICK *and* RAVEN] Let us drink some beer to those who love each other and kiss each other—these are what the politicians call the future of Zimbabwe!

ALL: [*In Shona, English, Ndebele, Nyanja, etc.*] THE FUTURE OF ZIMBABWE.

CURTAIN

Alien to the People

Characters:
Mr Jack Boyd,
Mrs Jane Boyd
BOBBIE, their son
LESLEY, their daughter
TINORWA, a neighbour
WHITNEY, a neighbour
HENRY, a friend of Jack
Various citizens, neighbours.

Place: The Boyds' veranda and sitting-room in a new Harare low-density suburb.

Time: The near future.

The Boyds' veranda and sitting-room. Enter BOBBIE *and* LESLEY, *supporting each other;* LESLEY *is sobbing and angry.*

BOBBIE [*warning*]: Now, don't make a fuss. You're not the first or last girl to be called a bitch. Just don't let mum and dad know. Okay?

LESLEY: Bobbie. . .

BOBBIE [*smiling softly*]: You know I love you. That's why I beat the guy up when he insulted you.

LESLEY: But won't they gang up on you when you have to go to school? You know they always lie in wait for dad when he is going to work.

BOBBIE [*defiantly*]: Dad is a fighter. Dad can take care of himself. [*Draws himself up*] I am a fisticuffer. Can take care o' m'self, Les. You saw what I did with that guy.

LESLEY [*doubtfully*]: But what about mom—what about me? I mean when you and dad are away somewhere.

BOBBIE [*thoughtfully*]: That could be a problem. [*Seriously*]: Do you know dad's given mom a gun?

LESLEY: A gun. . .?

BOBBIE: Yeah. A revolver. For when *they* come to attack the house when he's at work. [*Imitating his father*]: You're learning kid. It's fear teaches you your deepest self-respect. Your *own* deepest self-regard.

LESLEY: I never know what father means when he says that. [*Pause*] But couldn't we get away from this awful suburb or get out of the country? To somewhere we don't have to live fighting off the neighbours and their ghosts?

BOBBIE: I know what you mean. [*Slowly*] But even if there were somewhere to go we don't have the money. Daddy's broke as it is.

LESLEY [*without thinking*]: He's African like them—that's why we'll never get anywhere. He's only a nigger, a kaffir. [BOBBIE *slaps her twice. She screams*] Mama! Mama! [JANE BOYD *rushes in, separates them, wanting to know what the matter is.*]

BOBBIE [*furious*]: She said—she said dad's a nigger, a kaffir, an African!

JANE: But Lesley, I've told you over and over that he isn't. . .

LESLEY [*screaming*]: HE IS! I HATE YOU! I HATE HIM!

BOBBIE: You little bitch. . .!

[JACK BOYD, *his overall torn and face bleeding, has come in from the other side of the veranda. He leans on the beam and takes out from his deep pocket a rumpled parcel.*]

JACK: SHUT UP! [*They freeze. Softly*] Lesley. . .

LESLEY: . . .yes daddy?

JACK: I brought you something. Something you always asked me to get. Remember?

LESLEY [*thinks, then brightens*]: It isn't. . .? [JACK BOYD *nods.*]

JACK: Catch! [*He throws, and she catches the parcel. As she rips it open, he extracts from his pockets two other parcels*] That's for you Bobbie. Catch! [*Pause*] Jane, yours will break if I throw it. Come here. [*She does*] It's just a little thing but these are lean times for the heart, yours and mine. You kids go inside. [*Pause.*] We—ll, how are you Jane?

JANE [*taking out a porcelain vase from her parcel*]: It's beautiful, Jack. [*Kisses him.*].

JACK: Careful, you'll get blood on your lips. On your—shit Jane you're as wonderful looking as ever.

JANE: Sit down—I'll go get the first aid kit. [*Over her shoulder, as she turns to go out*] Who was it ambushed you this time?

JACK [*tired, nods to the left offstage*]: Tinorwa, our neighbour. I just can't figure out what he's got against me.

JANE [*steadily*]: Jack, are you blind?

JACK: I love you and I can see you.

JANE [*more steadily*]: It's *me* he's got against you. [JACK *is about to say something but she silences him with a gesture*] Wait. I'll get the first aid kit. [*Exits.*]

[*Children's voices are heard off-stage singing*]:

Football Piggy

Titball Tsitsi

Behind the bush

Kiss kiss kiss

JANE [*offstage*]: Will you two shut up. This is not a brothel.

BOBBIE: A brothel is where Lesley belongs.

JANE [*offstage*]: I suppose you are her pimp.

[*Voices fade. Enter* WHITNEY.]

WHITNEY: Hello Mr Boyd. I hope I'm not disturbing you.

JACK: Not unless you've come to make another disturbance, Mr Whitney.

WHITNEY [*smiling thinly*]: No. Actually I've come to save you from one.

JACK: What do you mean?

WHITNEY: May I sit down? [*Jack nods*] This heat—a drink would be in order, don't you
think?

JACK [*rising, going to the bar in the sitting-room*]: What will you have?

WHITNEY: A cold beer

JACK [*opening the bottles at the bar*]: That's all I've got. [*Comes out, hands him a glass.
Silence for first tentative sips*] Now, what disturbances have you come to save me
from? As you can see I've just met one coming from work.

WHITNEY [*smiles*]: You are a hard man to talk to, Mr Boyd.

JACK [*drinks; then, calmly*]: Come to the point, Mr Whitney.

WHITNEY: Right. I'll give it to you straight from the shoulder. [*Pause*] They want you to get
out of this neighbourhood.

JACK: Who? And why?

WHITNEY: All of us. Your presence is stirring up trouble here. The blacks don't want you.
The whites don't want you.

JACK: Me, or me and my family?

WHITNEY: The lot. [*Pauses. Drinks thoughtfully*] You know, Mr Boyd, you don't belong
here. This community only holds together because certain niceties, certain sub-
tleties, are observed by both the blacks and the whites. I have lived here in Zimbabwe for a long time; was born and raised here in fact, and I've seen all the political
changes right up to now in the eighties. Politics change but people here do not
change. People here have always observed certain rules about relationships between the races. [*Pause*] Politically and legally we all have the same rights—those
are the results of political changes on our public life. [*Significantly*] Right now I
am talking about people's privacies, their right to a certain security of private codes,
those private certainties which give the individual an identity different from the

public image. [*Pause*] You have infringed on those certainties and the community wants you to go. [*Silence.*]

JACK: Have you finished?

WHITNEY [*smiling*]: No. [*Takes out sheets of paper*] If you take a look at these papers you will see how serious all this is and I think you will take the sensible course. [*Gives Jack the papers*] You will see it's been signed by the majority of the residents of this suburb. [*Pause*] They mean you and your family no harm. They merely want to preserve the tranquillity which was there before your—er—sudden arrival. But [*sternly*] if you refuse to move, they have delegated me to tell you that there will certainly be trouble.

[JACK and WHITNEY *have not seen* JANE *freeze and listen from just within the sitting-room. She is carrying the first aid kit.*]

JACK [*looking up from the papers*]: What sort of trouble have I and my family caused?

WHITNEY: To you it may seem a trifling matter. But to us it's now only the little things we've got to preserve dignity.

JACK: In what little things have I offended, Mr Whitney?

WHITNEY: For instance, you and your wife have been seen several times walking arm in arm to the shopping centre.

JACK: What's wrong with that?

WHITNEY [*relentlessly*]: Wearing nothing but swimming gear and hers is practically non-existent.

JACK: But, Mr Whitney, there's nothing wrong. . .

WHITNEY: The blacks think you are showing off to them that you are [*leering*] screwing a white woman. And the whites think you are deliberately tweaking their nose and rubbing it in shit. Oow! [JANE *has hurled the first aid kit at his head and is bearing down on him. He retreats spilling his beer, breaking his glass. He exits but can be heard from offstage*] You give me no alternative! You'll regret it.Who are you? L et me go!

VOICES OFF: I will not. Let's see what you're running away from. Come on!

[*Enter* HENRY, *holding* WHITNEY *in an armlock.*]

HENRY: Jack, Jack, what's going on here?

JACK/JANE: Henry!

HENRY: Who's this fellow?

JACK: Whitney. Let him go. He's got some lunatic petition to throw us out of here.

HENRY [*taking the papers from* JACK, *glancing at them, then at* WHITNEY]: The petition. That's what I came about. [*Releases* WHITNEY, *almost spitting on him*] You. . .fuck off. Beat it.

WHITNEY: But you, you're white—you should understand.

HENRY: Precisely. Now get out of here. [*Shoves him off-stage. Wipes his hands as though he'd been holding a snake*] Phew, Jack, any beer around? I've only brought that sickening brandy I bought in Beira. [*Takes out two bottles from his jacket*] Better add them to the stock at the bar. [*As* JACK *does so*] I need not ask how you are Jane. I can see.

JANE: When did you get back?

HENRY: Couple of hours ago. Haven't even been home yet.

JANE: But Marie will worry.

HENRY: I phoned her from town. Told her I was going to check on you. Heard the rumours as soon as my plane touched ground. About the trouble you've got here. I'd dropped into Meikles and there was this group of Rhodies muttering diabolical threats about you and Jack and the kids. [*Accepting a beer from* JACK] Thanks. Have they started or was that Whitney the beginning?

JACK: It's been rumbling for a few weeks now.

HENRY: Did that Whitney bloody you like that? Better go wash it off.

JANE [*as* JACK *goes off to wash*]: No, that was much earlier on his way from work. Some blacks in the neighbourhood.

HENRY: Blacks. But I would have thought they would defend him from the likes of Whitney.

JANE: It's not as simple as that. It's like we've become aliens of the people. Or they are trying to make us become like that. An alien growth on their black and white skins. I don't know if I can stand it for much longer, Henry. [*Pause*] Lesley is becoming terribly confused. I don't think she knows whether she loves or hates Jack. One moment she's calling him nigger, kaffir; the next she is hugging him, kissing him, calling him daddy. I don't know about Bobbie. He's mature for his age. And you know what that means when combined with all that terrible sensitivity which adolescence entails. [*Pause*] He gets into fights every day but he tries to hide it from me. Like trying to explain a black eye by saying he ran into a lamp post. Or that the blood on his shirt is from the biology dissection class. [*Smiles wryly*] Sometimes I wish I had his courage; though it's a courage that sees the whole world as The Enemy. And you know that kind of toughness arises from a horrifying terror of the world.

HENRY [*nods*]: You don't know this country very well, do you?

JANE: No. [*Thoughtfully*] But it's always been like this wherever we've tried to make a home. It started in London—first my parents more or less disowned me; then most of my friends gradually shed me from their skin. It became very difficult to make new friends or just acquaintances. You see, whoever you were with you were always wondering what they were thinking. A whore, an easy lay, a communist fanatic—everyone seemed or looked like they thought Jack and I were weirdos. Loonies. The leers, the pitying side-glances. It was Jack who gave me strength. I can't say how, but it's a silent torn-out self-respect. Nothing that wants to live can touch it. Everything that wants to die is attracted to it. [*Pause*] I'll get you another beer.

HENRY [*rising*]: I'll get it. You sit down—you've been standing since I arrived.

    [*As he is getting the beer, lighting a cigarette, she continues*]:

JANE [*softly*]: It's terrifying, Henry. It's made me understand exactly how a mercenary becomes what he is. . . If he is to survive, an alien of the people must become absolutely mercenary.

HENRY [*drawing on his cigarette*]: And the gain?

JANE [*laughing bitterly*]: The terrible beauty of a desperate peace of mind. Accepting nothing, rejecting everything, but always the eye of the storm. The still centre of a cyclone.

HENRY: That comes close to Buddhism.

JANE: Call it what you like, but it has the lethal potential of a split atom.

HENRY: Yet you're afraid.

JANE: Not for myself. I'm afraid for Jack and the kids.

HENRY: Ah, the kids—where are they?

JANE: I'll get them. [*Exits through sitting-room.*]

HENRY [*looking straight ahead, sighs*]: Christ!

              [*Enter TINORWA, drunk.*]

TINORWA: Hi!. . .You're not Jack.

HENRY: Mr Boyd—no. He's inside. I'm Henry.

TINORWA: I'm Tinorwa. Know what that means, white man?

HENRY [*without hesitation*]: It means we fight!

TINORWA: I was in the Struggle. But we're still fighting traitors, sellouts.

HENRY: There's such a thing as overdoing it. Of course with South Africa's programme of destabilising the front-line states, it's a necessity.

TINORWA [*slyly*]: What do you know about destabilising?

HENRY: As a journalist I cover some of those events.

TINORWA [*quickly*]: Who do you write for?

HENRY: For ZIANA and sometimes for *The Herald* on a freelance basis. Here. [*Throws him a card*] That's my accreditation.

TINORWA [*disappointed*]: So you are a comrade. . .

              [*Silence.*]

HENRY: What do you do apart from getting drunk and fighting people?

TINORWA [*proudly*]: I'm training to become a magistrate.

HENRY: Christ!

TINORWA: That's me. A magistrate.

              [*Pause.*]

HENRY: What do you want to see Jack for?

TINORWA [*in a harsh whisper*]: He's a sell-out.

HENRY: Look here—what's all this about. [*Realising*] Are you one of the bastards who beat him up?

TINORWA [*drawing a pistol*]: Keep your distance, comrade. [JANE *is frozen in the sitting-room doorway; the kids are peering from behind her*] We don't want you, comrade. We want Jack.

HENRY: I'm from the Ministry of Information. Show me your credentials.

TINORWA: Shut up. [*He sees* JANE, *his glance lingers on her*] My dear Jane!

HENRY [*kicks the gun spinning away, and fells him with a karate chop. The kids are shouting. He picks up the pistol, examines it*]: It's a Tokarev. [*He looks down at the body, searches it, finds and scrutinises a plastic identity card*] I'm not sure but it could be a forgery.

JACK [*rushing in as he struggles into a Sierra Leonean shirt*]: What the hell's going on?

HENRY [*pointing down*]: Isn't he the one who attacked you?

JACK: That's him, yes. What did he want? He's not dead, is he?

HENRY: Said you were a sell-out. No, he's not dead. I only tapped him though I'd have done a real whack. [*Casts a puzzled look at* JANE] You saved me but I don't know how.

JANE [*grimly*]: I gave him a full look of lust. He's been waiting for it for a long time.

HENRY [*looks quizzically at her and* JACK]: It's like that, is it. Well. One learns something new every minute. [*Grabs the kids*] And how're you, Bobbie—Les? [*Draws them into the sitting-room*] Tell me what's new—what have you been doing with yourselves?

[HENRY *and the kids talk, while on the veranda.*]

JACK: What was that you said, Jane?

JANE: A full look of lust.

JACK: That's what I thought you said. [*Slaps her hard.*]

JANE: Not in front of the kids.

JACK: They were there when you gave that [*points at* TINORWA] a "full look of lust". [*Slaps her again.*]

JANE: I told you the next time you hit me I would. . .

JACK [*slaps her twice*]: You would what?

JANE [*swiftly kicks him in the crotch; as he crouches, lands him an uppercut which sends him sprawling backwards*]: This. . .THIS!

[LESLEY *has run out of the sitting-room and is ineffectually raining blows on* JACK; BOBBIE *is cursing and struggling with* JANE *who finally throws him sobbing onto the floor.* HENRY *is opening another bottle of beer, lighting another cigarette, and reading the names on the petition. A loud-hailer offstage*]: ARE YOU COM-

ING OUT OR DO WE MOVE IN? [*Pause. Loud-hailer from the audience*]: MR
AND MRS BOYD THIS IS NO MERE THREAT WE MEAN EXACTLY WHAT WE SAY!

HENRY [*grabs the phone, dials*]: I'll call the police!

LESLEY: Oh daddy, daddy, I'm sorry.

JACK [*getting up painfully*]: It's all right, my darling. [*She gets off him*] Now, listen, you
remember that hiding place I made for you? [LESLEY *thinks.*]

HENRY: I can't get any response. I think they've cut the telephone wires.

TINORWA [*getting up, dazed*]: Where the hell is my gun? [*Sees* JANE] Sorry, sorry.

LESLEY [*kisses her father and dashes into the house*]: I remember, daddy!

HENRY [*banging the phone down*]: We're cut off.

BOBBIE [*dashes into the sitting-room, dashes out brandishing a poker*]: I'll kill them,
daddy. They won't touch you—I'll kill them. Kill them for you!

JACK [*grabs* BOBBIE]: Remember what I told you about tactics? [BOBBIE *nods*] That's what
we've got to do. Tactics. Is the boiling oil ready, Jane? And in place? Good.

HENRY [*to* TINORWA]: Here's your gun and your I.D.

TINORWA [*to* JACK]: I'm a security officer. It's my duty to maintain law and order. I'll go and
try to speak to them. Who's got guns to cover me if they go berserk? [JACK *and* JANE
nod] Now remember, as far as the law goes you have the right, the legal right to
kill or maim in defence of your life and property. Good luck.

BOBBIE: We're mercenaries. Mother said so, good luck.

TINORWA: Good luck, kid. [*Exits.*]

> [*The rest deploy themselves at various points on the veranda and at the
> sitting-room windows. Silence.*]

LESLEY [*entering, cross*]: Daddy, how long am I to stay in that hole? It's getting hot.

> [*Several shots ring out.* LESLEY *falls dying.* TINORWA *leaps over the veranda
> parapet, rolls over. Blood is pouring out of his left shoulder as he fires
> marksmanlike.* JANE, *her lips bleeding from biting them unconsciously, also
> maintains steady fire.* BOBBIE *throws away his poker, rushes to his sister, heaves
> her into his arms, a tracery of bullets cutting a swathe towards him.* HENRY *leaps,
> bumping* BOBBIE *who is holding* LESLEY, *into safety, but is himself shot in the throat.*]

TINORWA [*his voice a harsh scream*]: Jack! Jack! Keep firing! With all this noise it's a matter of seconds before the army arrives.

    [*Even as he says it, the heavy drone of a helicopter approaches, and its demented scratching din shuts out all other noise. As the curtain closes slowly, the helicopter's searchlights break bright upon the audience.*]

CURTAIN

Killwatch

Characters:
First Watchman
Second watchman
Man
Woman

DAEMON

I walked all the way
Looking for Night's back door
It was locked it was barred
I heard you breathing...

I walked back all the way
Feeling for window and front door
There were none there were none
I heard you breathing

I combed my hair sparks flew
Revealing, stutteringly, grotesque
Human minds twisted in hideous pain
I saw you...

SCRAPIRON BLUES

SCENE ONE

In the park. A bench. A bush. A brass band playing in the distance. It is afternoon.
Summer. Enter WATCHMEN.

FIRST WATCHMAN [*consulting his watch*]: They will arrive any time now. Observe her closely.
I will concentrate on him. They are such an interesting couple.

SECOND WATCHMAN: I still don't see. . .

FIRST WATCHMAN: You are not supposed to. That is not part of the job at all. Don't worry,
you'll get used to it. At first, I used to ask questions myself. Then I found it doesn't
get the job done.

SECOND WATCHMAN [*thoughtfully*]: Who is he? [*Pause*] Who is she? Do they know you and
I are always watching?

FIRST WATCHMAN [*shaking his head*]: There you go again. I have told you already that the
moment we know them and they know us they are dead. They would have crossed
over to our side and that is dying. [*Grins*] I can't wait to greet them. Such an
interesting couple. You know they remind me of my younger days. I was in love
then. It was a day such as this. Bright. Laughter, music, somnolent, heady. . .

SECOND WATCHMAN: You? In love? I cannot imagine it. You are so. . .stern.

FIRST WATCHMAN: I know my duty, young man. I know my responsibilities. I am my job.
[*Waves at the sky and scene*] Do you see all this? It is a deliberate divine creation.
For it to stand and remain exactly as it is, the watchmen must watch. In their sleep,
in their waking, in their every moment, the watchmen must watch. Otherwise the
land, sea and sky will crack, boil and sunder and nothing but a tumult of chaos will
remain.

SECOND WATCHMAN [*boyishly*]: I would love to see that!

FIRST WATCHMAN: You're mad. Bonkers. Insane. You're off your fucking head.

SECOND WATCHMAN: I didn't mean. . .

FIRST WATCHMAN: Yes, I know you didn't. After all you've only just arrived this side. So I can
guess your spirits. . . I too when I started my tour of duty was like you, seeing my
complex nature hemmed in by this unshakeable structure. But early I learned the

pure simplicity behind all things—in a word, I learned to spell D-U-T-Y, to act DUTY, to think DUTY, to touch, smell, taste, see, and hear DUTY! [*Pause*] I don't suppose you understand that, but soon you will. We all learn in the end. How the foundation of all is only four letters. D-U-T-Y.

SECOND WATCHMAN [*sulkily*]: I'm not altogether an idiot.

FIRST WATCHMAN: I know. [*Smiling*] I teach you all this because I like you.

SECOND WATCHMAN [*startled*]: Really. You like me? [*Pause, happy, puzzled*] But, I thought. . .

FIRST WATCHMAN [*caressing* SECOND WATCHMAN]: I know what you thought. It hurt me. Your generation thinks mine has no feelings, no spontaneous outbursts of passion. But I can tell you we are no different from you and yours. [*Earnestly*] We fought hard to create all this, you see. I watched death and dying for years ravaging all this. It was a time of brutal sickness. You did not have to think but *knew, simply knew*, terror. It was terrible time. [*Pause*] That is why I do my duty to sustain the structure of all life.

SECOND WATCHMAN [*kissing him shyly*]: I did not understand. You are so good, so upright. [*Impulsively*] Let me kiss your feet!

FIRST WATCHMAN: It pains me to deny you that. Duty demands emotion step aside.

SECOND WATCHMAN: No! You said you liked me. [*Accusingly*] You said. . .

FIRST WATCHMAN: There is a moral foundation to the health of the landscape which in conscience—nothing but conscience—I cannot break.

SECOND WATCHMAN: There is nothing immoral about what I feel. It is such a joy. It is such an exaltation, it is so. . .

FIRST WATCHMAN: In years, the field between us is a great wasteland, you on one side, and I on the other. In the intrinsic virtues of which our duty is the chief among them, you are the North and I the South Pole. In emotional climate I am as deadly and as disciplined as the lightning which outspeeds its own thunder—I would tear you apart with passion. Let me once unleash what I feel for you and you'll scream and shriek, so painful the pleasure of our union.

SECOND WATCHMAN [*awed*]: Do I mean that much to you? Tell me again. Tell me.

FIRST WATCHMAN [*thrusting him down*]: We must watch. [*Pause*] Did I hurt you? I did not mean to.

SECOND WATCHMAN: I know what you did *not* mean.

> [*They exchange anguished looks.*]

FIRST WATCHMAN [*turning away*]: It is time. I can see them coming. Let us hide in this bush.

> [*They conceal themselves. Enter, from opposite wings of the stage,* MAN *and* WOMAN. *They hurl themselves into each other's arms. Hold for a minute; then* CURTAIN.]

SCENE TWO

Cafe Terrace. Gaily coloured tables. Sunlight. It is morning. SECOND WATCHMAN *has a pair of binoculars strung round his neck. They are drinking tea.* SECOND WATCHMAN *looks as though he has been crying or is about to.* FIRST WATCHMAN *sternly ignores this, talks as if there is nothing wrong in the world.*

SECOND WATCHMAN: First you wake me up at an ungodly hour. Then you try to make me feel a fool about the binoculars—after all we are watchmen and binoculars are for watching.

FIRST WATCHMAN: We are not watchmen in the literal sense.

SECOND WATCHMAN: In what other sense are we?

FIRST WATCHMAN: You would not understand. I am speaking of the universal structure. I am speaking of permanence. Of the fixed stars. Of the music of the spheres. I am speaking [*pained pause*] of you and I—especially of you. [*Tenderly*] I want to protect you. I want to shield you. I want to kiss you under the safe shadow of duty and responsibility. [*Pause*] You are your own hurt. You are your own worst enemy. I have been observing you these past few days and have noticed a dangerous tendency within you. I mean the spirit of rebellion. You must curb that. You must wring it out of you. If you persist in it I will have no choice but to report you. And you know I would rather perish in purgatory than ever give you hurt.

SECOND WATCHMAN: I? Rebellious? You must be joking.

FIRST WATCHMAN: I am not joking. And you know very well what I mean. I mean your impulsive indifference to anything outside your feelings. That, need I remind you, is subversive. [*Waves at the street and the sky*] If we let but one crack start in this glorious structure, all will tumble down in a whiplash of thunder.

SECOND WATCHMAN [*puzzled, awed*]: That would be very poetic, Dan.

FIRST WATCHMAN [*shocked*]: What did you call me? How did you find out my name? Tell me, you little fucking shit.

SECOND WATCHMAN [*afraid, puzzled*]: But you said I could call you Dan.

FIRST WATCHMAN: When and where?

SECOND WATCHMAN [*realising*]: Last night, when you. . .came into my bed.

FIRST WATCHMAN: I never came to your bed. I never told you to call me Dan. [*Threateningly*] Whatever happened last night, I never came to your bed. Never! [*Pause*] Do you understand? Never. [*Shaking* SECOND WATCHMAN'S *collar*] Did I ever come to your bed?

SECOND WATCHMAN: But —you did. I was so happy. . .

FIRST WATCHMAN: DID I EVER COME INTO YOUR BED?

SECOND WATCHMAN: Your body was inside my body. Your arms great chains tightening around me. Nothing existed but you inside me. . .

FIRST WATCHMAN [*incredulous, then angry*]: You must answer and answer correctly. DID I EVER COME TO YOUR BED?

SECOND WATCHMAN: You want me to say no you never came to my bed. [*Hurt*] But it was so good how can you and I deny that moment [*Seeing* FIRST WATCHMAN'S *face*] All right. [*Pause*] You never came into my bed. I made it all up. I made it all up. I made it up. I was lying through my teeth. I was giving you goat's wool. I was telling fibs. I was being a dzakutsaku to my own conscience. I was. . .

FIRST WATCHMAN: Shut up, you little twit! [*Pause*] Drink up your tea—it's getting cold.

SECOND WATCHMAN: But you have not touched yours for the last few minutes.

FIRST WATCHMAN: I'm your senior, in age and service. I have prerogatives.

SECOND WATCHMAN: I'm talking about tea for Christ's sake!

FIRST WATCHMAN: In every particular, however insignificant, there reside cold hard truths.

SECOND WATCHMAN: There is nothing to tea but water and a minor stimulant.

FIRST WATCHMAN: If you persist in being literal I will not be responsible for your. . .

SECOND WATCHMAN [*curiously*]: You do want to report me, don't you? [*Silence*] You want to report me, don't you? [*Silence. Standing up*] I know when I am not wanted.

FIRST WATCHMAN: Sit down, you fucking fool. [*Pushes him back into his chair*] I cannot explain very well. I love you. I fear for you. But I love and fear my duty more. [*Almost desperate*] Can you not see? Open your eyes wide—can you still not see, you, a watchman, can you not see?

SECOND WATCHMAN: Is that why you're so. . .brutal to me? Like making me deny last night with you ever happened. And you always talk to me as if I was a village idiot. You try to make me ashamed of my love for you. You make me question everything I feel is holy. And now you justify yourself by the argument of being two worlds in one body.

FIRST WATCHMAN [*resigned*]: You do not see at all.

SECOND WATCHMAN: In my own way I see you too clearly. I may not have much up here [*points to his head*] but [*points to his heart*] here I have something infinitely more worthwhile than all your eyes. [*Pause*] In the other world I was a scholar of note. I majored in mathematics and philosophy. Perhaps you have read some of my so-called controversial theories?

FIRST WATCHMAN [*distractedly*]: You must not tell me your personal details. That will put obstacles in our path. Even if I know you I cannot acknowledge it. It is not in the rules. [*Angry with himself*] You must not do that. It is not in the RULES!

SECOND WATCHMAN: But you told me your first name. And you told me something else too. Something. . .

FIRST WATCHMAN: What—I never—well, what am I supposed to have told you?

SECOND WATCHMAN [*hesitantly*]: You said. . .you said Duty was all nonsense and you said [*he waves at street and sky*] this was. . .was disgusting.

FIRST WATCHMAN [*unable to say anything—shocked, stutters*]: I - I - I. . .

SECOND WATCHMAN: Shut up, idiot! I will never report you. [*Kisses him*] Never. [*Pause*] Pick up your newspaper—here they come. [*Pretends to read his.*]

    [*Enter, from opposite wings of the stage,* MAN *and* WOMAN, *eyes only for each other. They embrace hungrily—there is a touch of sadness about the em-*

brace as though something in their lives had died and each wanted to console and love the other. Hold for a full minute until Curtain.]

SCENE THREE

The Cemetery. The Watchmen *are hiding behind a large tombstone. They watch as the* Man *and* Woman, *both dressed in black, enter carrying wreaths, holding on to each other, the* Woman *weeping silently. The* Man *and* Woman *approach a newly filled-in-grave, laying their wreaths. She convulses in sobs. He stands helplessly. It is a dark humid afternoon. Thunder rolls. The* watchmen *watch.*

Second Watchman: Emotions in another are always unconvincing. In fact they are utterly ridiculous. Don't you think?

First Watchman: I don't know. [*Pause*] In you they are and they are not. I want to laugh at you. Cry with you, muck about with you, and give you delicious pain. [*Pause*] It is a matter of life—and death.

Second Watchman: Were you afraid of it?

First Watchman: Of what? Oh, you mean death?

Second Watchman [*nods*]: What else could I mean in this [*he waves at the scene*] atmosphere?

First Watchman [*regards him curiously*]: I hated every minute of it. Even to think and remember it kills me a thousand times. [*Pause*] I envy them their world. I never wanted to leave it. There was so much I wanted to do, to feel, to think out for myself. There was so little. . . Here, on this side, everything is thought out for you. Here everything has been prescribed and defined to such a fine point you cannot be anything other than what you are supposed to be. It goes against the grain of all I was in their world. [*Nods at the mourning couple.*]

Second Watchman [*anxiously*]: I know so little about you. I want to know everything about you. So much. Your body, your mind, your dreams, your whole imagination. And when I know, I will still cry out demanding to know to the last ounce what I can never possibly ever know.

FIRST WATCHMAN [*touched*]: Your passion—I cannot possibly equal it. You make me feel unworthy of you. I mean there is, in the last resort, very little in all men. But life demands that we make a mystery of that little. You are more than a million riddles to me the closer and more intimate we become. . .what's that?

> [*The* MAN *and* WOMAN *are quarrelling. She picks up clods from the grave and hurls them at the* MAN *who stands there helplessly. He is pleading something but it is all incoherent.*]

MAN [*flinching from a blow on the cheek*]: Helga! Don't!

FIRST WATCHMAN: You see, it's all the same, whether here or there. It is all the same. [*Pause*] I think for the first time I have grasped the meaning of tragedy.

SECOND WATCHMAN: Oh—we learnt that at school. Something about pity and terror. A purging of our souls.

FIRST WATCHMAN: That is not what I meant. [*Silence, watches the* MAN *and* WOMAN] I long to greet them, to just go up to them and say "It is all right". I want to comfort them.

SECOND WATCHMAN: But that's not in the Rules.

FIRST WATCHMAN: Fuck the Rules!

SECOND WATCHMAN [*stunned, then a boyish shout, cheering*]: Hurrah! I knew you were not all old and stuffy.

FIRST WATCHMAN: Ssssshh, they'll hear you.

SECOND WATCHMAN: They'll only think we are ghosts.

FIRST WATCHMAN [*with resigned finality*]: We *are* ghosts.

SECOND WATCHMAN: I don't want to be a ghost. They scare everybody. I'm terrified of them.

FIRST WATCHMAN [*laughing*]: Get it into your head. You're a fucking ghost like me.

SECOND WATCHMAN: I don't want to be a fucking ghost. I don't care whether I'm one or not—I just don't want to be a fucking ghost! So there.

FIRST WATCHMAN: Okay, okay. [*With tender understanding*] That's what I felt too when I started my tour of duty. We are bound to this rung. With no hope of ascending or descending. [*Nods at the* MAN *and* WOMAN] They are our rung until their time comes. And it will come. Then we will be assigned to some other couples. That is the personal meaning of Hell for you and me. Having to watch couples eternally. [*Pause*] I'm sick of couples. I am sick of watching people living out the illusion that their feelings and emotions are permanent. Look at those two, dying of love—grieving for each other. [*Puzzled*] It's their little boy who has died isn't it?

SECOND WATCHMAN: Yes, Damien.

FIRST WATCHMAN: He should be coming along nicely into our world. Such a wretched idiotic churl of a child. [*Thoughtfully*] I never did like children. I consider them the inescapable permanent nightmare, a secret steel trap waiting all who believe in this illusion of love.

SECOND WATCHMAN [*hurt*]: You mean you don't believe in our love?

FIRST WATCHMAN: Of course I do. I meant. . .

SECOND WATCHMAN: You were politely telling me that my powerful feelings for you are all illusion. You were politely telling me that I am a child, that I do not understand, that I am a fool, that I am an ignorant riddle to all intelligent minds. . .

FIRST WATCHMAN: Oh don't start. Please, don't start.

SECOND WATCHMAN [*shouting at the top of his voice*]: I will—I will!!

[*The* MAN *and* WOMAN *jump into each other's arms, looking fearfully around them. They hastily, cautiously leave the cemetery, holding on to each other.*]

FIRST WATCHMAN [*caressing Second Watchman*]: I know I love you. Want you. If the only way possible to have you was by the total disruption of all this universe, I would take the irrevocable step, like Samson among the Philistines—we are living among Philistines. All these fucking Rules and Eternal Constitutions and bloody Duty. Even a Philistine would not design such rigidity for his worst enemy. And we have to be *like* this forever. [*Almost sobs, but stoically refrains from the luxury.*]

SECOND WATCHMAN: We have each other.

FIRST WATCHMAN [*embracing him*]: Yes! Yes! It is the one and finest thing of all. We may be the guardian spirits of wretched souls in love but we are also the owners of a love as tormenting and lurid as even the Devil—did he exist—cannot dream of.

SECOND WATCHMAN: Guardian angels—did you say we are guardian angels?

FIRST WATCHMAN [*grimly*]: Of a sort.

SECOND WATCHMAN [*puzzled*]: But we are not protecting that couple from anything.

FIRST WATCHMAN [*even more grimly*]: That's not our job. [*Pause*] I used the phrase "guardian angels" in a deliberately metaphoric or symbolic manner. We are something simpler but more deadly than so called guardian angels.

SECOND WATCHMAN: But what exactly are we supposed to do to them or for them?

FIRST WATCHMAN: The Rules say I must not tell you. The Rules say many things. So [*looks around and at the sky*] FUCK THE RULES. [*Pause*] You really want to know?

SECOND WATCHMAN [*nods*]: Yes.

[*Silence.*]

FIRST WATCHMAN: We are going to kill them.

SECOND WATCHMAN [*startled, terrified*]: What did you say?

[FIRST WATCHMAN *remains silent, turning into stone.*]

SECOND WATCHMAN [*whispering, on the edge of hysteria*]: Tell me you did not say it.. Please, you are just joking, fooling around, aren't you? We can't! I won't. There is not a place such a horror can happen. What have they done?

FIRST WATCHMAN [*turns away. Fixes his eyes on the newly filled-in grave, points at it. A hand is coming out of it, then a head, then the whole body of a small boy chuckling*]: Look!

CURTAIN.

First Street Tumult— More City Stories

First Street Tumult

SUNLIGHT stencilled her image in the big gleaming shopfront window. Like a photograph negative held up to the light, her image lingered among the pink harlequins dressed in velvet, silks, corduroy, lingered long and longingly among the latest fashions from London and Paris, a hazy gold-shot silhouette of a tall graceful Afro-crowned single woman, a teacher at Blake High School in Fourth Street, Harare.

It was early February; the days brutally hot and the nights a sudden, unexplained chill. It was late afternoon. She had just left the school.

Bright blue and gold-yellow figures criss-crossed her motionless image, each passing to and fro on secret assignments. She was in the First Street Mall; sharp watercolour strokes of pastel-shade people sliding gently in and out of each other; bright whorls of African cloth, Afghan jackets, Indian saris, and the odd English blazer and boater. A colourful tumult parading itself before the sun went down.

Some construction work was going on at the corner of First Street and Gordon Avenue—the strong skeletal scaffolding providing a modernist element to the too sunlight-clean Mall.

A white matron in a polka-dot finish was politely waiting for her poodle to finish its ablutions by a bright green lamp post. At the restaurant tables by the QV Pharmacy, young men and women were drinking coffee, sipping Coke, cajoling out of each minute the maximum fashionable gesture to entice, to enrapture.

The heat made you dozy. The languid late afternoon hour made you wish for anything but.

Up and down the Mall the dizzying, dazzling fresh linen—in the shop-windows and out here in the streets, casually walking to and fro—a concertina of human movement in the glass-shot sunbeams of fantasy.

She still had not moved. In the shop-window she was like a mosaic of colour on a new postage stamp. A still photograph from a film on the horror of commonplace events. A hastily scrawled drawing in a five-year-old's scribbling pad.

And there was that about her which reminded you of the blind man who, when cured, said he could see men like trees walking. She would not have been out of place in a painting by Monet; one of those boulevard scenes where the paint leaps at your ear rather than your eye, and the crowded delirium of people massed together at a dance, or at a spectacle, would split a ripe tomato slowly into two.

She was in no hurry to get back to her flat. There were too many silent and invisible things going on in it for her to seek its comforting texture. There was the light grey carpeted sitting-room, one wall of which was devoted entirely to her expensive and very complex but up-to-date hi-fi stereo system.

Another wall with its ceiling-high bookshelves was her library. An old but elegant mahogany desk, small but compact, casually graced the space immediately by the batik curtains of the big window. The chair was straightbacked, hard.

But in a riot of colour on the grey carpet was a throng of handmade cushions strewn carelessly everywhere; the effect being like that when a wanton child on a bright grey moonlight night throws all his favourite toys into the milk-grey sky.

In just such a way she had thrown all of herself at Dan.

She taught art: drawing, painting and sculpture. Life, form, were lines. Squiggly lines. Spiralling lines. Straight lines. Zigzag lines. Dotted lines. Squeezed, enmeshed, fused, entwined together to make shapes that became a mealie cob, a matchbox, a face struck down by grief.

Light and shadow too. It was terrifying the way in which a flicker of a shadow could transform a commonplace object into a horrible notion. As if the eyes of a portrait on the wall suddenly moved, making you hastily draw back, afraid and ashamed of being afraid.

In the same manner the fabric of day-to-day events—weaving its lines, its lights, its shades, through the texture of her moods and thoughts—would, like the sun, dip over the horizon of the things she took for granted and all would be eerie, a tale of twilight.

Ideas would split into unidentified atoms; known faces would doff their masks to reveal the flat, fleshless monotone underneath. Unblinking daylight would turn into dream. The freshly mowed grass would be the small print on her living contract. Green seedlings, suddenly the matter of the morrow.

It was no use saying: give me strength. It is not strength life needs. Neither weakness.

Would the open gateway, creaking with the fury of wind, star, and rain, continue to bang against the inside wall of her days making her listen too anxiously to her heartbeats, listen too anxiously to her indrawn and outdrawn breath, making her aware of how her arms swung whenever she walked, how the right foot lifted and the left foot prepared to take upon itself the pinnacle of her weight?

And would this have been the matter had the wanton child not cast her treasured toys into the piercing moonbeam glance of a passing stranger?

In the distance, an ambulance wailed, the siren going on and on. She was aware of it only as a submerged cry in her own consciousness.

At the corner of First Street and Speke Avenue a group of people were watching a chess game between a white man in safari shorts and a black man in jeans. The chess pieces were two feet high; the two had to walk onto the set to make their moves.

Twenty paces from this group, three Buddhist monks were holding forth on the wealth of the inner spiritual life of man; their audiences listened inscrutably. A young Swede was calmly taking pictures with her Instamatic.

In and out of the teeming, resplendent and gay crowd, police officers in neatly pressed khaki and brilliant white armbands strolled two by two looking seemingly at no one in particular. By the rose bushes near CT Stores a bearded Australian teacher was playing his violin, watched by two Norwegian girls who carried under their arms five canvas paintings which they were selling to any who cared to buy.

The sunlight, however hard it tried in the vivid shop-window glass, could not stencil the luminous tears streaking down her cheeks. She still had not moved. And still the harlequins had not moved an inch: their smiles were still three-and-a-half centimetres long.

There was no breeze to gently swirl the gold tincture of the radiant air. She was a sylph, caught in the effulgent halo of earth-shine; caught in the chiaroscuro of mood and mode, movement and stillness, the mezzotint of a subtropical February late afternoon.

And how all too late seemed her mood! Not a moment lost but had bound her with invisible twine to this spot.

A group of young university students, dressed in white chef's uniforms cycled into the Mall on a six-seater bicycle; cycled slowly round and round, ringing a Holy Communion bell, so tiny and tinkling it startled the polka-dotted lady's poodle.

At last they slowed to an undignified halt, half falling, so clownishly that the promenaders gasped and laughed and pointed with painted fingernails, and a squalling baby in mid-howl stopped crying and plugged its mouth with its thumb and stared.

Now the student chefs were taking out sheets of paper from their pockets and one by one reading their poems. They were poems, not of revolution or of struggles or of history or things political. They were poems to the sun and to the air and to the fire in people's hearts and to the stone which is the material of our strong houses.

They were simple, straightforward poems, sometimes elliptical, but with truth; the truth that resides in the material of manners on a late afternoon day when the sparrows and the doves and perhaps the chaffinches are tuning their instruments for the coming of twilight.

> I am what you see, said the cat.
> What you see is in your head.
> Am I in your head, or am I me.

And the fierce pulsing rays of the sun could not penetrate to the glittering secret tears coursing one by one down her cheeks.

The Skin of Loneliness

COLD, crisp, sunlit. Snuffling into tissue paper. Earl Grey's twenty-something storeys towering over the seedy jacarandas whose equally snow-grey trunks serenaded me into Fourth Street. Lighting another cheap cigarette, the pile of marked exercise books under my left armpit.

Army trucks droned to and fro down Fifth and Fourth. There was something big—a political conference—going on at the Holiday Inn. I could see the winter sunlight glinting off the automatic G3s of the guards far down the street. Make it tonight but not too soon. Overhead three scrawny crows cawed, swivelling their black glass eyes to inspect the traffic below for some putrid tidbit. I wondered if it was me. Bacon rind, once crisp, now cold, books tucked underarm, going to teach.

I cut the cheap pork into bits. My head was thinking: tonight but not too soon. I carefully washed the bits of meat under the hot water tap, letting the grease shuffle under my fingernails, watching the water turning grey and thick like soup from a paved gutter. I scooped the meat into the already boiling pot and listened to the sharp hiss of drops falling on to the hotplate.

Every inch of movement was orchestrated by the impatient snarl of the traffic outside the ground-floor flat. I washed my fingers in the hot water. A cockroach was watching me from the other side of the fridge. It was the knife after that, shaving the potatoes bald, one by one and washing them and cutting them into pieces and dropping them into the now seething pot. Through the open kitchen door I could see my bed, the desk laden with books and typewriter, the poster for the skydiving national championships, and her poster entitled "Expressions".

My cold fingers, both hands, cradled the ice-cold beer tankard. I had finished the newspaper. Finished the worry and the worn-out purpose. The evening stretched out before me like an endless tabloid whose contents I had read and re-read long before I was born.

To jump out of the skin of loneliness. To measure the sightlessness, the creeping deafness. H G Wells trying to ponder on the possible course of morality with the development of civilisation. There between her silktight legs. There is this loneliness, a level teaspoonful of it to be taken three times a day.

> Will the church and its hymns
> Bless the drunken distance between me and her I love?

Nine-thirty in the evening means another glass of Castle; wormy things float in it. But my friend is speaking: "Like one of those slimy things, you know, capitalism, when you have cut off its tail, simply grows another one. That's what is happening. Mind you, I don't say I know the names which make up the new tail but," he winked, "we all know, don't we?"

I grunted.

She had uncrossed her legs, slowly, watching me and I watching her. A long bony face, large black eyes that glittered obscurely, firm straight nose and lips that seemed on the point of advertising a melting bar of chocolate. That's who she was, my eyes said. What unnecessary quirk of fate had discovered her here? Discovered me here? Watching. She and I, even as we watched each other, waited patiently for the inevitable sordid encounter.

> What extremely sublime feelings
> In a dog howling at the moon!

113

I smiled. She smiled back like my lips were chocolate on the tip of her very pink tongue. But my friend tugged impatiently at his stiff brush of moustache and continued: "When I filled in and sent back the six forms, I received in return twelve more of the same, and when I filled them in and sent them back, I received twenty-four. . ."

At my back, time's muddy chariot, sputtering my greying hair. Straight ahead, running headlong into my sight, her smile teasingly tasting me.

The lights flickered off-on, off-on. Closing time. I said goodnight to my tedious friend—but then aren't we all tedious just by being what we are to ourselves? I brushed past swaying shoulders, stood silently by the long line of taxis, wondering what to do. A hand from somewhere in the foully drunk crowd touched my shoulder. It was her. I nodded grudgingly. In the taxi, she sat far away from me.

"I'm Grace," she said quietly. Her voice was the rustle of silk curtains on a calm twilight moment.

"My name is Heat," I said.

"What?"

"Heat," I repeated. They always asked me again—for as long as I could remember.

"Oh."

I twisted the key in the lock and we went in. Mine was a bachelor flat: bedsittingroomstudy, bathroom and the tiny kitchen.

"Get into bed. I'll make us some coffee." I said, already filling the kettle and wondering whether she needed food. As the water began to steam, I cut slices of cheese and tomatoes.

She sat up for her cup and nibbled at the cheese. I sat at the desk drinking my coffee, reading Peter Wildeblood's *Against the Law.* Except for the occasional drone of a car, it was very quiet outside, though we could hear the movements of the people in the other flats. I washed our cups and the Chinese plate.

"You go to sleep," I said. "I'm going to read for some time."

She looked at me oddly and began to say: "Don't you want to. . ."

I shook my head. I switched on the desk light and switched off the rather disturbing overhead one. I read for a long, long time. When at last my eyes were tired out, I took the spare quilt from the wardrobe, switched off the desk light and slept in the armchair.

THE SKIN OF LONELINESS

She woke up while I was in the bath. I dressed.

"I'm off to teach, Grace. The keys are over there and there's some money on the desk. See you at lunchtime," I said and went out.

She was at the stove, in a clutter of pots and pans. Something smelled very good.

"Hello," I said, "that smells very nice."

She only smiled, but in her eyes there was a crossword puzzle. I dumped my students' exercise books on the bed. The flat was spotless. It irritated me but in a pleasant way. When I went into the bathroom, the bath was full of my shirts, socks and pants, all soaking in a blue pool of Surf. As we ate, the plates on our laps, she in the other armchair, I told her: "I don't teach in the afternoons. Can I help you get your things?"

Her eyes met mine calmly; that obscure glittering had receded into the black depths. And she said, quietly: "I don't have anything."

I munched a pickled chilli and said nothing. Afterwards, as she washed and I dried the plates, I said: "Let's go shopping, some dresses and jeans and t-shirts for you." I looked at her shoes. "And some shoes."

It was bright, cold and crisp. Cars rattled down wide Rhodes Avenue. The occasional CD plates softly hummed through the traffic. And behind the tall jacaranda trees, Earl Grey building towered into the sky. Around it, on the lawn, civil servants were eating their lunch, mostly fruit and sandwiches. She looked at everything as though everything had just been conjured out of thin air. She was wearing my jeans and the Greek shirt I had been given by a friend last Christmas. Her thick black hair combed straight back from her forehead emphasised her long lean face. For the first time I noticed she was slightly taller than myself. The sky was like a Chinese bowl of a delicate gunmetal-blue colour; and the strands and whorls of cloud were like the paintings on a Spanish ashtray for sale to tourists. There was no need to say anything. It would all have sounded artificial, strained, a bit off-side. We strolled on as if we had done this together for years; a casual and tormenting deliciousness, the result of long association. We passed Earl Grey II, passed CABS and leisurely made our way down Central Avenue.

From Second Street, we turned into Baker Avenue and then into the Mall. The strangely exhilarating Mall—the colours, the glitter, the quaint buildings, secretaries chattering away, the beggars loudly singing strange hymns and, in the distance, the solemn clangour of the Anglican Cathedral bergfrith. And in the smart shop windows, those enticing harlequins, showing perfect legs, perfect faces, perfect busts, and all of the feminine frills planted in pleasantly outlandish settings, each stuck with the price you had to pay to be just like them. I trailed after her from shop to shop as she bought this and that. Afterwards we went into OK Bazaar where I bought a bottle of Chateau Burgundy.

I opened the french windows, set the little mopane table with glasses and slices of cheese. It was pleasant to sit there, drinking the wine and nibbling away and watching the cars and pedestrians driving and lopping by. I thought I might as well mark my students' exercise books while drinking.

Her voice reached me from out of the blue: "I was in the war," she said. "ZANLA. I cannot believe it's all over."

I felt I had to say something. "Combat?" I asked.

She looked at her fingernails, then slowly nodded.

My hands trembled as I refilled our glasses.

The next four nights, she slept badly. Dreams, nightmares and, I think, recapitulations of her war experience would make her wake suddenly, wide-eyed, looking wildly around her and I have never seen such terror fighting to burst out of someone so frail. That first time, it must have been well after midnight, I was reading and marking more exercise books. She was asleep, breathing easily. She leaped out of bed, landing on all fours, her face starkly lined with determination and her hands were searching for something on the floor. Her eyes were firmly fixed on me. I looked at her, astonished. I started to get up.

"Don't move," she hissed.

The tone of her voice sent chills down my spine. I started to get up. She lunged at me, her fingers tautening for my throat, her knee coming up to smash me between the legs. We both crashed to the floor. Thin animal sounds erupted out of her bared teeth. I don't know what saved me, don't know what mechanism in her head suddenly made her realise what she was doing for she suddenly released me and without looking at me, quietly crept into bed and was soon sound asleep.

The other nights were mere variations of this.

On the fifth night, we bought six bottles of wine and drank till morning, when I slurped cold water on to my face and went off to teach. I didn't go home at lunchtime but went straight to the International Hotel and drank and fought somebody for some reason, and I woke up in Parirenyatwa Hospital, to see Grace sitting on a chair by my bedside.

I looked questioningly at her.

"That Billy skunk beat you up," she said, "but I fixed him up good."

So it was Billy I had had a fight with. Billy was the friend I had been drinking with the night Grace came back with me to my flat.

"What do you mean, fixed him?"

"I beat him up," she said. "He's also somewhere in this hospital."

A doctor and a nurse approached my bed. The nurse was carrying some x-ray photographs. The doctor grinned. I knew him; we'd been at university together.

"The x-rays show there is nothing seriously wrong with you," he said. "But you'll need painkillers, I think, for the next forty-eight hours. Nurse will give you some."

"Thanks, Don", I said, as he and nurse walked to the next patient.

Grace bit her lip: "Well, let's get out of here. I don't like hospitals," she said.

I bathed and changed my bloodstained clothes. I could hear Grace tinkering away in the kitchen. After we had finished dinner, I felt a bit like my usual self, though I still don't know what that is. Grace was very silent, too silent.

"What's the matter?"

But she got up and began to rummage in the drawer.

"Where's the corkscrew?"

I found it under the bed. She opened a bottle.

"Sit down."

She began to giggle. This was a Grace I had never seen.

"Well, tell me," I said impatiently.

Her hand reached out, touched my knee. She was suddenly earnest. "I've bought a shop, bookshop in Gordon Avenue."

I remained silent.

"I saved all my demob. money and I didn't know what to do with it until I met you," she continued.

I laughed. She leaned over, kissed me.

"Honest"," she said. "The papers are in my briefcase." And she got up. She unlocked the new briefcase and there were the papers. I read them through three times. It was true. A cold breath stirred the hairs at the nape of my neck.

"But, Grace," I stammered, "it's all in my name."

"Of course. You are the one with the education" and she gestured at the bookshelves, "you know all about books."

"But. . ."

"Let's talk about the details later. Right now we are going out. I want to dance."

We went to the Causerie at Meikles Hotel. She wore a low-cut light brown velvet dress which accentuated her colour. She looked beautiful. She was light on her feet in my arms. And as she sat across the table from me, the candle flickering between us, the music a forgotten but delicious background, I thought, amazed, that she was the incarnation of a myriad transformations. I ordered a half bottle of the dry white and a salad and cheese.

"Except for your name, I don't know anything about you," she said.

"Do you want to?"

"Not particularly." The candlelight, reflected back to me, made her eyes even larger than they already were. "All I know is you are a good man, though you seem always to be denying that."

I lit a cigarette.

"It's all silly, you know," she said. "One way or the other."

She waved at someone, who waved back. I could not see who it was. Her long thin eyebrows drew together, half-closing her eyes.

"You don't want to know where you are going, do you?" she asked.

"I have already arrived and see no point in scrutinising the horizon. But you. . .?"

She smiled, a hint of cynicism.

"Why do you still sleep in the armchair?" she asked.

She held my gaze as I inhaled the cigarette smoke.

"Are you frightened of me?"

It surprised me, this question.

"No."

But then how could I explain? That sex always planted some barrier between me and the woman. That all my life I struggled to master myself so that I would be able to look at any woman without desire unless I really wanted to. That a subtle change would shift our relationship—if it was that—to some other humiliating level. That in any case I seemed always to associate sex with the expression of power and all its disgusting uses.

She was waving again. A minute later a couple I did not know joined our table. Grace introduced us.

"Sally, this is Heat. Heat, Sally. And hey, Mike, it's good to see you again. Heat, this is Mike we fought together in the battle zone. Sit down." She looked round. "Waiter! Two chairs please."

Mike and Sally sat down.

Mike was of average height, stocky and slightly balding at the temples. His face was square, the eyes always half-closed, nose small and flat, and the mouth sensuous. As he talked, you noticed one of his incisors was missing, giving him a kind of imposing handsomeness certainly one who was used to giving orders and seeing them carried out. After the polite talk, Grace turned to me: "Mike was my commander."

I nodded. She added: "Sally, like you, is a teacher."

She was a diminutive, oval-faced, helpless-looking woman, probably about thirty. Mike, I guessed, was in his early forties. He laid his arm round my shoulders.

"I've heard of you, young man. I've just returned from Bucharest—one of those aid conferences. Security, you know." He paused to nod at a passing waiter to order a beer for himself and a "glass of red" for Sally. From his profile I suddenly remembered him—one of our finest commanders. It made my mouth dry, just to be sitting with him.

I looked at Grace and could only feel a sudden, but painful, elation at the thought that we had such resilient individuals among us. I looked round the room. Most of the dancers—if not all of them—seemed suddenly to emit that aura of harsh and sheer brutal battle experience. I felt out of place, as it were, superfluous to our history. I looked back at Grace and she must have been watching me for she reached out and her fingers interlaced with mine. At that very moment she subtly shook her head and before I could register it her whole face lit up with a stunning joy. And I knew. Yes. I knew.

Mike and Sally gave us a lift in their dark blue Mercedes Benz. Before they drove off, Mike said to Grace: "Remember you are not on indefinite leave." Then he turned to me. His was a firm handshake as he smiled: "And you, young man, take good care of her."

He closed the door, rolled down the window a few inches and with an infectious chuckle, started the car.

"Good luck to both of you."

We stood on the pavement till the car's crimson rear lights disappeared.

I switched on the lights. Gasped. The flat had been turned upside down, the pillows ripped open, the mattress slashed, my books and papers in total disarray and the money I had left on the desk was still there but neatly arranged in a pile of notes.

"Shit! We've been burgled, Grace," I swore, stooping to pick up a painting which had been torn from the wall. Her silence finally made me turn round. She was biting her nails—and, no, trying to hide a smile.

"What on earth. . ."

She couldn't help herself; she burst out laughing. Looking at her, a dreadful, terrible suspicion overwhelmed my brain.

"You!"

Between bouts of laughter she managed to say: "It's just security. We were worried you were not with us. We now definitely know we were wrong!"

Before my fist could smash her face, she had caught it in an iron grip and sent me flying over her shoulder.

"Don't be a fool," she said quietly. "Don't you see, it was just a job? You're cleared, do you understand? Mike's cleared you."

Though full of blind resentment and anger at what she was saying, I brushed myself up from the floor and as calmly as possible said: "I can't stand the sight of you right now, Grace. I'm going out. Maybe I won't be back tonight, but then I've got to teach tomorrow."

As I fumbled at the door handle, she came up from behind and kissed me.

"Don't get beaten up again."

I went to a shebeen in Union Avenue. I tried to arrange my thoughts between several beers. I could not get drunk. I suspected everybody in the room of being "security". But then security against what? We were all for Zimbabwe, all in it together. My resentment was ridiculous—unless I was against Zimbabwe. It was the invasion of my privacy that left me with a bitter taste. And Grace—she worked for Mike—that was obvious. I finished off my beer and returned into the brisk night air. I could smell a whiff of rain; would the drought break now?

She had cleared up everything. The flat, unless you looked too closely, seemed as it always had been. She sat in the armchair reading one of the books I had published some years before. She ruffled my hair as my fingers slowly felt her small firm breasts.

"Why did you stop writing?" she asked softly. "I've read your books over and over."

"I didn't stop," I said. "It's just that I've only been back three years and I think Zimbabwe takes some getting used to. Like you."

She dropped the book. Her hand came up from somewhere holding out a card. It said she was something in the Prime Minister's office. I breathed hard; she was looking at me earnestly.

"The Struggle never stopped," she said, rising to her feet, drawing my arm around her waist. "You understand, don't you?"

I nodded. She went on: "Another thing is I can't have children. I was captured once and the enemy soldiers—well, they did things to me. Mike rescued me before they could take me to their base camp."

She was looking down at my chest, fumbling with the shirt buttons. A searing terrible realisation flashed through my head. I cupped her chin in my fingers, tilting her

121

head back so she could look at me. Her eyes were wet. A fatalistic sadness shone through the tears welling up. I began to kiss them away. She held her breath.

For the first time since we had been living together, I kissed her full on the lips. It was just the beginning.

The weeks rolled by, ponderously. A sharp tang, an elusive tincture and, in the squares of blue sunlight, a momentary pause. You had to look at the calendar to convince yourself that the days were passing by. After school I took long slow walks all over the city. Pausing before the elegant harlequins, the monuments of Smith's bygone era, the Indian bazaars that perpetually announced Best Bargains, the publishing houses in their discreet retreats and, from the heights of the Monomotapa Hotel, the slumbering music of the cityscape over the Harare Gardens, blocks of flats and the imposing embassy residencies.

Sometimes, Grace would come with me. The recapitulations of the Struggle had vacated her dreams; she slept easily now, almost like a baby, her body cuddling mine as though I was a precious doll she dare not lose. I became almost sociable; got to know the Police Support Unit guy who lived next door. Each time he returned from active duty in Matabeleland, we would drink morning to night in his flat, listening to his stories which invariably were about the women in his life. Apparently he had to do a juggling act with them so that they would not tumble to his infidelity. I liked him. Grace did not mind him; though, of course, she warned me about the whiskies and the brandies which Chris liked to drink.

I even started to write a series of sonnets under the overall title of "The Cemetery of Mind", on the general theme of the demon lover. The city as demon lover, its visitations into my paranoid imagination, night after night of terrifying embraces which in the cold light of day would retreat into the netherworld of stark clarity. Of course, it was also an attempt to come to terms with the shadows and fluorescences in Grace's effect on me.

The beginning. Of what?

Black Damascus Road

THE mind of a man who has seen too much too soon. Jagged, sharp, a flinty edge to things. That is how I remember Paul. Perhaps I mean an enduring simplicity, direct, precise. He came back from the war the way he had gone into it. Without regrets, without questions. There was an iron sunlight constantly flashing out of his eyes. He took off his uniform and put on the dog-eared garb of a librarian—he had been one before the war. It was not much of a library, mostly donations from well-intentioned philanthropists. The pay was not good but then Paul was single and lodged quite cheaply in an ugly room in Mbare. He only drank on Fridays and Saturdays. He got married the day he killed himself.

I see myself sitting on his bed, this creaking fourposter. On the wall facing me is a poster. It is of a barren thorn tree sprouting out of the harsh stony soil, the sun rising directly behind it. There are no words. Just this thorn tree and the suggestion of blurred fingerprints. To the right of the poster is the wardrobe, a cheeky devastated affair whose secrets are a pair of patched jeans, three shirts, a shabby black suit, three pairs of dirty socks, and underwear. To the left of the poster is a bookcase he must have bought at an auction. I peer at the titles: detective thrillers, love stories, cowboy tales, war novels. Of the last type there are such titles as *Kamikaze, Dreadnought, Strike Force Flag*, etc. All bear the signs of having been read again and again.

Without any warning, a key turns in the door. The door opens. The hairs on my head stretch and stand on end. He comes in with an empty suitcase and begins to pack. He does not see me at all. He dumps the clothes from the wardrobe into the open suitcase. I stand up automatically as he rips the sheets and blankets from the bed, folds them, stuffs them into the suitcase. It is a cheap hard cardboard one. He is about to close it when he remembers something. On tiptoe he can just reach the top of the wardrobe. He takes from there a small package from which he extracts a live grenade. Suddenly he seems overcome by total despair. I thought then he would crumple up and cry on the floor. But, no. He looks round the room, memorising all its ugly details. He does not look at the grenade, but his hand clutches it to his chest. Still looking hard at the mean little room (did he in the end have a mean little soul?) he rips the trigger out and for those three deadly seconds from within his human frame shines a blinding luminosity. It thrusts a dagger right through my heart.

When I look again, he is no longer there. There is no suitcase. The door never opened to let him in. Does it ever open for anyone? I remember many like him, but Paul wrenched all my certainties apart, taking to the grave with him my more sentimental pictures of humanity.

Evening Star over 28 Highlands Avenue

YOU let it in and throw away the key. Those outside can hear only the muffled screams, the heartbreaking gibberish, the quiet shriek of desperation. The simmering pent-up heat of a soul about to explode. Is it like this for all those others? The book dropped from her lap. She did not move. She was fast asleep. The empty bottle of gin and the full ashtray were at her side. From a record player near the french windows von Karajan was conducting Schumann's Third Symphony. It was a quarter past six in the evening.

I threw my briefcase on the floor by the door. In my room I changed into jeans and sweater and sandals. I plugged in the shaver and trimmed my beard. There was a pimple above my right eyebrow. I grabbed a bottle of whisky and went out into the lounge. I sat opposite her, drinking, smoking, wondering what Bosman thought he was doing filing in such a damned report. Some of these younger executives were the end. In any case, I would be retiring soon. Then. . .?

I looked at her. She was just waking up. I crossed the miles between us and kissed her gently on the lips. She cried a little on my shoulder, muffled sobs. I gave her my handkerchief. She dabbed at her face. I nodded at the bottle.

"Not now, not when you are here," she said.

Painful cramps flickered across my belly. I eased out of her arms and went to the toilet. I was in there a long time. It was, the doctor had said, a mild case of food poisoning. When I came back she was at the piano, her fingers restless over the ivory keys. She had been a more than average pianist. But the arthritis had set in early. I was not in good shape myself. My face was a mass of wrinkles, my hair was grey and I was bald at the back of the head. How fragile she looked—but actually she was not. I refilled my glass.

"Let's call some people over," she said over her shoulder.

"Fine," I said, and walked to the phone.

Morgan and Hilda were the first to arrive. We had arranged candles and easy chairs on the verandah and thrown open the french windows. Bach was playing. We chatted about nothing and drank a great deal. Morgan had been a film producer, Hilda a teacher. They had both retired.

It was one of those evenings: a great big shining moon, glittering stars scattered across the grey veil of darkness, the swimming pool lights a shimmering wonder. Mellow. Perhaps at times it felt like the evening that had crept into our lives, stage by stage, till death was no longer an idea but a certainty. Our two children had long since left home. There was Mike, an architect, and Jill who had tried to paint. Both had married, had children and dutifully came to visit at Christmas.

Malcolm, a grizzled bachelor, something of a senior novelist, arrived around nine o'clock. He staggered onto the verandah, two wine bottles sticking out of his coat pockets. His eyes were always half-closed, a thin creased veil over startling blue. He sprawled onto a chair and fumbled with the corkscrew. There was more chat about nothing. Iris, my wife, was already halfway down another bottle of gin. She and Hilda were deep into the merits and demerits of a recent Shostakovitch concert. Morgan as usual had nothing to say and did not say it. Malcolm was telling me about his new novel which he had not written yet. That damned report. What exactly was Bosman trying to do?

The next day I threw my briefcase on the floor by the door. I shaved and changed. I grabbed a whisky bottle and joined Iris in the lounge. The book had fallen from her lap. The empty gin bottle and full ashtray. . .

Fragments

HE woke up to find all his sisters pregnant. He was, perhaps, still dreaming. It was other people's sisters who got pregnant. A dark rage, like a puff-adder, coiled itself at the base of his skull. But then how can you look a pregnant sister in the face? Let alone look yourself in the eye. His first instinct was to get drunk, blind drunk. But the beerhall laughed, sniggered, whispered, pointed him out. Mug after plastic mug of beer gurgled down his throat. The great Hymn to Beer surged up his throat; drums, bass drums, steel drums. He felt himself catapulted into the sky, looking down at creation whose brightness was marred by the listless shadows of three pregnant sisters. The beerhall watched, analysed, evoked gnomic analogies, waiting for him to wreak vengeance on the three men responsible. Poverty was poverty, but poverty was warm and snug when it could still cover its nakedness with the woollen blanket of honour. Family honour. The family name.

He called Barbara, the youngest, first. She was tall, thin, gawky, twelve years old. Probably didn't even know what was happening inside her body. A nut-brown angular face, eyes large and brown—always lowered, except in sudden bursts of pain or laughter. Before she even knew what he wanted, a series of hard backhanded blows had thrown her all over the room. Her astonishment acted as an anaesthetic. Through the blood, spurting clear and bright red, her large brown eyes stared at him questioningly.

"Who fucked you?"

The obscene word recalled her to his drunken anger. The shocking, insane out-rage in the features of his face, in the cracked crystals of his eyes. She blurted it out: "It was Tom."

"Who?"

"Tom," she whispered.

Tom was his best friend. They had grown up together, fought for each other, shared the same desk at school, been beaten up together. Tom was practically a member of the family.

Shove it!

I don't want to know.

But the scene, pulsing brighter and brighter against dark memory, returned. He watched. The mortuary attendant drew open the big drawer. Something long and bulky was underneath the stained sheet. The too-bright lights seemed to increase their inten-sity. The long thing began to move—

Shut it!

The battered skull swivelled to face him directly. He scrunched his eyes shut. Refusing. Denying. Shaking his head furiously.

No!

He woke up to find himself confronting the empty chair by his bedside. There was no one in the room. Except himself and the rivulets of sweat and the deranged hammer-ing of his heart and the smell of fear. He switched on the light. He turned on his record player. He lit a cigarette. He sank back into the pillow and started to read.

That was father, the voice inside him whispered.

Shut up!

He checked his watch. 3.25 a.m. He read. It was Wambaugh's *Onion Field.* The knocking woke him up. Bright sunlight streamed in. The knocking was repeated. He ignored it. Whoever it was finally went away.

In the bathroom Harold gritted his teeth and lowered himself into the cold water. Later, on the phone, he could hear the number ringing repeatedly but no one answered. He opened a carton of yoghurt. As usual there was nothing in the newspaper. Outside he sat and smoked on the fire-escape. The caretaker, a thin wiry old man in khaki overalls, was doing something to the flowers. The sky was a watercolour pale blue sparsely painted over by snow-white traceries of cloud. A whiff of music like a hesitant breeze hovered ahead. Harold was not thinking of anything.

Soon it would be time to walk down to the office. Harold was a minor functionary in the Ministry of Construction. He sat at his desk waiting for work to come to him. Most of the time it didn't. When it did, it was a flood of queries and he would spend hours in the Ministry's library and then more hours at his desk typing out his reports. Sometimes he would have to step over to the Treasury but that used to be all right because Virgo worked there. He looked forward to the nights she spent with him, not because he loved her (he did) but because of his growing fear of being alone at night in his flat. He tried to put off going back to the flat by drinking late in the bars, dancing crazed dances in the night-clubs and (though rarely) persuading some lone woman to take him along to her place. Harold liked to think he had given up on people. He liked to think they had no hold on him; that nothing they did or said surprised him. This meant he was free of them and they free of him, which made anything possible and everything impossible.

His flat, the castle of his personal life, balanced the office. Each depended on the other. Off-tangent situations, like Virgo, were irrelevant, though in a heartbreaking way they seemed necessary. Relationships, however firm, were a source of irritation, not happiness. The irritation could be intimately bittersweet, almost a condition of endearment, but it also signalled an incurable indifference which Harold interpreted as a source of strength when the inevitable break-up occurred. This pessimistic inevitability Harold applied to everything and everyone. He may as well have worn a t-shirt emblazoned with Abandon All Hope. . .

In his dapper charcoal-grey suit Harold crossed Rhodes Avenue and strolled across the large parking lot where already learner drivers were being put through their paces. Schoolgirls in olive green and some in navy blue uniforms, and schoolboys in their invariable khaki were hurrying to school. Soldiers in camouflage and police recruits strode by, each to his own destination. A nurse in crisp starched white waved to Harold. He smiled back. She was one of the nurses who had taken care of him when he was last in hospital. He did not want to remember the awful pain, the blood transfusions, the urine bottle, the bedpan—the terrible realisation that one's body could not always be counted

129

on. Harold already knew that the mind cannot be relied on. He had a "breakdown" in his last year at boarding school. The experience had left him with a wonderful realisation of the mind's fragility: it must be defended against certain "things". Even at a cost to himself. This was the germ of his definition of personal courage.

His slightly effeminate face had been corrugated by experience. At moments he looked like a small boy who had just survived a fight in the schoolyard. He was five foot seven, walked with shoulders hunched and eyes scanning the ground for answers. In the strong light he looked somewhat ridiculous in his neat charcoal-grey suit.

The work was welcome. It cut out other considerations. Those "things". He set to with a will. But he would have to get certain statistics from the Treasury. Virgo was the records director there. He had to get the nitty-gritty on foreign exchange for several construction firms that had responded to various tenders put out by the chief.

She kissed him warmly. Everything about her exuded warmth, friendliness, generosity. Her face had the capacity to enfold all and everything with an easy smiling grace. You could imagine her giggling on her way to certain death. If this was a mask, then all masks are true. She scanned his list and began to scribble numbers on it.

"That's stack H2001," she mumbled. "That's stack Q3457. That's stack. . ."

Harold lit a fresh cigarette from his stub and crossed his legs. It was not the usual ministerial office. There was something personal. Yes, it was decorated by her own things, her own taste, her own impetuous disarray.

She reached across. "Here you are."

At last he was back at his desk—he had missed lunch—and typing his report. He neither loved nor hated his work. It was just another necessity. And when everything moved effortlessly, that was a boon, no more. His duty was simply to do it right. He did not tolerate mistakes in himself though he expected them of others he worked with. Other people were not his responsibility; they were their own lookout. Virgo was not a mistake in himself: she was her own contradiction. Harold was thirty-five but already he conducted himself as an aging invalid whose hold on reality depended on an extreme refusal to acknowledge his sickness. Self-respect, without regrets, only came with this, and only this, specific gravity. He finished typing, stapled and filed each report separately and, with a light heart, dumped them in the "out" tray.

When Rainwords Spit Fire—A Township Novella

When Rainwords Spit Fire

THE boy peeked his head round the door resentfully.

"What is it, mama? They're waiting for me."

His brother stood by the cheap cupboard, grinning. Morgan sidled into the room. Mother was holding several parcels and that could mean only one thing: the new clothes and the new shoes. Morgan was instantly, curiously, happy. There had been too much uncertainty about where the fees and the money for the clothes were going to come from. Mother had managed somehow. She was smiling secretly, warily, as though she was wondering whether it was all worth it. Thomas leaned against the cupboard which creaked.

Mother cleared her throat. "I suppose you'd better try them on," she said ripping at the plastic covers of the parcels, extracting khaki shorts, khaki shirts, socks, green ties, green jerseys, and brown shoes. She looked around wildly. "Did you see another smaller parcel anywhere, Tom?"

Thomas strode to where mother's big quilted bag stood, by the big window with its cracked pane through which you could open the window from outside. Another one of Morgan's tantrums was responsible for *that*.

"It's tucked away in here, mama." Thomas said, handing it to her. He always managed to do things for her as though she deserved nothing but the best. A mother deserved respect, honour. Thomas had very early seen the harsh poverty that encircled

132

them, the wolf at the door whom mother had till now shooed from the door. As she extracted the cotton singlets and cotton underpants, he bit his lip wondering what all these purchases had cost her and what it would mean for the rest of the family. Probably less to eat, no more luxuries like bread and sugar. He looked at her, squinting his eyes. Mother was thin, wrinkled, her eyes careworn and blurred as if she no longer wanted to see anything too clearly. Morgan had already taken off his tattered shirt and trousers and, totally nude, was waiting to try the new clothes. Thomas slowly did the same.

Some minutes later, Morgan strutted up and down the room, looking down and smoothing his new clothes, chuckling like he was on stage. That was for his own benefit. It was the shoes which delighted him. They were his very first pair. Brown and shiny. And the black socks that almost reached to his knobbly knees, made him feel very grown up. "Wow!" he exclaimed, coming to attention directly in front of his mother.

"My darling," she laughed, but close to tears. He was so wilful, impulsive, fearing nothing, only concerned with his own wants and not their expense. She did not think he would long survive in the harsh realities out there. She looked at Thomas. He was standing stiffly, afraid to crease his new clothes. There was a sadness whose fingerprints were clearly marked on his face. He was only thirteen years old but looked thirty. And he held himself like one used to the blows of life—used to them but quite ready to fight back with all his coiled-in strength. She had never really been close to him: he seemed so self-sufficient, so manly, so independent. He left no room for her to feel she could help in any way. She knew he was calculating what all this had cost and what it would cost the family. It drew him to her, but also exasperated her. After all, this was her small triumph, after the skimping and saving and slaving away as a nanny and, in her free time, spending hours at her sewing machine making dresses and quilts which she would sell in the township from door to door, and sometimes keeping a stall at the market selling the clothes together with vegetables, boiled maize, sweet potatoes and fat cakes.

Someone cried out. There was the sound of running feet and Debbie burst into the room all wet and in tears.

"Mama! Look what Violet did to me. A whole bucket of water, mama!"

The sisters had been watering the garden. Morgan was at once at her side, all concern—he liked her best—but she pushed him away. Mother gave her a penny and she gradually quietened and went out.

In the garden, Debbie stuck her tongue out at Violet and wiggled her thin hips. "Hah!" she said, showing the penny. Violet put down the garden fork with which she had been weeding and threw a fist of mud right into Debbie's face—smack! The little girl howled. Violet laughed in disgust and was about to turn back to her weeding when a strong arm grasped her wrist.

"Caught you," mother said. She snatched a long stick from the dry peach tree and quite savagely, but only for a few seconds, her hand swung down hard on the bigger girl's back.

"No, mummy, NO!" the girl cried, twisting and turning to get away.

Debbie laughed. Behind her was the euphorbia hedge that encircled the garden. Beyond the hedge were the streets and side lanes and other houses, also hidden behind hedges. It was a scrawny, strident township. Always pregnant with dust when the rains did not come, always slushy and marshy when the rains did come.

Morgan stood on the brick steps of the front door, smart and cocky in his new clothes. In his very first pair of brown shiny shoes. He was smiling boldly at his three friends who were peering through the gate, amazed at the transformation in his appearance.

There was Bobby, who lived with his mother in a tin, cardboard and plastic shack down by the Rutendo River, where they would all go to bathe and swim and fish or just lie on the soft sand basking in the flushed warmth of the brilliant winter sunlight. Bobby did not go to school; there was no money for his school fees. But he had such a clear, infectious laugh and could imitate Charlie Chaplin, and knew how to make the best catapults and wire motorcars, that Morgan could never think of life without him at his side. Also at the gate was Charles, a thin quiet pimply boy who had more brains than anyone else and whose father was a teacher at the local school. Then there was Silas, a puzzled, strange boy who always joined them without any invitation.

"Morgan!" mother cried, "go right back in there and change those clothes."

"But, mama. . ." Morgan sulked.

Mother took a threatening step. "I said get back in there. . ."

"Awright," the boy said, "but can't I wear the shoes just for today?"

"No."

Thomas came out, already changed back into his own old dirty clothes. He gave Morgan a push and the boy hit him in the stomach. Thomas gripped the boy by the throat, shaking him. He slapped him twice with the back of his hand. Mother rushed forward and grabbed Thomas.

"Do you want to kill him, heh? Let him go, you lumbering ape!" she hissed.

Thomas let go. The boy was crying. Mother tried to smile: "You take the clothes off but you can wear the shoes, but only for today. And I don't want them ruined before you get to that mission school. Okay?"

Morgan nodded, disappearing into the house. Thomas looked grimly at his bare toes and went and sat by the peach tree, picking his nose. It was always like this, he thought. The little shit always got away with everything—there was nothing she could refuse him. He looked up. The cold white winter sunlight had only a little warmth in it. Some pigeons flashed across the sky; his eyes smarted. There was this uncontrollable hardness in him, a fatalism he could not shake off his shoulders. What was it in him which made all of *them* give him only the minimum of everything, and reluctantly? He watched Morgan join his friends at the gate and had to suppress the sudden urge to run after them and play with them. They would only be uncomfortable in his presence, waiting for him to leave them alone. Anyway, school was just round the corner and he would be back in the happy company of his books. But then the little shit was coming too. Well, I'm his senior if he tries anything funny. . .

Mother licked the tip of the thread and fitted it through the eye of the needle. On her lap were the sheets she had taken from her bed. The school letter had said the boy, Morgan, must have sheets. There was no money to buy new ones; she was mending these for him. She was thirty-five years old but already looked fifty. There were the four children and, she smiled, the fifth child—her husband—whose horizon was his wages, beer, his cigarettes. She finished threading the needle, tied the knot and picked up the worst sheet. She sighed.

In the garden at the back, someone whistled softly. Violet looked round, knowing who it was. "Jim, is that you?" she whispered.

135

"Yes."

She put down the watering-can. Her right cheek was caked with dust and her legs were muddied right up to the knees. She wore an old pink dress which she had hitched up and her black plaited hair swept sharply back from her wide forehead. Her eyes, wide apart, were black and somewhat large, but her nose was small, thin, too thin above the wide sensuous purplish lips and the narrow chin. They could not see each other through the hedge but their hands somehow found each other and he was squeezing hard and she moaned a little.

"You're hurting, Jim."

He eased the pressure but she could hear his sharply drawn breath, his impatience. All their meetings had been like this. There was something violently unfair in it all, she felt. Something about her own growing body and the way it burned all over whenever Jim was near, touching her, squeezing from her fragile palms a futile but dangerous passion.

"Please go now, Jim," she whispered, afraid of him and of all the others and what could happen.

Bobby, Silas, and Charles lashed furiously at the horses. The wagon lurched forward. Silas's ten-gallon hat whizzed off, struck by an arrow.

"Holy Jesus!" he swore, thrusting shells into his shotgun and firing coldly, deliberately, knocking off the Red Indians one by one. At his side, Bobby shot the whip again and again, barely holding onto the flesh-tearing reins. But the pursuing Indians were drawing closer and closer. The situation was hopeless. Charles, the dude from the useless East, was crouching beneath his top hat and firing uselessly with his Derringer.

"Ugh!" Silas grunted, an arrow drilling through his heart until it protruded from the back. The shotgun clattered onto the moving ground.

Bobby winced, watching Silas leap into empty air and fall like a stuffed oversize doll. Through the stark cacti and bare boulders on either side of the trail, the angry Red Indians galloped closer and closer to the wretched mail-run.

Like a weird illusion, a bugle sounded from somewhere. It sounded again and again. Charles whooped with sudden glee. "The cavalry! It's the US Cavalry! We're saved!"

And indeed, the skyline was suddenly a-gallop with uniformed riders, swords drawn and, at their head, in his distinctive white Tuxedo, rode that fearless scourge of the Wild West, none other than Captain Morgan, firing steadily, accurately, with his two six-guns, while Honky-Tonk, his famous stallion, whirled him like an avenger towards the cowardly savages.

Morgan jumped from the car-wreck, shouting: "Its coming! Look, its coming!" The others, surprised from their game, looked up. There it was, the horse-drawn Town Management garbage wagon bearing down on them. The boys could see that it was more than full—there would be pickings for everyone: comics, toys, books, anything that could be treasured, horded. Morgan laughed. Silas looked more puzzled than ever. Debbie, with her tongue, deftly pushed the "blackie" into her right cheek. She was leaning against the table where Johnny, the grocery boy, was weighing out and packaging mealie meal. He was powdered white all over. They were in the same class at the local school. She was something of a tomboy and Johnny liked to frolic with her, racing her, baiting the township dogs, fighting the other kids, and often playing war games, stalking each other with AKs and grenades, and tracking down enemies of the country. The most persecuted victim was Amos, the cobbler, a Malawian whom they suspected of being a South African spy.

Debbie was too tall for her age but very thin. Her black hair was turning brown at the edges, probably a sign of malnutrition. Most of the kids her age also had hair that was turning reddish but no one noticed. She was very like Morgan, but through a disturbing shyness found it difficult to stand her ground when conflicts arose. From childhood she and Johnny had always been close—Johnny lived next door—playing together and sticking up for each other. But now Debbie felt slightly uneasy. He seemed to be turning away from her, noticing too much the woman she would be, and right now, as he weighed the mealie meal, he insisted: "Either you are my girl or I don't play with you any more."

"But we've always been together. What difference does it make?" Johnny looked confused, stubborn.

"All the other boys have girls. I want one too," he said, pouting his lips.

Debbie's brown eyes widened. "Are you talking about the dirty things?" she asked timidly.

Johnny laughed uneasily. "You're really the end, Debbie. There's nothing dirty in kissing and maybe we could hold hands too. And. . ."

"Oh that," she said seriously. "I don't do that sort of thing. We're buddies and we've always played together. Besides, I am just like you and it would be so confusing to think you think I'm just there for kissing and holding hands. I'm not a girl and you know it, Johnny. Can't we be just the same as we have always been?"

"Not a girl!" Johnny scoffed. "Of course you are a girl."

Debbie looked at him with the beginnings of resentment. She was trying to see into his eyes but he kept them lowered and they were filmed all over with the mealie meal. He was asking her something, not as he had always done but in a way that had nothing to do with her person. She tried to see him as a boy, to see herself as a girl, but it was unreal, it was impossible.

"Maybe with the others its different," she said carefully. "With us you know it has never been like *that*. So there."

Debbie picked another blackie from her small bag of sweets. Without tasting it, she shoved it round and round her mouth, perplexed. "Its just kissing and holding hands you want?" she asked.

Johnny felt he should disappear from the face of the earth. "That and other things too," he said finally.

The blackie popped out of her mouth, thumping onto the floor. She picked it up wiped it on her dress and popped it back into her mouth. Very carefully she said: "You mean making babies?"

He turned angrily on her, twisting her arm and snarling until she cried: "Johnny, no!"

But he continued to twist her arm and suddenly she was angry: her foot came up into his groin. He cried out and they circled each other, Johnny screaming: "I'm going to kill you!"

She laughed grimly, and they would have fought had not Thomas entered the shop and slapped both of them. Their anger was transferred to him. But he was so big they could do nothing about it except wait until they had grown up and he was an old man and then they would make him bleed like a pig.

"Or like a goat, its throat cut at Christmas," Johnny said later to Debbie who still felt the total unfairness and indignity of it all.

Mother had finished sewing the sheets. Violet was washing her face, arms and legs at the pump. When she finished she went into the kitchen to prepare the vegetables and the meal. It was late afternoon and father would be coming from work. She was thinking of Jim, how anxiously hot his desire was for her. Mother carried the reed mat outside and there she sat, sticking pins into the materials and wondering whether *he* would come home drunk and violent. She was pregnant again, which was against the doctor's advice but, of course, *he* did not care.

He arrived soon afterwards, accompanied by Max his workmate at the mortuary. He grunted a greeting in her direction and went inside. Violet brought him his washtub of warm water. He washed, shaved and changed from his khaki uniform into a white shirt and grey trousers. Then he was off with Max to the beerhall.

Mother watched them go as the crimson twilight dipped and the firm hand of darkness opened out to hold the whole sky in its palm.

"Cheer-up," said Max. "It's not the end of the world."

But Joe was thinking about the bodies in the mortuary. It was his usual job. He had been sacked from being a messenger for the Town Management Board after being convicted of stealing bicycle plates from another messenger. He had been sentenced to three months in jail. After that there was no job until he got the one as a mortuary attendant. That was the beginning of the end. He was still thinking of the bodies in the mortuary.

"Nasty business," he said.

"Someone has to do it," Max said.

"But, Christ, what I mean is I have fallen so low, that's all." Joe's voice was bitter.

They sat on the cement seat, their plastic mugs of beer on the cement table before them. There were all these cement seats and tables and everywhere there were groups of people drinking, talking, arguing, or sitting around waiting for someone to buy the holy drink. Thick stubby fingers rolled cigarettes. A cowlet of snuff was sniffed delicately.

The Herald was read all over again. Dust filtered into everything: dust in the drink, in the face, on the clothes; dust on the policemen's uniforms; dust, and the overpowering stink from the toilets.

"Its a joke," Joe laughed, staring at a very fat well-oiled matron coming out of the Ladies. He called her over. She sat between them, a boulder of flesh, sweating like gelignite. Her name was Blessing. And the blessed early evening hours would roll, mug after mug of thick cereal beer, wiping the thick lips after each long sip, spitting out the grain, nuzzling the noise with ears that no longer knew silence. The beerhall band was playing an old Beatles' song.

The beerhall was the size of half a football field, all enclosed by thick cement walls studded at the top with broken bottles. Men's territory. The women in there were for sale, like the beer. Joe, with the mountain of female flesh beside him, felt a sudden urgent desire. He gripped her hand. She nodded. The two of them disappeared behind the toilets. There were three other couples doing business there but what the hell. She pulled down her panties, waiting for him. He slowly unzipped his trousers.

"Turn around," he said huskily.

Max was thinking of nothing but the beer. All this business about women did not touch him. He had recently married a local girl called Tsitsi and was still full of her enclosing him in a self-satisfied vision of the delights of life. He was not too bright, but this gave him a literal straightforward attitude to everything. Right now he was watching a drunken young man prowling around this or that group of drinkers, insulting and abusing any who met his eye. Max, without thinking about it, said: "He is an accident looking for a chance to happen." And without exaggeration, Max added to himself: "We are all accidents looking for a chance to happen."

He licked his parched lips when he saw Joe and Blessing coming back. All these people would one day be carried into the fridge feet first and locked away in metal drawers. It was rather interesting, watching them all drinking and fucking and then turning up in his mortuary. A very neat plan. You had your one chance to happen and that was all. Only a neat creator would think up such a maliciously neat joke. Accidents waiting for a chance to happen. The sand dune of female flesh sank beside him, giving him a hopeful look. Joe was muttering to himself, already drinking from the plastic mug, sweating, lost still in the agony and delirium of her flesh. Max shook his head ruefully. She smiled at him; it was all one to her whether he wanted to or not. Men! she thought, they were all the same. Little boys who easily gave in to the simplest pleasures. She was not thinking about the venereal disease she had just charitably given to Joe. It was their own lookout. And they paid for it. He will probably give it to his wife tonight, she thought, giving Joe a crazily tender look.

Joe was on fire, smouldering low, somewhere in his brain, watching the local primary school teachers who always sat together, sharing cigarettes and talking very loudly in English. A sort of aristocracy. They were never short of money, those teachers. After all, like the ads said, education was the gateway to Success. And Success was never short of Money. There were all these girls and you could have all of them if you had it. That monetary chance to happen. Joe took out his pouch of tobacco and started to roll. He thought wistfully of his wife. That was another joke. You thought you were in love. You thought you were marrying a delicious dream, but then you woke up and she was just an engine programmed to create babies by the dozen. You looked at her and you saw a female engine that dripped monthly and spewed out babies every nine months. The jobs were a joke too. Dealing in life and death for a miserly fifty dollars a month. It was the sheer hypocrisy of the relatives which rankled in Joe's mind. In the fridge. They came in, with their hats off, their faces set in a defiantly dignified look. And Joe would open the drawer and turn the sheet down, revealing the ugly details of death. He had lost his temper only once when a widow had dragged in an eleven-year-old boy who was screaming: "I don't want to see him, mama!"

But she had grabbed his head and forced him to see the "last of your father" and the boy had looked, and looked, all the noise and protest blown out of him by the sight of his terribly mangled father.

"You are killing him too," Joe said pointing at the boy.

But the woman gave him a scornful withering glance and Joe retreated behind his mortuary attendant's mask.

"It's all a cynical joke, Max," Joe said.

And he stood up to get another plastic mug of beer. He wanted to get sickeningly drunk. Max stopped him and gave him more money.

"Get two big ones," Max said.

The big ones really gave you time to talk. Beer was not beer without a little honest-to-god dust in it. Max shifted. It was rather hard on the buttocks, this cement seat. He let his hand fall on the woman's knee. She slinked her eyes at him. He was suddenly very aware of her bright red lips. Christ, I'm not doing this, he thought, shutting his eyes. Her hand was lingeringly fingering the front of his trousers. "For fucking sake, Max, go with her and get it over with," Joe said. Max stood up. They disappeared behind the toilets. There were six other couples there. Everyone seemed to be in business. She knelt down and unzipped him. With his eyes tightly shut he felt the hot wet blindingly moist tongue on his centre. He gave a long drawn-out groan. Jesus H. Christ!

It was the women corpses who were very important to Joe and Max. They had long discussions about it, mostly off the point, but each knew what the other was alluding to. "Its all shit," Max muttered, sitting down. Joe nodded. "Finished already?" Max's mouth slid to one side. His very first fall. And he had enjoyed eating his half of the apple. Tsitsi did not know half the tricks of pleasure this woman knew. Maybe there was something in it. All this infidelity. But then, what if she was doing it to someone else right now, he thought. It's not right. And the thought of Tsitsi gave him another erection. But she was watching him and thinking "Men."

Blessing smacked her lips, wiped them with the back of her hand and started to sing:

> "Where have all the men gone
> He's shrunk out of sight and I'm alone. . ."

Joe gave her another four dollars.

"What's that for?" she asked, winking.

Joe winked back. "Another two rounds later," he said.

She was quiet for a moment. Well, if they have the money to fool around with, what the hell. Money for handling corpses. For a fraction of a second, her mind blacked out, thinking: *Money from living corpses.*

Tsitsi sat by the fire on a reed mat. She was knitting a baby's jersey. The burning logs rustled, glowing, encrusted with bright blisters of fire. The paraffin lamp hung on a wire from the thick wooden rafter. On the other side of the fire in two white metal plates was the food she had cooked for Max. Sadza and stew. The walls were black from smoke, though here and there the whitewash still showed through. She had finished five years of primary school when Max asked to marry her. He was steady, had a job, and was saving money—traits that were now rather rare. She did not like the sex much but it seemed to give him great pleasure so she felt she ought to see it through. Now there was a baby coming and she did not know how to deal with it. But, as all the women dealt with it, she felt she would too. Taller than her husband she was heavily built and had the large-boned features of those not very bright but was handsome and sensible. If it was a boy she would name him Joseph. If it was a girl she would name her Josephine. She shrank a little from thinking about the pain and probable horrors of birth. But, then, since every woman had to go through it, maybe. . . Maybe it did not hurt very much if you did not think about it. And there was a lot to do *really.* She sighed. She thought of her father's house. Nothing much really. She did not miss it at all.

It is very silent tonight, she thought. On most nights, there would be shrieks and shouts from children playing, men fighting, the wailing of police sirens, the thunderous songs of some obscure religious sect, the hue and cry of "Thief! Stop thief!" But on this night, everything seemed dead, too silent. It made her afraid, listening to every rustle, waiting tensely for the sound of human feet approaching and passing on. Or had they stopped? She stood up heavily, trimmed the lamp and went into the bedroom. An iron bedstead; the blankets blue and grey. A calendar from some wholesaler was nailed to the far wall. In the corner was the gaunt wardrobe. What was it? The vitamin pills. Martha, their neighbour, had said it's the vitamins that make a good pregnancy and a good birth.

Tsitsi's bare feet made no sound on the cold cement floor. One of these days she would ask him to buy carpets. He never refused her anything, but then she was timid about asking him for things. It's not much of a life, waiting and sitting at home. But mother had done it all her life and the chance to sit and gossip takes out some of the boredom. Her friends Tina and Martha could be quite outrageous in the things they said, talking about the men and the sex thing and how to cope when you suddenly heard rumours your husband was straying. It could be useful too. Like the medicines that made your man yours for life, and how to get rid of a pregnancy. She shuddered, feeling good in scaring herself with the old wives' tales. Right now he was drinking, probably with Joe. She winced, thinking of the whispered rumour about Joe's morals. But Max was sensible. He would not do a thing like that. He always shut his eyes to things like that. There was a blind side to him, which made him do the right thing automatically. But with Joe at his side she could not be sure of him. Always this fear of desertion, this fear of some scarlet woman turning his passion and her life into a nightmare. Not Max. He wouldn't. Tsitsi returned to the kitchen, washed down the vitamins and started to sew. What time was it? *This awful silence.*

Morgan, at the dining-room table, was reading *The Collected Short Stories of H G Wells.* Debbie and Violet had spread their blankets on the floor in the kitchen. Debbie was reading a girls' magazine but her mind was still on Johnny's perplexing change. She had asked Violet but the other girl had laughed: "They all want one thing."

Now Violet was in her own kind of stupor, pouring over the letter Jim had smuggled to her. It began: "My darling Phantom of Delights. . ."

That was a good thing about Jim, this flair for words, making even dirt beautiful. But then, like Johnny, he only wanted one thing and he would not get that until after the wedding. She did not want to lose him. She thought of him as her boyfriend, indeed loved him in her own strange way. Maybe. . . What if he got it from another girl? He had even hinted as much but had later said he had only been joking. That's what I don't get, how they can *joke* about it. A subtle cruelty, a veiled threat. But his letters were always honey, a soothing distant caress that lulled you, cajoled you into responding.

Mother was fast asleep in the one bedroom. She was snoring gently, one arm flung over the top of the blankets. Beads of sweat studded her brow. In the dream she was a man riding a bicycle down Makoni Avenue. From all sides there came a hail of stones and she cycled faster but the stones seemed to come from everywhere. A big stone smashed the back of her skull. Blood and bones flew everywhere and she was falling. Falling.

Morgan raised his head sharply, hearing the scream from the bedroom.

"What's wrong, mama?" he shouted.

There was dead silence. But then she spoke: "It's nothing. Just a bad dream."

Thomas stood against the street light, hands deep in his pockets. He was looking down at his feet, bare and caked with dust. A deep frown creased his face. There was so much to think about. The moon in its final phase was directly overhead. Something was going out of his life. What would come next, he wondered. Darkness? Oblivion? He had reached that stage where he was no longer a boy and yet was not an adult. There was nothing apart from the books. And it was all hard work ahead. He wanted to get into the university, but that was still a long distance away. *Why all this loneliness!* Coldly white, like a fleck of ice painted against a wall of blackness, the moon beyond the street light glinted at him. But the distance. . .what a great leap it takes to be other people, their insane triviality, their tightly coiled uniqueness—as if they knew something he would never know. That was what there was to think about tonight. Grace. He had finally written her a letter, in despair. She was Jim's sister. He had worshipped her for a long time without ever approaching her. He had asked her to meet him where he was now standing, waiting hopelessly, knowing she would not come. She had already shown my letter to everyone and they were all laughing, he thought bitterly. He usually expected the worst from other people. *People are so unreliable.* Not mother though. And she must not ever know about father. That would kill her. The pinpoint of light approached very slowly from the other end of the street. As it drew near, he saw it was a girl on a bicycle. He looked hard at the face. It was Grace. His heart stood still. She got off the bicycle and, holding it upright between them, she waited for him to speak. Breathing painfully, from some unknown crevice in his soul his voice came out cracked. Passion and joy and the weakening uncertainty of what to do or what not to do.

."Hello, Grace," he said.

She was looking straight into his eyes. "Hello, Tom. What made you wait so long?"

She offered her hand. He clasped it tenderly. Still not believing. "I was. . .afraid." He was very much aware of the bicycle between them. That great distance of darkness. She wore a white sweater over a white skirt. And tennis shoes. He was aware of his own shabbiness. Most boys of his age already wore trousers and shoes.

"There was no need," she said. She saw his difficulty.

SCRAPIRON BLUES

The words hissed through his clenched teeth: "I have always loved you, Grace."

She looked at him and he understood. A great joy like galloping mustangs drummed in his breast. He could not speak. She reluctantly withdrew her hand. "Come," she said. "Walk me home."

He took the bicycle and they walked together down the street. They stopped a few yards from her home. He was suddenly afraid of losing her. His mouth trembled. From inside her sweater she took an envelope. This too he understood. He thrust it into his shirt pocket.

"Will you come with me to the cinema tomorrow?" he asked.

"Of course," she replied. She thought a bit. "Tell Violet I will come to ask her out. I will be with Jim. That way there won't be trouble."

"Won't Jim be angry with me, about you and me?"

She smiled. "No, he won't. Don't you know he is courting your sister?"

He shook his head, confused.

"Violet?"

"Yes?"

They were silent awhile. Then very gently she said: "I must go now. I will see you tomorrow at half past seven."

And she was gone before he had scarcely said goodbye.

Jim and Violet? He started to laugh. He had never thought of her as a girl all grown up.

In the lounge bar, Blessing and Joe were dancing the quick complicated rhythms of smanjemanje. They were right in front of the stage. A big grin split Joe's face. *Fuck the corpses. This was life.* A great big hunk of it. Like this woman. Everything easy, not unnaturally complicated. Max sat on a hard chair at the end of the room among other friends, talking, gesturing. The overhead lights shimmered eerily through the thick cigarette smoke. But that was all right. The music boomed, pounded the white-washed walls. Max took a swig from his Castle. A girl, smart and sleek in jeans, denim jacket and Afro-wig, started to dance. Max could see she was dancing from inside her own dream,

146

not from outside the music. He smiled shyly at her but she could not see him from within her trance.

"Of course the driver was drunk," Max was almost shouting in the drunken din. "Me—imagine it if I went to work drunk and having to cope with all those corpses. I only drink in the evenings. But it was terrible, all those people who died. I saw them. Terrible."

"There's nothing wrong with drink, only the time for drinking it in," someone said. They were all silent for a while, thinking deep philosophical thoughts about death. Max smiled at the girl again. She caught his eyes and came over, sitting on his lap.

"What will you have?" he asked.

"Castle."

"Waiter!" he shouted.

There was something nagging at Joe's mind, something his wife had said. Through the fog of alcohol and female flesh and the stale stink of beer and sweat he tried to remember. Something about another baby. He smiled wryly. *That's the povo's lot.* And those two who are going to secondary school. It always came down to Money. Money earned from the dead. *Now if I had any education.* But the thought was too big. He began to dance furiously.

Tsitsi dropped the knitted things. She looked wildly around her. Something, someone had just smashed the dining-room window. She grabbed the poker and rushed out of the kitchen. A hooded head was peering through the shattered pane, one arm trying to unlatch the window. She screamed, throwing herself forward, lashing hysterically at the arm. She screamed as the window shoved open. The figure, all in black, was jumping over the sill, grappling at the poker, the other arm swinging up and pointing the revolver at her. She screamed, hitting out blindly with the poker, but the blast of the gun echoed and re-echoed. As she fell, he leaped over her, looking round with slow precision. He picked up the poker and again and again smashed at the woman's body.

Thomas heard the shot as he walked past the house. A black figure leaped over the gate and started to run towards him. The boy screamed as the gun scrunched onto his head. The figure swept on like an arrow down the street. For a moment there was total silence. Then doors and windows creaked open everywhere, faces peering out. Men hushed and hustled their wives and children back. They were armed with sticks, axes, knives, anything that could be used as a weapon. From all sides of the street they erupted into Thomas' fading consciousness. A man reached him just before the boy passed out. In the distance, a police siren smashed the silence.

"In there," the boy gasped, pointing. A flush of blood seeped down his face.

The man spoke sharply to the others. They peered over the hedge, over the gate—an ominous angry crowd. The police car screeched to a halt, blue lights flashing. A constable rushed to the boy. He ran back to the car and tensely radioed for an ambulance. Then he ran into the house. He came out vomiting, but soon recovered and once again snarled into the radio.

Silas vigorously stirred the steaming sadza. The vegetables were done; the little pot was simmering by the side of the fire. The only light in the black grimy room came from the squat sweating candle. He shoved more sticks onto the fire, then blew gently at the coals till flames leaped up. His dark red eyes glowed, squinting at the sadza. He breathed heavily. Father would arrive any time now. He clanked the lid onto the sadza pot, and waited, listening to its hissing steam.

On the walls around him—there was only this one room—were coats and trousers, shabby and tattered, hanging from rusty nails. A shaft of steam hit his face as he took the lid off and gave the sadza a final twist with the big wooden spoon. It was ready. Ash and grit from the mud floor grimed his knees and elbows. The metal plates rattled as he scooped out the sadza and the vegetables into two portions, the big one for his father, the small one for himself. He stood in the doorway, looking up at the waning moon, puzzled; his thin frame slouching slightly to the left, like a malignant animal discovering the vast empty night for the first time. He was very hungry. He turned back into the room and sat on the small reed mat. He began to eat, slowly and deliberately. There was silence. His eyes smarted from the fire smoke.

The man stood in the doorway, breath rasping, taking off the black hood using it to wipe the sweat from his face. Silas looked up.

"Good evening, father," the boy said.

The man grunted, then padded to the bigger reed mat and sat down. Silas took the dish and hurried out to the tap some distance away in the dark night. He returned, panting, balancing the dish on his head. He placed it before his father. The man washed his hands. He wore a black sweater, black trousers, black socks and black shoes. Silas set the food before him. The man began to eat, fingers digging into the mound of sadza, snatching, moulding it, dipping it into the vegetables.

Debbie whipped her dress over her frail shoulders. She yawned. Wearing only her panties, she crawled into the blankets. Johnny was no longer there. No one was there. She felt her body, heavy, drifting into an inexplicable languor. What was that last thought, like the sound of distant gunfire? Yes, why was Johnny so changed? She was fast asleep. *Let go! Johnny let go.* She turned fierce eyes on him. But even as she watched, Johnny quickly changed into a spitting snarling cobra, the luminous green hood as wide as the winter night. The long needle-point fangs obscenely protruded from the night's black gums. *No! Johnny no!* Her purple lips drew back over her teeth. The scream tore through the house as a terrible pain ripped her body inside out.

She was sitting up, trembling, shivering, encased in ice so tight she could not stand the heat.

Violet was hurriedly lighting the stub of candle, frightened.

"What is it, Debbie?" she asked.

The younger girl said nothing. *What is happening to me? My god, what has happened to me?*

Mother's face floated into view. Prying, poking, peering into Debbie's eyes. *That's mother.* Making her drink something that tasted like whitewash. Debbie threw up. Mother's voice—the old wrinkled hands wiping something with the towel—was gentle, afraid.

"Debbie, try and keep it down," mother said and without pause instructed Violet how to make another tumbler of the medicine.

Debbie's body writhed, shuddered, but she managed to keep the second dose down. The spasms gradually died down and the girl drifted into an uneasy sleep.

What's wrong with her, mama?" Violet whispered.

But mother shook her head, not really knowing.

149

Morgan wandered back into the dining-room but he could not sleep. He lit the candle and tried to read himself to sleep. He was thinking and not thinking.

Max was silently crying into his beer glass. He was precariously perched on a barstool. He and Joe had finally drifted into the cocktail bar where it was quiet and the smartness of the place was spooky. It was not at all like the beer garden or the lounge bar. Here were only the pillars of society. Conversation was quiet and low. The women were the cream of their sordid trade. *Why am I crying?* There was always this sentimental part of each drinking evening. Inexplicable bitters tears would scald out of his eyes. Everyone pretended not to notice. He did it every night. Where was Joe?

Joe was sitting with young Charlie's father, the teacher. They were talking about the two rascals, Morgan and Charles.

"Those two are inseparable," Charles' father was saying.

Joe nodded, proud that his son should be the intimate friend of a teacher's son; proud that he himself should actually be sitting with that teacher on equal terms, discoursing on matters philosophical and critical. For once, Joe felt, I will have something to chat to my wife about. He did not know how but the two of them, before they became man and wife, had always found something to talk about—this, that, or simply nothing at all. *How we talked! She was young. I was young. The world was young. Our love was brand new.* Each day death expands the space it occupies in our hearts. What was it Max said before he started blubbering? We are accidents waiting for a chance to happen. That was it. You waited and waited but nothing happened. Nothing has happened today to drag my inner core into luminous being. Maybe that whore, Blessing, but it cannot be *her.* Growing old is the discovery of the means to keep the illusion going. The illusion of me, of the community, of the nation. All endlessly waiting for a chance to happen.

But Martin, the teacher, was saying something about Thomas. "A very hard-working boy. I am proud of him."

Joe smiled, nodding.

"We must all try to see he gets into university," Martin added.

"Yes, yes," Joe nodded vaguely. University was something outside his imagination. It was so big he believed and did not believe *his* son Tom could find a place in it. "We'll see," he said.

"All he needs, like most of us, is direction and encouragement," Martin said reflectively, knowing the boy would never get *that* from the likes of Joe. He slowly filled the bowl of his pipe.

The knocking, gentle but firm, persisted. Morgan woke with a start.

"Who is it?" he called.

"Police."

Morgan put on his khaki shorts and knocked on mother's door.

"What is it?" she asked drowsily.

"It's the police, mama."

She said nothing, but he could hear her dressing resignedly. It was not the first time the police had called. She came out, finger against her lips, asking him silently. He gestured towards the door. She squared herself up, facing the door.

"Who is it?" she called.

"Police."

"What do you want?"

"We've brought your son from the hospital."

She hurriedly opened the door. There was Thomas, his head bandaged thickly, looking sheepish and small between the two policemen.

"What happened?"

"He was attacked by some maniac," one of the policemen said. "We have to go now. It's not a bad gash. All he needs is rest." He turned to the boy. "You still have those painkillers, don't you?"

Thomas was clutching the little bottle tightly in his left palm. He said, and it was hardly a whisper: "Yes."

The policemen left.

Mother looked at Thomas. "You better come in, Tom," she said.

Joe and Max were back in the beer garden, drinking the thick cereal beer, singing their favourite tune:

SCRAPIRON BLUES

No need to knock me down
I'm no more than a clown
God in his Grace wears a frown
My human fridge holds all the town.

What was it in wine and song that washed away all of a man's sorrows? Why worry about the answer when the nice neat joke of it all held them fast in its little jaws? Joe and Max held each other tightly.

"You're the only friend I've got, Joe," Max said.

"Well, there's Tsitsi," Joe replied.

Max released himself. "A man can't be friends with his woman, you know what I mean."

Joe nodded, thinking of his own wife.

Max pointed all round the garden

"And there're all these crooks," he said, "they could murder a man just like that for no reason at all."

"No. That is work. And a man is not a man until he works and works it out of himself at night."

"You've got something there, Max," Joe said, slurring his words. He was looking round. "Wonder what those two policemen are looking for?"

Max turned. "Some poor bugger, I bet," he said. 'They don't know how to leave us poor buggers alone. They're always bad news for the likes of you and me. You know that, Joe."

Joe gripped Max's shoulder and whispered: "They're pointing at us," he hissed, hauling himself to his feet. "We better get out of here fast." He was dragging Max towards one of the exits. Max, baffled and puzzled, followed meekly.

Once past the gate, Joe and Max began to run. Several yards behind them, a voice shouted: "Hey, Mister! wait!"

The streets as usual were not well lit. There were large patches of darkness and Joe, leading, kept to these. They dashed into a side lane, crashing and clattering into a heap of metal dustbins.

"Shit!" Joe cursed, rubbing his shins.

They limped along the lane. Something was puzzling Max.

"I say, Joe, what are we running for? We've done nothing wrong. Or have we?"

"Shut up and keep running. A policeman at your heels always means you're in the wrong somehow."

They ran.

Behind them two torches were weaving among the upset dustbins.

A rough hand woke Silas.

"What is it, father?"

"I can't sleep, so why are you sleeping?" The man's voice was curt, reined in.

Silas sat up, thinking: It's going to be one of those nights.

"Is it your head again, father?" the boy asked timidly.

The man grunted assent.

"Then I'll sit up with you, as always," Silas said softly. The massive silence outside was drumming against the walls. And beyond that silence there was the piled-up thunder of the tumultuous planets and stars. And beyond that there was. . . What? He did not know. But father had always said *he* knew and that was what gave him the awful headaches, the painful moods. Silas could not understand it all but when his father said it he knew it was just as he said. The headaches had started after his mother had left his father for another man. The father had become withdrawn, but constantly demanded from the boy a scathing attention which the boy did not understand. There was no need to understand. He is my father, Silas thought.

A helicopter thrashed its pinpoints of red and yellow lights across the winter nightscape. Silas raised his head. His father had crouched over, holding his head tightly between two clenched hands, swaying sideways with the pain.

Grace, in her nightdress, swung herself to and fro on the swing in the back garden. She could not sleep. Jim was playing records in his room—reggae music. Their parents had gone to some party and were not yet back. They would return, father slightly tipsy, hanging onto his cane; and mother would be cross, not speaking to him. She planted her feet onto the lawn, then arching backwards, she heaved herself forward into the air, Jim's music ringing wildly, frenetically, through her head. To and fro. She did not hear the helicopter though it was passing directly overhead. Swinging to and fro. Burring, thrashing its bright lights across the stark streets.

Jim shut the fridge, clutching yet another Coke. He was bored. In his room, he poured the Coke over a generous measure of Baccardi. Then he sank onto a pouffe, shut his eyes, and drank, holding the drink in his mouth for a long time, savouring the bitter sweetness, waiting for the moment when he would no longer be bored. The walls of the room were covered with posters of Bob Marley, Peter Tosh, The Wailers. Novels and comics were scattered everywhere on the floor. He lit a cigarette, drawing the smoke in deeply, holding it, finally letting go.

"Fuck it all!" He strode into the living-room. He dialled. "Hello? Is that Roger Taxis?"

Grace heard the steady drone of the taxi and was not surprised when it stopped at their gate and blared its horn once. He's going to Willie's Nightclub, she thought, swinging to and fro. The helicopter had long since gone to its unknown destination. Swinging.

"Are you all right?" Silas whispered to his father.

But the man did not stir. Silas could hardly keep his eyes open. He did not know whether it was early or late; time had left only its overpowering shadow in the room. And the shadow was darkest where the man sat.

The man's head jerked upwards

"What are you thinking, Silas?"

"Nothing, father."

"That's right," the man chuckled. "You must not ever think."

"Yes, father."

"You must only do as I tell you." The voice was soft, too soft.

"Yes father."

"Thinking leads to death."

"It is as you say, father."

"So death leads to thinking."

"Yes, father."

The man grinned, but the boy could not see.

"Was I thinking just now?" he asked the boy.

"Yes, father."

"Why?"

"Because you are death."

"That's right."

They were silent for a long time in that dark grimy room. Martin, the teacher, had cycled away from the cocktail bar out of the township. He wanted to be alone. He clattered across the stone bridge and, sweating profusely, pedalled up the steep slope that led towards the Rutendo Mountain. He hid his bicycle in the bushes and, panting, struggled his way up to the mountain peak. Now and then he stopped for a rest. *I am old.* It was sparklingly cold but that is how he liked it. On the peak. Sitting on a ledge of rock. Thinking his thoughts. Looking down, with bitter tenderness, at the township he had faithfully served for twenty-three years. In the vague distance he could see the lights of a helicopter.

The slit of moon shone with a last, almost profane, clarity. The glowing bowl of his pipe was warm in the cup of his palm. *Let the music of time play what it will.* This will endure. But was endurance all? A certain inner refinement of spirit, a mellowing, that rare quality which could only be cherished and nourished and at the last regretfully bidden farewell. And, like a diver looking down at the distant rippling pool of life below, this one thought poised itself for the final plunge, the nerve-wrenching shocking suicidal dive into the unknown of his community's heart.

The boy's head snapped back, ringing from the blow. His father, dressed all in black, his eyes glittering at the boy, towered over him.

"Could you not watch with me?" the voice was muffled, sulky.

Silas spat out a tooth, tasting the salt of blood welling up in his mouth.

"I am sorry, father."

"I forgive you this one time, Silas."

"Thank you, father."

The man stuffed a gun and knife within the folds of his clothes. "I am going out."

The man padded out of the room.

Silas held himself in, listening to the footsteps growing fainter and fainter. Then, when he was sure, he rushed outside and retched out of himself the blood and mucus of the blow. He rinsed his mouth with water drawn from the dish his father had washed in and, with a long sigh, fell into a painful sleep. The nightmares would come in the morning.

The Concentration Camp

Part One
The Camp

IN a narrow winding valley in north-west Zimbabwe, there lived two families: the Makoni family and the Murehwa family. Once there had been a big village there with more than two hundred families; but the Rhodesian soldiers came with guns and bombs and most of the villagers were killed. The rest were taken in trucks to concentration camps many miles away.

It was hard and harsh, life in the camp. No one had been allowed to bring maize or anything from their village. There was no water nearby; you had to walk a very long way to get to a river. That water was brackish but it was the only water near the camp. Five years old, Rudo Makoni used to walk with her mother to the river. They fetched water in the early morning. The guards at the gate had rifles. They were Africans. These guards always searched Rudo's mother very carefully whenever she and Rudo were going or returning from the river. Rudo did not like it because the men would put their hands inside her mother's dress. Though there was nothing she could do, Rudo was learning something important about the world in which she lived.

Summer followed winter, and winter followed summer; the years slowly walked through the sky. But the camp was always there. The river was far away and their bare feet hurt going and returning to and from the river.

After fetching the water, the women and the children of the camp went to the piece of land outside the camp where they were allowed to grow maize and vegetables and some pumpkins. It was hard work because few had hoes. Many had to use sticks. Some of the men, like Rudo's father, also helped in these fields. The others were taken away day after day by white soldiers for questioning and sometimes they returned bleeding and unable to walk. Several of the men never returned and were reported killed.

Nine boys had to herd the cattle each day; among them was Tonderai, Rudo's friend. The cattle were few; the rest had been taken away by the soldiers as a punishment for the village. Though it was tiresome living on roots and wild vegetables, the prisoners did not want to kill their cattle for meat. The cattle were now their only wealth.

The prisoners lived in huts made of sticks and grass. Sometimes these were plastered with mud to keep out the cold. There were not enough huts in the compound; many large families squeezed into one small filthy hut. "It's your own fault," the commandant said, "you breed like flies!" The commandant had a round pink face, very small slit eyes set close together, a nose like a sparrow's beak and a small "o" for a mouth. He was completely bald. He was short, fat, with a beer paunch; his palms sweated. "Isn't that so, s'geant?" the commandant asked the African soldier. "You breed like flies, don't you?"

"Yes, sir," the sergeant replied. 'We breed even worse than flies, sir.'

The commandant chuckled.

The two of them walked slowly towards the office. The African soldier looked back over his shoulder at the Makoni family huddled around a cooking fire. Tonderai, who had been watching the commandant, looked away before the sergeant could catch his eye.

His father, Tonderai could see, had been beaten again. One eye was closed and seemed to throb through the fiercely swollen flesh; the other was half open. The right arm was in a rough sling; *they* had broken it for him the week before. Through the rends in the dirty khaki shirt, Tonderai could see his father's weakening ribcage. How thin, how terribly thin he is, Tonderai thought, watching his father's gaunt bulbous knees perched on the dry maize stalks of his feet. The heels and soles were split in many places. When he looked up at his father's bowed head, he realised in shock that his hair had turned completely white within the last twenty-four hours. Or am I mistaken? Tonderai wondered. Surely only yesterday it was. . .

A bitter darkness flashed past his eyes—the beginning of a terrible knowledge. But he did not yet understand. He saw again the sergeant turning, and himself turning his gaze away. The sergeant was tall, heavily built, with a very black, cruelly rectangular face set squat on a disciplined neck. The combat uniform made him look like the fearful face of law and order. But whose law and whose order?

The boy was learning little by little from the horrifying stories whispered around the concentration camp. Dawn followed darkness, and darkness followed day. Heat turned to cold; rain departed, making room for dry frosty days, which in their turn made room for the time when rain chose to return.

Tonderai and the other boys let the cattle wander from tuft to tuft of grass. He missed his exercise books, left behind in the burning village. He tried to remember his arithmetic; tried to recall the English grammar. There was nothing to do while the cattle grazed. Even fighting the other boys was now boring. The games were boring too. Standing on one's head was stupid. Hunting for birds' nests was tedious. Whistling, or blowing through the cow horn of interlaced thumb and fingers, left the mouth dry and horribly thirsty. And there was no clean water nearby. To kill time, Tonderai tried hard to remember his school lessons. But it was hard to do that when the swift night would flash through his brain and he would know with certainty that his father was dying.

As these thoughts drew his mind away from the world, his hands, all unknowing, plaited fresh bark to fresh strip of bark, ceaselessly. He was eight years old, with an oval face the colour of rich dark-red soil, large brown eyes that sparkled suddenly with hidden pain, a flaring nose too mature for his age and a wide sensuous mouth always on the brink of bitterness or poised on the edge of a smile. He was tall for his age, somewhat gawky, conscious of the dirty vest and shorts he wore day after day. His teeth, once clear milk-white, were yellow with plaque. Two of his lower teeth were missing, the result of a kick from the sergeant when the commandant had questioned him about his father's "friends". He had said nothing because he knew nothing; and when they stuck the bayonet to his mother's throat telling him that if she died it would be his fault because he was not telling them about his father's "friends", he had writhed into an epileptic fit and they had to hold him down as his eyes rolled back and his tongue spurted blood. . . The boy's hands worked ceaselessly, plaiting fresh bark onto fresh strip of bark. At that moment he did not know he was making anything. He did not know for whom he was making it. Only when the other boys shook him—it was time to round up the cattle—did he know with a lingering smile: it's for Rudo.

As the boys fanned out, carrying sticks, stalking the stray cattle and cajoling them back into the ranks for the return to the camp, a Hawker Hunter spun out of the bright last rays of the sun, dipping its wings in a metallic flash towards the group of boys and cattle in a strafing run. Tonderai was hurled to the ground and, even before he thudded onto the hardpacked clay, his ears were filled with shrill screams, maddened bellows and, as he hit, his vision encompassed a panoramic scene of horror.

It was a long time before a boot turned him over. He opened his eyes. The sergeant towered over him.

"Get up!" the sergeant barked.

The boy tottered to his feet. His eyes were coming into focus, but it was as if he was seeing the whole world through a thin screen of fresh blood. He still clutched his present for Rudo. He looked up into the sergeant's face. All the darkening twilight of the universe was streaming into the sky from a point at the back of the sergeant's head. Getting darker and darker, minute by minute, month after month, year after year. Century after century.

"Move!"

Tonderai walked forward, staring with amazement at his feet. Four other boys were also on their feet, walking, staring around them with a deep refusal to acknowledge that it had happened. The five survivors mechanically rounded up what was left of the cattle and began to herd them back to the camp kraal. Tonderai, without registering anything, saw that four of the soldiers were carrying four mangled bundles in their arms.

When at last the five were marched up to the gates, the arc-lights from the gunpost towers blazed down on a throng of mothers, fathers and children massed behind the guards in an eerie silence. An anguished hopeless silence; a lethal silence that in an instant transfigured the faces into grotesque masks. A guard began to body-search Tonderai.

His mother's voice rang out: "Tonderai!"

She sprang forward, then stopped in midstride, staring at his face. She sprang forward with a despairing wail and had almost touched him when the rifle butt knocked her spinning backwards. Tonderai looked up at the guard. The sergeant, with a curse, punched the guard aside and pushed the boy in. He rushed to where she lay unconscious.

"Mama! Mama!"

He barely noticed his father hobbling forward. A small hand brushed the back of his neck. He did not notice. He was barely aware of the screams of mourning and the cries of relief as the other prisoners recognised among the bloodstained survivors the face of a son or a nephew or suddenly identified one or two of the dead. This time the sergeant joined the guards in striking again and again with their rifle butts into the howling confusion until all was reduced into a surly acceptance of futility.

"Well, s'geant," the commandant beamed, "a nice bit of work. Got to hand it to the air force, eh?"

"Yes, sir," the sergeant replied.

"Living here safely out of the hands of the terrs, these munts were forgetting there's a war on. . ." The commandant patted him on the shoulder. "They'll appreciate us more, don't you think?"

"That they do, sir."

The commandant frowned. "Well, what I think. . .ah! Tell mess to hand out to all our—er—guests a slice of that cake. Yes. It promotes that necessary community feeling we're trying to instil into them, eh?"

"Yes, sir. Right away, sir!"

Rudo sat down beside him. Her brother, Fani, had not been seriously hurt and she had crept away to the Murehwa hut to see Tonderai. No medicines or bandages had been given out. Tonderai's father had cleaned the wound with the leftover water and greased the horrible gash with the family's Vaseline and had, without hope, finally bound the boy's head with a strip torn from one of the blankets.

A strange sweetness splashed into Tonderai's heart as Rudo took his hand in hers and held it in her lap. It filled him with a mellow confusion that drove away from all around him the steady march of darkness and light; exorcised out of his otherworld the brisk inevitability of paralysis. Her eyes, in the flames of the cooking fire, were fully clasped to his and though they did not know it, the two were in the crucible of a tormenting first love. A love which would not declare love but would simply, giddily say: "You are alive!"

Death was no stranger. They had seen his foul and reeking work back at their village. Here in the camp, with guns bristling everywhere, guns in the sky, guns in the hardpacked ground, cordite in the air you breathed: here death was everywhere. The only thing these two perhaps still had to learn was that in conditions of brutish survival, affection was a luxury, a double-edged sword, a weapon for the enemy; it was anything but what it would be in peacetime. But then, there was something in these children which made them resist being changed overnight into little cynical adults. Perhaps this was the pleasurable pulse rippling through their joined hands. It was a terribly sweet thing to live for. This realisation rushed through them into a certainty: the two of them would never die.

Part Two

The City of Anarchists

HE broke off the bit of nail that had split, inspected it and flicked it onto the ground before him. He up-ended the bottle and the beer slowly slid down his throat. Warm beer. He flung the empty bottle into the dustbin. A splintering crash. He had missed the bus to the funeral; but do the dead miss the living? He took off his coat, placed it on his knees and unbuttoned his shirt. He wiped at the sweat, but that did not help. It was very hot. The heat was in everything. The heat was in the sky. The heat was in the ground. The heat was in his heart. There was nothing to do about it. Except bake; cook your brains with it.

Directly across the square was the girl in a white dress. She sat on a white garden chair at a white garden table. She sat with what seemed to be her parents. He had seen them sitting like that—at exactly that hour—for the last nine days. Not wondering who she was, who they were. There was no curiosity in his seeing. It was just happening. The physical act of seeing. The automatic act of the brain incuriously counting the hours and days of their sitting on white garden chairs around a white garden table. Sipping what looked like Perrier water. But this day the heat of her presence was sneaking into his heart, swelling it, introducing a tenseness into his movements. It was an uncomfortable feeling. They seemed to talk little, like a group fated to be together, without need of speech. But then there was the dog—there it was, sneaking along towards the table. It stopped before the girl, conscious of her but only looking at her feet as though to lick those slender feet with a tongue unused to tenderness. And she, as on the other days, reached into a brown paper bag and started to throw meat and bones at her hairy suitor. A grateful whine and an acknowledging grunt—the dog snatched at the bloody snacks and retired to a distance to eat its tea. At this point he should have risen and left—as on the other days—but the girl in white was running towards him—the parents looking on in astonishment—and—her face a twisted mask of beauty—she looked down at him, earnestly: "Will you come tomorrow? Please."

That voice! He nodded.

She was immediately off, running back to her table. The dog trotted towards him. He smiled encouragingly and it let him pat its back.

It was time to leave. The dog followed him out of the square. When he looked back he saw the father slap the girl and she shook her head in defiance, like one refusing to cry. He walked on.

When he entered the tavern, Jimmy the Dwarf and thin Larry Long beckoned to him. The dog curled under the table. Larry shouted at the waiter for more beer. Jimmy lifted his glass to propose a toast: "To the revolution!"

Larry and Otto echoed the fine sentiment. Otto asked the waiter to bring a bowl of water for the dog. As the dog slurped under the table, the three drinking companions carried on an animated, though whispered, discussion—even walls have ears. Otto declared he was ready—the approach had been made. Jimmy rasped that he had finished the bomb. Larry smiled affirmatively when they asked him about his end of the job.

The tavern was in the very poor section of the town. It was at the end of a filthy alley graced by similar establishments at whose doorways dirty ragged urchins tried to sell not only themselves but the oddest kind of junk. There were brothels offering little boys and little girls. There were opium dens more decadent than any low visions the depraved mind could imagine. At all hours it was business as usual. Men in female garb roamed the area for clients; women dressed as men paced up and down looking for women to prey on. Small-time gamblers plied their dice on the grubby pavements. Lewd ditties deafened the ear from all sides. Muggers, pickpockets, drunks, army deserters and all those who through some quirk of fate had become habitués of this slimy skid row—they all rubbed shoulders, knifed each other, acted out their nightmares together and, not infrequently, broke out in hysterical riots that would leave everything devastated, snarled and in smoking ruin. It was a difficult area to patrol; the law enforcers could never wholly penetrate the maze of alleys and indiscriminate hovels. None here believed in law and order—it was dog eat dog. You made money even over your dead mother's body.

Larry Long and Jimmy the Dwarf eked out a grubby income by presenting themselves to the public as a two-man freak show. In between shows, they supplemented their income by burglaries which left none but the patrols baffled. But now, with talk of the "revolution" all over the country, Jimmy and Larry had seen the chance to accumulate a tidy nest egg for their old age. Now there were all these foreigners ready to finance a bit of bombing and the odd assassination. The funny thing was: Otto seemed to take the "revolution" seriously at its face value.

Otto was the educated one, yet he had this impractical idealism. Not quite education, because he had been expelled from the university for some unexplained crime. Jimmy tried to find out what the crime was but Otto remained tight-lipped. Well, well—Jimmy was saving that for later. The three of them had grown up together in this neighbourhood but it was Otto who had had the only chance to escape from poverty. Maybe that was what had crippled him: all those books he read—even in the bar—must have unhinged something in his brain. But he was useful in that he could fluently compose the revolutionary pamphlets and speeches which were necessary if the foreigners were to be convinced of the trio's revolutionary sincerity. Ah, quite useful indeed. The nonsense was, he really believed the shit about class warfare and the inevitability of the revolution—sometimes it made Larry ill. After all, it's money that oils the wheels, money that lubricates the inevitable stiffness of old age, Jimmy was sure. You had to watch yourself when talking to Otto—like this dog, snuffling under the table. As far as Jimmy was concerned, that dog would do nicely as a steak with mushroom sauce and fried onions, and you could even sell the skin as a sort of furry scarf for some of the transvestites. But there was Otto, talking *seriously* about the rights, the fundamental rights, of living things. Living things were only okay if they put something in your belly, and a bit of coin in your pocket. Jimmy knew about struggle; he had had, all his life, to struggle to survive. Not that he was bitter. You had the measure of your fate according to the size of your cloth. He understood that. But with a patch here, some trimming there, you could bend your fortune somewhat to your taste. Jimmy thought of himself as a realist: no room for dreams, though with the right application the imagination could be compelled to serve the ends of realism. The imagination was not there to serve the illusions of dream and fantasy; it was there to serve life, and life was, though temporal, a very practical phenomenon indeed. For Jimmy, of course. This talk about starving peasants and workers was all very well but all of them, like Jimmy, looked to number one where the belly and its comforts were concerned. Altruism did not exist in Jimmy's vocabulary; if it did, it was the insincere mumbo-jumbo that ultimately led to one's own personal advancement. We are artists of the dark, Jimmy thought sadly, working like manure underground to exploit seed and plant to our own enrichment. Otto is a plant, ready to wilt and add to our resources.

Jimmy, looking at Otto, proposed another toast. "To the success of our mission!" Jimmy, though buoyant still, kept his voice down. True, the place was nothing but a thieves' den among other thieves' dens in Vice Mile. But still, you can't be too careful. After all, even a sodding informer is only after what we're all after: MONEY.

Jimmy beamed at Otto who, as usual, seemed abstracted. "Surely, Otto, you have not fallen in love?" Jimmy chuckled, hedging his eyes.

Otto blinked, wiped his brow. "You don't know how beautiful she is," he replied. "But that does not mean I have fallen in love."

He was seeing her again, seeing her the way he had suddenly seen her and how it had swollen in his heart. The girl in the white dress sitting at the white table sipping, perhaps, a mild but very expensive cocktail. The thought brought him up short. "But she does not belong to the revolution," he said a little sadly. "She is only a sympathiser. Only a rich middle class princess going through a tantrum of rebellion against her parents. And only against her parents. So I say she is beautiful because that is the truth. But it is also true that even though she will help me I know she is part of the problem we are trying to eliminate."

Larry Long leaned forward, leering. "You could just fuck her though."

Otto bit his lower lip and chewed. "That shows me, Larry, that you did not read my last pamphlet-but-one on the alliance between women's liberation and the revolutionary struggle." He paused, biting his fingernail. He banged the table with his fist. "DID YOU!"

Jimmy tentatively touched him on the shoulder, looking warily round the bar. But no one had noticed anything untoward. "Otto. . ."

Otto's temper immediately subsided. He drank for a long time without pausing for breath. At last he looked at Larry, a faint smile flickering at the corners of his mouth. "You must understand those pamphlets. Right. Order some more beer and I will explain to you the details of this alliance," he said. He shuffled off his chair. "Carry on, Otto. I'll just take some air for a bit."

Jimmy the Dwarf shouldered his way through the crowd of thighs and knees. At last, panting slightly, he reached the door. His sneering lips became almost a smile as he scanned the depraved activity of the alley. About two yards to his right, a couple were in the throes of ejaculation. At their feet two little girls dressed in nothing but G-strings were fondling a cackling old degenerate who was squirming luxuriously. Across the alley, a skinhead and a very weird Hell's Angel were lashing at each other with brass knuckles, bicycle chain, a trident, and what looked like a steel wire net.

Jimmy chuckled. He let loose a piercing whistle and shouted: "Ten dollars to the winner, you two! But mind you observe the rules. I'll be at my usual table."

The two gladiators set to with a will as Jimmy, rubbing his hump and still chuckling, made his way back to the table. Larry, beer untouched, was sitting bolt upright staring at Otto with glazed eyes. Otto seemed to have reached a triumphant but sober conclusion: ". . .and in countries like Cuba, the Soviet Union, China, the Democratic People's Republic of Korea and the German Democratic Republic this necessary and inevitable alliance has worked."

Jimmy climbed onto the chair. A feeling of awe swept through him whenever he heard that note of inevitable victory in Otto's voice. He could sometimes envy Otto for it. After all, Jimmy liked to think that there was something more to life than grubbing for money. It was a poetic feeling he sometimes had when money was no problem. It didn't do to dwell on this poetry too much but it's sweet to scratch oneself when the itch is there and one's hands are not in handcuffs.

"Well, Jimmy, how's it outside?" Otto had cheered up.

Larry was fast draining his beer.

Jimmy winked: "All's well for the peasants and the workers," he said, running a pink tongue over his dry lips.

Part Three

The Camp

Characters:

Two deserters from the Bishop's paramilitary Pfumo Revanhu :

HANNES

BOLT

Thunder and lighting. A thick forest struck into sight by the flickering of the electric storm. A cloaked figure, desperate, skids across the stage. The growl of jackals pursues him. Heavy tread of sudden rain. Change to: A room in which two nasty-looking characters are conversing.

HANNES: No, no.

BOLT: Why not?

HANNES: I don't know. It's just no.

BOLT: I'll kill her myself

HANNES: You can't.

BOLT: Why not?

HANNES: Stop saying "Why not?"

BOLT: Why?

HANNES [*shouting*]: Shut up!

BOLT: Why should I shut up?

HANNES: There you go again—WHY WHY WHY Why?

BOLT: You're saying it—

HANNES: I wasn't.

BOLT: But why—

HANNES: My boots.

BOLT: What?

HANNES: I don't know.

BOLT: You don't know your boots?

HANNES: I didn't say that.

BOLT: But you said you don't know your boots.

HANNES: Boots cannot be known.

BOLT: I know mine.

HANNES: What intelligence do they have?

BOLT [*shaking his boots*]: Listen.

HANNES: The Bishop will arrive any minute.

BOLT [*shaking his boots*]: Did you hear that?

HANNES: I've seen better ventriloquy.

BOLT: Right, wise guy. [*Shakes his boots*] Listen.

[*Pause.*]

THE BOOTS: You fool, the Bishop will arrive any moment now.

[*Pause.*]

HANNES [*awed*]: Did you say that?

BOLD [*shakes his head; points at his boots*]: I didn't. They did.

HANNES: I don't like this.

BOLT: Neither do I.

HANNES: Let's get out of here.

BOLT [*shaking his head, looking around him*]: Out of where?

HANNES: Here!

BOLT: Where's that?

HANNES: Your boots are talking. Let's get out of here.

[*They rise.*]

BOLT [*looking down at his boots*]: I say, Hannes. . .

HANNES: What now? Come on.

BOLT: They said the Bishop is somewhere out there. Nearby.

HANNES: Where's that?

BOLT: How should I know. We've got to stay here because he isn't here. If we leave here we'll meet the Bishop.

HANNES [*puzzled*]: You've got a point there but I don't see where it is.

BOLT [*shouting*]: Right here!

HANNES [*even more perplexed*]: Where? [*Looks round and round*] I can't see it here.

BOLT: Of course you can't because it's not there.

HANNES: Well, if it's not there and it's not here then I don't see what you are getting at.

BOLT: I'm not getting anywhere.

HANNES: Maybe your boots will tell us.

BOLT [*shakes his boots*]: Maybe.

THE BOOTS: You guys can stick yourselves up your. . .!

HANNES [*looking up*]: There's nothing to stick ourselves up.

BOLT: There's the sky—but I'm no astronaut.

HANNES [*sitting down like Rodin's Thinker*]: I've heard it before. . .

BOLT: Heard what?

HANNES: That voice.

BOLT: What voice? [*Straining his ears*] I don't hear anything.

HANNES: In your. . .boots

BOLT: In my. . . [*Jumps.*]

HANNES [*significantly*]: See what I mean? [*Pause. Nods.*]

BOLT [*sitting down, staring at his boots*]: He said we know where to stick ourselves up.

HANNES: He? Who?

BOLT: The voice in the boots.

HANNES: Take them off and we'll see what's inside.

BOLT: Take him off. . .?

HANNES: Your boots!

BOLT: You know he's always talked like that after a good. . . [*He winks.*]

HANNES: But I thought he was gay.

BOLT: He is.

HANNES: What?

BOLT: What you thought. [*Thinks*] Do you think he wants us for. . .er. . .that sort of thing?

HANNES: I don't see anything. [Pause] There's the ceiling. [*Pause*] And there you are. But you're not a thing. [*Thinks*] Which the ceiling is

BOLT [*yawning*]: There are the walls. If these things were not here how would we know where we are or that we are at all?

HANNES [*whispering*]: We're here because of the Bishop.

BOLT: She said he is a walking dead. A zombie. A werewolf. But then you can't trust hystericals, can you?

HANNES: What hystericals? [*Looking round*] Where?

BOLT [*pointing at the floor*]: She's in there.

HANNES [*puzzled*]: Did we give her food and water today?

BOLT: I don't know. I'm not very good at acting a jailer.

HANNES: You mean we are jailers?

BOLT [*nods*]: I think we did. [*Pause*] I think we didn't. [*Pause*] But again it's all beyond me. [*Pause*] Isn't it?

HANNES: What is beyond who?

BOLT [*fiddling with the trapdoor lock*]: Her. In there.

HANNES: But she is not beyond you. [*Looking down*] She is under you.

BOLT: Beneath me?

HANNES: The Bishop said all women are beneath one.

BOLT: Which one?

HANNES [*thinking*]: He didn't elaborate. He just said they are all beneath one. [*Pause*] Maybe he meant God. And since she is under you right now then you must be God.

BOLT [*scared*]: Don't say that.

HANNES: I didn't say that.

BOLT: No. No. I don't mean. . . You didn't say it.

HANNES: I didn't say *it*.

BOLT [*with relief*]: Then we must shake hands on it, comrade.

HANNES [*looking round*]: I don't see him.

BOLT: Who?

HANNES: The comrade you want to shake hands with.

BOLT: That's a thought.

HANNES: A comrade is a thought?

BOLT: Sometimes. Yes. . . No. I think we didn't. I mean feed her. [*Pause*] Did we feed her yesterday? And all the days before?

HANNES: I suppose it's her concern. I mean she's the one who needs feeding so she must know the answer to that one. [*Thinks*] A jailer is not a waiter, is he?

BOLT: Who?

HANNES: The waiter is not the jailer.

BOLT: I see.

HANNES: No, no it's your eyes which see. Not you.

BOLT: Not me?

HANNES: Eyes are eyes.

BOLT: I see. . .

HANNES [*thoughtfully*]: You're a funny one.

BOLT [*brightly*]: Like Groucho Marx? Eh?

HANNES: He's dead.

172

BOLT: You mean I'm possessed.

HANNES: It's the voice I seem to remember.

Bolt: Voice—where?

HANNES: The voice in your boots. [*Pause*] Boots which smash down doors at the crack of dawn.

BOLT: Is that a movie?

HANNES: No. It's. . .military. [*Pause*] Boots which thump up and down the pavement.

BOLT: Sounds like a rendezvous.

HANNES: Boots which lurk by the staircase.

BOLT: Hitchcock.

HANNES: Boots which kick your teeth in.

BOLT [*scared*]: Ssssh. That's either crime or politics.

HANNES: Dragged by your boots into the mortuary.

BOLT: Ssh. That's horror.

HANNES: Black market boots. Concentration camp boots. Strike me blue if the stars are not forgotten loot.

BOLT: Singing in the rain.

HANNES: Like I dream of the Dust Bowl, of Oklahoma, of how boots make the man.

BOLT: Not the child.

HANNES: Know what we're doing?

BOLT [*thinks*]: Damned if I know. Do you?

HANNES [*whispers*]: Are we waiting for the Bishop or are we hiding from him?

BOLT [*pauses*]: Waiting is hiding, isn't it? Like jailing.

HANNES: Hiding from God?

BOLT: Maybe that's what all this is.

HANNES [*points at the trapdoor*]: She said the Bishop is the Devil.

BOLT: Is that why my boots talk?

HANNES: Don't talk about your boots, please.

BOLT: Not the boots but the talking.

HANNES: There's an artist who specialised in portraits. Know what he did to portray the character of his clients? [*Bolt shakes his head. Pause. He studies their boots*] If he was here right now he'd study your boots to find out everything about you. Like the others study palms, and the others study the shape of your skull. Phrenologists. Others read the tea leaves at the bottom of your teacup. And there are all those others who study your dreams and the consistency of your shit and the mucus running down your nose and the map of pimples on your face and backside. [*Pause*] Life. Like we are all hidden from God and he has to study us like that to discover the nature of the bastards he created. If you create life out of yourself, is that incest? That's what he did, rubbing himself up to ejaculate us into the world.

BOLT: That's interesting. . . [*Looking round*] What world?

HANNES [*staring round and round and down at the trapdoor*]: This, I suppose.

BOLT: A room is not a world.

HANNES: You can't get out of it. [*Pause, strangely*] Haven't you noticed about this room? [*Whispers*]: There is no door.

BOLT [*checking*]: You're right, there's no door anywhere. [*Thinks*] No, there is. [*Points at the trapdoor*] The trapdoor. We can go down into there.

HANNES: But she is in there.

BOLT: And we are up here.

HANNES: Do you think the Bishop did this to us?

BOLT: I don't know. But don't you remember he gave us a lot of liquor and a lot of those drugs he said were very good for the soul?

HANNES: I don't remember. Christ, I don't remember.

BOLT: Maybe we are not supposed to remember things.

HANNES: But the voice in the boots reminded us of the Bishop.

BOLT [*staring at his boots*]: You mean my mind, my memory, is all in my boots?

HANNES [*critically*]: Not all of it, I think.

BOLT: I remember the Bishop.

HANNES: Don't!

BOLT: Well, he. . .

HANNES: For God's sake, don't!

BOLT: But if God is the Bishop. . .

HANNES: Or the Devil. . .

BOLT: Right. [*Pause*] It wasn't a still small voice, was it? You said the voice in the boots reminded you of something or someone.

HANNES [*frightened*]: Worse than that.

BOLT: Then I don't want to know.

HANNES [*pointing at the trapdoor*]: I think it's something to do with her being there. [*Pause*] Was I ever married?

BOLT: I don't remember.

HANNES: And weren't you her brother?

BOLT: How would I know?

HANNES [*striking the wall*]: I think I was, but as soon as I think that I become certain that I never was.

BOLT [*clicks his fingers*]: That's it! You were. And you were not.

HANNES: That sounds about right.

BOLT: And you played the mbira like the Devil himself.

HANNES: I did?

BOLT: And when you played, all the rats, cockroaches, mosquitoes, bees, wasps and fleas came out to listen at your feet. [*Pause*] You were the devil himself with that mbira. . . [*Smiling*] Those sure were the days.

HANNES [*struck by a massive thought*]: So I'm here to rescue her, take her up?

BOLT: I'm not a marriage counsellor.

HANNES: Did the Bishop take her away from me?

BOLT: He did worse to her than that.

HANNES: Then I don't want to know. [*Pause*] You mean he. . .?

BOLT: Worse.

HANNES: I'm getting out of here!

BOLT: The only way out is down.

HANNES: I see what you mean.

BOLT [*ear to the wall*]: Can you hear it?

HANNES: What?

BOLT: The hurricane of silence out there.

HANNES [*ear to the wall*]: Christ, yes. It's mind-boggling.

BOLT: Then where are we? [*Pause*] Like this is all the world there is. And the rest is silence.

HANNES: That sounds like death.

BOLT: Maybe we are. . .

HANNES: Dead?

BOLT [*nods*]: Or [*hopefully*] we have merely strayed into the land of the dead.

HANNES : You mean we're lost somewhere in the underworld?

BOLT: Well, you did insist. I told you it was. . .weird.

HANNES: I wanted to come here?

BOLT [*points at trapdoor, nods*]: You talked a lot of nonsense about how much you loved her, how you'd bring her back to life. [*Pause. He thumps the trapdoor with his boot*] Listen.

[*An enchanted mbira melody issues from beneath the trapdoor. They listen. BOLT's eyes are riveted on HANNES who gradually falls into a paroxysm of grief until, thrusting himself down on all fours, he bursts himself inside out in a demented but strangely silent scream.*]

Part Four

A Cast of Cadres

A path in the forest. Intermittent drumming is heard from a distance. A group of recent refugees enter and squat wherever on stage like an expectant audience. Enter a fat black SLAVE TRADER in khaki and topee carrying a rifle. He begins to sing:

I wouldn't believe a Kimberley bootblack
A Jo'burg tsotsi, a Durban squatter
I couldn't believe a Cape gardener
A farmer's floozie, a DC's flunky

I couldn't believe an office boy
A kitchen boy, a lady's chauffeur
I couldn't believe—hey comrades
I couldn't even think
I couldn't even perceive—comrades.

A CHORUS OF COMRADES *enters guarding five white* WOMEN SLAVES, *singing:*

I couldn't believe—couldn't believe
A Kimberley bootblack
A Jo'burg tsotsi
A Durban squatter
A Cape gardener
A farmer's floozie
A DC's flunky
An office boy
A kitchen boy
A lady's chauffeur.

SLAVE TRADER: I couldn't believe.

CHORUS OF COMRADES:

A Soweto schoolboy
A woman of Crossroads
A Marxist miner.

SLAVE TRADER: We couldn't believe.

CHORUS OF COMRADES:

We could all get together!

SLAVE TRADER: We couldn't believe.

CHORUS OF COMRADES:

We could all pull together!

CHORUS OF WHITE WOMEN: We could all change it together!

SLAVE TRADER: I don't believe my ears. What did you all say?

Both CHORUSES:

We could all pull it down

Pull it

Down!

For the better.

SLAVE TRADER [*pointing at a boy in the stage audience*]: Name?

FIRST BOY: Peter.

SLAVE TRADER: And we are here to pull who down?

FIRST BOY: Botha.

SLAVE TRADER [*to another*]: You. Name?

SECOND BOY: Themba.

SLAVE TRADER: To pull who down?

SECOND BOY: Botha.

> *The* SLAVE TRADER *(singing) asks five other boys and girls while, behind him, the* CHORUS OF COMRADES *and the* CHORUS OF WHITE WOMEN *interweave their voices starting from the beginning but this time the* CHORUS OF WHITE WOMEN *enumerates in sequence their professions, if any, when still in South Africa.*

* * *

> *The* SLAVE TRADER *has changed into camouflage. He is now the* CAPTAIN. *He has the* CHORUS OF COMRADES *in formation before him. He drills them in between the following verses:*

CAPTAIN:

Apartheid is an ideal
That twinkles only in gutters.

Apartheid is an ideal
To perverts behind closed shutters.

Apartheid is only real
To faggot Afrikaners
Who fuck their daughters

* * *

CHORUS OF WOMEN [*behind large TV-like frame*]:

This is the South African Broadcasting Corporation.

Among the latest government reforms are the following:

Fifteen blacks have been reclassified Japanese.

Seven Chinese have been reclassified Indian.

The white who turned black last June is now officially black though
a decision about his specific tribe still has to be ascertained.

Nineteen whites have been reclassified coloured.

A government spokesman also added that three Eskimos who were
discovered living on the immoral earnings of white women sought
political asylum in the Dutch embassy which as you all know beats the
best whorehouse in Texas. [*Pause.*]

The minister of foreign affairs is reported heartbroken following the
defection to SWAPO of his favourite black Dobermann bitch while on
a working visit to Windhoek. [*Pause.*]

The notoriously racist, Marxist regime in Zimbabwe has dared to send
a congratulatory telegram to the first non-racial couple to be married in
South Africa. This blatant subversion of our postal services. . . Sorry,
the rest of the bulletin is unprintable, I mean, unbroadcastable.

That was the SABC NEWS BULLETIN. Now there follows a unique guest
commentary by the former prime minister of Zimbabwe-Rhodesia who
was ousted in a coup plotted by the British on behalf of Moscow.

Part Five

The Intellectual's Revolt

TWILIGHT by the lakeshore. An uncertain breeze worried the tall grass and msasa
branches. Piles of a giantchild's playrocks loomed in the distance. A clear twilight, cloud-
less, not too warm, bringing to eye and ear and nose—and to tongue—the resonance of

a distant purity.

Domain of the manfish.

An undistinguished block of flats in the avenues. It is twilight. The meal of dull minced beef and bread is over. The toilet is flushed. The pages turn slowly but surely as the eye follows the tale of India's midnight children. A cockroach creeps in from the kitchen. It crawls along the wall. It stops and begins again to watch.

Watching Craig.

Craig drops the book. Drops the present. He concentrates on his anger. He watches carefully, concentrates, watches it grow. From a dull insignificant baby, thumb firmly in mouth, it grows into a morose-looking youth who does not know why he is there at all; it then grows into a bespectacled faintly smiling student on graduation day; and finally into the shape that is sitting in the armchair, a book on the floor.

Craig.

The body of the spirit of the air. The birdman, wings of brass stirring heavily from the muscles of his shoulders.

If there is a soul and it is for sale, where is the buyer? And there are all these concentrated possibilities of emotion which find no attainable confirmation out there, no buyers, no takers. And the empty honeycomb within the heart—who or what out there will arrive with the pure liquid gold and the motor pulse to life again?

Craig's mind swivels to the distant lakeshore, to the probability of the manfish. Though the waters ripple, no message washes gently on the tide towards him. He shivers; the breeze has become stronger, colder. He looks up, and the stars are fixed in their own chilly realm.

The cockroach raises its antennae. Questioningly.

He picks up the book. Somewhere above him, a woman screams. The scream is cut off suddenly. Craig throws the book onto the bed. He pours himself a shot from the fifth of whisky on the bookshelf. His face in the bathroom mirror is puffy; there is a cut above the right eye. The eyes are a transparent but dark shade of brown; their inner lattices show emotion too easily, but he does not consider that a weakness. He switches on the radio. Some choir is fervently singing a revolutionary song. He switches it off. On the television, a broadcaster is describing in footnote detail the topic of dialectical materialism. He switches it off. Only the cheap gramophone is left; he plays Mick Jagger's latest solo album, *She's the Boss*. He pours himself a big one, stands in the middle of the room, drinking. He has stopped asking himself what's wrong. If this is how it is, then that's how it is. It's years since his graduation day. What's wrong? It's three years since he came out of jail. He had killed his wife. He notices but ignores the cockroach. What's wrong with a cockroach anyway?

I killed my wife, but what does that mean? But the manfish does not answer. Perhaps the manfish has no answer. There is no answer— is that how it is? The sun comes up. The sun goes down. Rivers flow into the seas, into the lakes. A cockroach watches. The cigarette is lit, stumped out. Another. Day. The dry dusty region when all iris-moisture, cheek PURPOSE, has evaporated. Spare me, O Lord, the evil eye of emptiness. It was not a bad brand, the whisky, a local brand hiding behind the label "Avion". There never seemed to be enough air in the flat; too cramped. It was the ground floor— the curtains always had to be discreetly closed otherwise all and sundry would have a free movie of his life. The newspapers had already done that, after his arrest and during his trial and sentence. But that was not the same thing. Everything is the same—the illusion of difference is caused by the varying degrees of emotion brought to each particular. Rot, of course. *She made me do it.* Even her letter, exonerating him, had been declared either a forgery or a missive diabolically extracted out of the "helpless" dying woman.

There was nothing helpless about Pamela!

He lit another Madison, took a long drag. While he exhaled, there swooped through his memories a flight of sparrows, swivelling, swerving, cutting across the dull gold afternoon when the two of them had sat under the wild date palm trees in the Gardens and talked about the funeral home in Rhodes Avenue. A mistake. It only reminded them of the one thing they had avoided for eighteen months: the death of Rita, their only child.

More whisky sloshed into his glass. He stared at the bed, remembering the rainy nights when the three of them would huddle on it under the great quilt, scaring each other with weird stories as, outside, lightning struck and thunder boomed across the cityscape.

Daddy, he had no nose and no mouth—only eyes with teethlights in them. That was Rita all right.

He saw himself lying on the bed inside a coffin inside some obscure tomb carved into the side of a mountain. It was warm, soothing. He curled up. Pamela wound her body around him, holding him so tight he could not breath. But who wants to breathe anyway? Such a hackneyed, mundane, stale, mindless occupation. Breathing. . .

Mummy, what is evil?

That was Rita all right. The corner of his mouth twitched; his fingers tightened round the glass. He lowered himself slowly onto the bed, punched the pillow into shape and settled himself. At that moment he knew it had all been his fault. About Rita. And maybe about Pamela too. But when was fault faultless enough to be right? He choked back the self-disgust at such a question. But shouldn't it be asked? Shouldn't everything be asked? And after the asking, to ask again—and again. Then perhaps, a light would interrupt the dismal horizon with intimations, notions of a pliant fate. Not this seemingly predestined, preordained, *fated* fate. He felt nothing. He wanted to feel nothing. But Pamela was an unfathomable hole in his heart. The wanting to forget was beyond him. But because it was beyond him, he could match the possible forgetfulness with a clarity that awed him. Making him shudder.

O Pamela, is that what I have become?

Mummy, daddy's drinking in the bathroom.

And later in bed—Rita fast asleep (or pretending) in her cot—the whispering and the touching and the final collapse into an uneasy sleep, clinging to each other like tendrils that have nothing but themselves to entwine with. When it was done, when he *knew* she was dead, he had lost control. He had reached out for the one thing, the drink. A slow but steady pub-crawl through the town, the suburbs, the ghettos. And when he could take no more—the sun was coming up—he had staggered out of a taxi and walked, not unsteadily, into the Central Police Station. . .

"Wait!" his secretary grabbed his arm. "It's too. . ."

But he tore himself from her and lunged into the rain, the fierce, blasting rain. His car was a matter of thirty yards away; but by the time he reached it, he was drenched to the skin. And the essays of his students were more or less no more. He paused by the car, tore the pile of essays into quarters, flung them onto the asphalt and wrenched the door open. A meaningless grin ripped his mouth as he drove, rather tore, out of the faculty car park.

Another fucking day over.

It was some minutes before he became aware of the figure sitting in the rear seat. All he heard was a voice moaning, trying to scream inarticulately: "Please! Please, slow down."

He almost lost control of the wheel, skidding, swivelling, the voice and the rain throbbing within his brain, and, within a foot of the deep gutter, snarled to a lucky halt.

"What the hell are you doing in my car?"

"My name is Pamela," the voice said.

And that is how he met the future wife he was going to murder.

Rita, on her way to school, stopped by the corner shop to buy ice cream. Mr Gray, as usual, grinned, winked: "And how's my girl, eh?"

As usual she did not know where to look.

"I'm not your girl," she said thumb in mouth. "I'm daddy's girl."

"Ho-ho-ho. . . So that's what's been going on behind my back."

She took a very serious lick of her ice cream and with confused dignity, walked out.

"Ha-ha-ha! That's a good one."

She tripped on a paving stone and ran all the way to the school.

"Daddy, what's wrong with mummy?"

"She's drunk!" he snarled.

"What?"

"I said she's DRUNK! Pissed, sozzled. Her boyfriend. . .O shit—get the hell out of here."

Craig downed his night gin and tonic. Who's this guy leering at me? What time is it? What town? What country? What—? Who cares anyway. It can be any time, anywhere, anyhow and anyway you please.

"You all right?"

Craig tried, vainly, to sneer. "What's it to you?"

"Sorry. Just trying to be friendly."

"What?"

"To be friendly."

"And what's that?"

"What?"

"To be friendly."

The bloke inched away. "Well, sort of sociable."

Craig blinked. "Are you hinting I'm part of this society?"

The bloke leaped out of range. Craig wagged his finger, a dignified admonitory finger.

"Now look, I won't give you any shit and I'll take none from you. Do you understand?" Craig, in royal blue dungarees, stared expectantly at his class. There was no answer. He inched forward, confronted a rabid-looking haystack student. "Do *you* understand?"

"Me?"

Craig sighed. "Never mind. Anyway, today we start with *Sir Gawain and the Green Knight.* I don't suppose you've ever heard of King Arthur and his Round Table?" He paused.

The haystack raised his hand. Craig nodded.

"Well sir, I saw the Monty Python film on the holy grain."

Craig smiled. "Grail."

The haystack smouldered a flickering snigger. "Exactly, sir."

"That should start us off. But before I begin I think you should read *Don Quixote*, the story about a guy who fights windmills, a guy sometimes known as the Knight of the Sad Countenance. In our time he goes by the name of Clint Eastwood. Reality's Minister of Home Affairs. Get it?"

Dull apathy receded even more into its vacuum. Craig took a swig from his hip flask. And I'm going to be with them for a whole fucking three years. But he did not let it show. He went on, calmly, fluently, all the time ironically observing himself.

You take on a foolish bet. Your honour, I thought it was a good thing at the time. You take on the Green Knight. Come the day of reckoning. . . O Pamela. Rita! Scrape off that lipstick! Lighting a cigarette. Who was that fellow who said cigarettes are more lethal than AIDS? Some comfort. The mind hurling itself

back:

Three Nigerians were beating him up right outside the Rock Garden. By the dustbins. He passed out sprawling among all the Covent Garden rubbish. It was daylight when he woke up. Christ. London.

Hurling himself

back:

He had drunk as much as his blood could take. That was the thing to do, wasn't it, if you were quietly but scathingly contemplating suicide. The time was 3.27 a.m. He staggered down to the Thames Embankment, clambered up and was about to jump when he noticed something wrong with the water.

Dirty.

That's what is was: filthy.

I'm not drowning myself in *that!*

A patrolling officer found him there raving with demented laughter.

Hurling himself

forward:

185

Into the class. "Ideals of honour, valour," cousin of the Knight of the Sad Countenance. Forcing himself into the centre of his dignified voice: "A trial of strength beyond mere physical endurance. Call it a test of moral resilience. A seemingly ridiculous challenge which, accepted, results in questions and answers that lurk beyond mere consequences of mortality. Of course, throw in that weird figment of the imagination which for centuries has been known by the label 'Christianity'. . ." He was staring out of the smudged window down at a group of students among whom was one dressed in batik t-shirt and baggy jeans. "Now, about gentillesse. . . No, we'll leave that for another day. At the moment let us think on lines 2510 and 2511:

"For one may keep a deed dark, but undo it no whit,

"For where a fault is made fast, it is fixed evermore.

"I want you to write an essay on the implications of those lines, with special reference to Sir Gawain's conduct throughout the book."

Through thin sickly mist, bloodshot street lamps cast their jaundiced thoughts at Craig slowly worrying his feet down Second Avenue towards the Terreskane Hotel. His protesting arms, like unwilling bodyguards, tottered on either side of his mind. Fed up, but why? Because—because, because, of course. On the other side of the street three drunk students were vainly trying to thumb lifts to the campus. On a night like this—good luck to you. Did it all come down to luck? To chance? To happenstance? If that is so, then why, O Lord, WHY? Thinking of Huysman's *Against Nature* and the futile attempt to shut out the ghastly realities of physical distress; descendant of Goncharov's *Oblomov*, cousin of Dostoevsky's fatal ennui. Himself worrying burnt-out thighs through the murky air of hope that there lurked some meaning beyond the shadowline of impossible intent. Now he was passing by the Chibuku shebeen, hearing through harassed ears the vague inglorious laughter of demented pleasure that whipped out at him from the dimly lit smudged windows. A voice scratched at him from the bus shelter: "Do you want to fuck? Only five dollars?"

He walked up to her. She looked a fearfully aged sixteen-year-old. He fumbled in his pockets. As she grasped the crisp notes his hoarse voice surprised him: "Right. Turn round and hitch up your dress." When it was over he slammed shut all the doors within his brain and, like an orang-utan in unfamiliar terrain, ambled into the hotel. The trick was to convince yourself (and accept) that this was all there was, all there was ever going to be. Like the slightly warm beer trickling down his gullet. You got on with it—the rest was without enchantment, without that enticing rubescence which for some is the aura of childhood, the tug of those salad days. Salad days? Or mere digression down Oxbridge lanes? Mentally, a down-and-out Gatsby in a rundown apartment, making do with tortured vision rather than a beguiling tenacious beauty. In Harare. Not full circle, for the point was only a dot, no point to it at all. Be a Manley's Man. Yes, waiter—another beer. For that's how it is, a parabola, endlessly.

The pale blue sky split in the east as the bright green morning rays cast a tracery of luminous bullets. Craig's dark brown eyes flashed awake, staring upwards through the acacia branches at the dappled heavens. Pamela beside him was still fast asleep, cradling her mass of bright black hair with her curled arm. The land was flat, stitched with young msasa and acacia bushes, rough tufts of brown grass and sudden outcrops of granite boulders. The shrill cry of birds sparkled like an enchanted voice through the crisp morning air. Soon the cicadas would weave their taut silver wires into the scarcely vibrant tapestry of this unfolding day.

Pamela's tawny sleepy voice filtered into his consciousness: "What time is it?" she murmured.

He shook his head. "There isn't any time, Pamela. Don't you remember?"

Her grey eyes blinked; she rose, leaning on a bruised elbow. "Of course," she said very slowly. "Time went away. . ."

He pointed. "Look at the sun—it's bright green."

It did not hurt to look at the sun; the green sunbeams, the green orb, the green light were a little strange. Not frightening. It merely evoked within her a curious wonder, a beauty that made all lips mute.

Craig scanned the sky. The Thing was nowhere in sight. Pamela, remembering, shuddered. "Craig, we can't stay here," she said, touching his shoulder. "We've got to get somewhere."

"Yes. But where?"

A dark spot, growing bigger and bigger, was flying swiftly towards the centre of all his thoughts. He stood, pulling her up with him. "It's still very close," he whispered. "I can feel it. . . Let's go."

Holding onto each other, the two youths stumbled westwards. Bits of torn-up stars spangled the western sky. To keep moving—the illusion of going somewhere—that was the thing to do. Perhaps illusion was the only destination. But to get there, you had to travel in your head and not on this green-tinged seemingly solid ground. To stop, to lie still and listen to the mad black dots which like wicked bats were tearing towards the core of their being—that was death, infinitely beyond any darkness. You fled, with no bearings, no direction, for the Thing was everywhere. . .tracking, charting his existence through the void of an absurd constellation of frozen star-thoughts. This glittering finery which, after all is said and done, proves to be bitter ashes, the bite of sour fruit. Neither heaven nor nirvana nor total extinction of thought and feeling. But the stout hand grasps the nail-studded knobkerrie, lips snarl back to reveal yellow fangs, and thunder coldly and precisely bellows from the remote area at the nape of the neck. Not black bludgeoning clouds but swarms of warrior locusts homing down onto those salad days. Salad days? You turned a trick and queued up for the penicillin the day after. That's all there ever was going to be. A smell of almonds, a whiff of ambrosia, the ridiculous softness of hardening nipples. Her thin cry at the sudden pain. This monstrous geometry of an architecture outside time and place and, looming from all sides, the physics of grotesque individuals savouring an out-of-key memory tune. Salad days? Rather loneliness experienced deliberately, intensely; an experiment into the hazards of being yourself. That lettuce-self, with niblets of raw garlic and fresh ginger. Carrots for quiet biblical meanings. Oranges for morning sickness after he "knew her." Tomatoes for terrace conversations after three hours of jogging down Julius Nyerere Way towards seedy Elizabeth Hotel and all the motor-snarling breathy way back to the Monomatapa. Weaving through incurious pavement crowds, to and fro, the sunlit blaze of shop-windows revealing the objects of material cravings. Odds and ends advertising a tourist Zimbabwe concocted out of the minds of tired hack copywriters. Jogging till not strength but the imagination was pounding like Stravinsky's demented drum toward a truth only for the ears of the soldier's return. Not exactly MacArthur's nor the cross-eyed puzzled look of the war veteran. The wild cat's eyes. Splintered convex lenses chiselled out of the back of the icy moon. Elizabeth Smart's mad look to the end of time. Or the strangled voice issuing out of the bell jar: "Dying is an art."

Craig sucked at the cigarette. Maybe a chaser will do the trick. He paved the whisky's raw roads with the bitter tar of raw green chillies. No, they did not have Gunter Grass's jellied pig's head. Wondering whether Pamela was still typing her newspaper article—and Rita in the bathroom experimenting with her mother's lipstick. And where, those trumpets of Jericho? "They marched around the city once each day for six days; on the seventh day they marched around the city seven times; on the seventh march they sounded the horns, the walls of the city collapsed, and the Israelites killed all the inhabitants except Rahab, the prostitute, and her family." What music!

Buried deep down the dark end of memory were shattered blackened buildings, streets gouged, dredged by the tremendous blast, agonised screams forever engraved on the copperplate of an astonishing vision, and the mangled demented howl of the hovering Beast unleashing a firestorm over the city. Pamela stumbled.

"Hurry!"

They rounded a huge boulder that looked like a large cat sleeping. Pamela could feel the stony whiskers swivelling towards them. A sound like claws ripping up the hard clayey soil assailed their ears. Ahead, beyond the pale yellow barrier of acacias was the river—a thin rippling stream of molten silver. They ran towards it. A blue-black metallic shape swooped from the top of the boulder, scratching the air, ripping out of the green sunlight a wind tunnel that sent the pair sprawling, panting, dusty, covering their heads with their arms. When at last they dared look up, the bird, ugly as evil, was regarding them with large red-hot eyes from the peak of the rock. It bristled its huge wings, turning its crooked beak from side to side. They rose cautiously, and waited. The bird did nothing. They warily inched away. The bird did nothing. They ran.

Raucous laughter screeched after them. The brutish dark green echo dimmed the sunlight, drummed through their minds, their lives fleeing recklessly towards the illusion of the river shimmering like a harmless watersnake. It was cool under the trees.

They slumped to the ground. Always this need to rest, to forget. A lone cicada was playing a razorsharp tune using paper and comb. It brought into focus—unaccountably—a glittering picture of Craig's chemistry set. He wondered whether the world was undergoing some litmus test, turning red, turning blue, turning green—perhaps disappearing altogether. No direction, no guidelines; nothing at all to take for granted. In other circumstances, it would have been exciting, intoxicating. A brave new world. But this was something else, the mad stampede of crowd after crowd through the streets and alleys smashing shops, looting, setting on fire buildings, parks, anything that was inflammable. The irregular thwack and C-CRUMB of bullets and bombs was a cacophony of the irrational come into its own. Craig did not know what was happening. He tore out of his hiding place—when the rocket-propelled grenade ripped the room apart, streaked down the stairs, and before he knew where he was he had scaled several gardens and backyards. Was it the South Africans?

A rattle of machine-gun fire cracked somewhere beyond the thick pall of oily smoke. Where lurked the danger? A dying scream—a body falling from a rooftop. The hellish burr, rumble of tanks, turrets swivelling, aiming, blasting shell after shell into the smouldering ruins. And high above the city, another daunting formation of bombers homing in, bomb bays opening, the dark shower raining down. He scrambled over another wall, a gash opening in his thigh and landed almost on top of the girl's huddled shape.

"Help me," she cried.

It was Pamela.

She had been in the kitchen, stirring the stew, while listening to a Rolling Stones' cassette. Her aged aunt, always sickly these days, was propped up in bed upstairs, reading Jane Austen's *Northanger Abbey*. The phone rang. It must be Craig, she thought. It was. "Are we still going to that film?" he asked. His voice was hesitant; boisterous and direct with the boys; but, with Pamela, shy, stammering, as though he could not believe she was actually listening to him.

"Yes, she is much better today," she replied. "I've just about finished preparing dinner. Why don't you come round in an hour?" She listened for some time. "What?"

"There's something going on out there," he was saying. "It sounds like guns."

The phone went dead.

He half dragged her up. They fled through back streets, helping each other over garden walls, jumping over rooftops, hastily brushing themselves through sparks and flames. Mounds of sinister smoke erupted over the city's skyline. Choking, coughing, they fled the hell of fire engines, sirens, air raid hailers, the screaming uproar of crowds teeming in total disorder. The stench of spent explosive, burst drains, the stink of fuel dumps on fire, the overwhelming terrible chorus of multitudes caught in the fierce clawing heat of horror; they fled, careless of distance, careless of the miles of horror—fled into the green sunlight verdant sunbeams like glistening coils of python, eerie scales of fishes long extinct, the green of a menacing evolution.

"Your aunt?" he asked, trailing his hand into the molten green stream.

But she could not look at him. She did not have the strength even to burst into tears. He held her face between his palms, peering into her: her once grey eyes had turned fluorescent green. When he looked at his own reflection in the water, his eyes, too, had changed.

The beauty of flowers lies in thinking thoughts that hurt. The path splits into several paths which must all be taken simultaneously. Glass (the fire, the air, the case of water) ridicules by reflection. Craig, draining his beer, thought: When I go to bed, do my ghost selves repeat the action, a hundred, a thousand times? (O beauty of flowers). Such a raindrop on index finger feasts threats of thunder from tense wrists sprouts cactus dreams do I remain when my feet have departed is it pain or revolt when the heart is forever silent Pamela is asleep grey daylight filters deep into grey memory at once is effaced the blank slate on which to chalk tomorrow's colours when rainwords spit fire and fire words spit blood a door behind the eyes slams shut does nothing remain of manfish birdman she is asleep timedrops gather in a pool paperboats glide downstream my storms squeeze painful symbols out of Hiroshima out of her in me smiles claw cruelty to bed in dream propose daylight a waking nightmare this rude rubescent (so raw) glow of fleshembers in bright midnight day's spade and hoe (to sculpt or torture) strike clutch HEAVY heart bursts into bloom O a sorrow of flowers stench pit of yesterday's aerosol silence of bullets straight ahead do I remain when character is clawed out by chance circumstance by sleep or perpetual pleasure cruise on winelake cheesescape lamb's heart rainwords flapping maddened sailing ship into simpler lethal direction to know is not enough more is demanded than I ever borrowed each finger is king holding down a string of thought stroking ear and lip to life and delight this bracelet of firewords my knuckleduster for night's bright innuendoes. . .thinking thoughts that hurt.

Craig was snoring, propped up at the bar. The barman clicked with disgust and picked up the house phone. Moments later, a security guard calmly strode in, yanked Craig by the armpits and more or less gently got him into the garden. The combination of heavy nocturnal mist and the hotel's multicoloured outdoor lights, and the several groups of late-night carousers created a startlingly impressionist effect. It was bitter cold now. Craig stirred, aware of the security guard at this elbow. A shock of clarity flashed through his brain—all this had happened before, several times. He checked his watch. He mumbled. The guard leaned closer. With effort he hawked the words out of his throat: "A taxi, please."

Part Six

The Camp

THE cattle had snuggled down to chew the cud. The cool after-rain breeze wafted to and fro, lingering over the msasa bushes and the green runner grass. Pale yellow sunbeams shimmered down from behind the retreating clouds. A wisp of light blue smoke trailed into the air slowly becoming invisible; the way the roasted juices of meat were inching out of the boy's satiated tastebuds. They sat, rather snoozed, around the dying embers. It was good just to lie there, slowly digesting the wild rabbit whose desperate surprise had been so comical as the rocks had rained down on it. It was Fani, Rudo's brother, who had discovered its hideaway some days before. And the boys had, like seasoned hunters, been patient, waiting for the right moment.

Tonderai wanted to make a purse out of his share of the skin. Rudo would be pleased. He took a long deep breath; it was sweet, this after-rain smell. Not that there had been much rain; something less than a drizzle. You didn't even have to seek shelter. It was an undulant plain, here and there dotted with outcrops of granite, mounds of termite hills, and idle but world-wise msasa trees. As the probability of rain became a reality and the expectations were not in vain, the land had overnight put on its multi-water-coloured gown: flame lilies, wild violets, tiny daisies, clover, mushrooms, wild ginger, and (over there!) the flash of flamboyants whose firebuds were as a cluster of heavenly embers.

He scuttled over the fire even as Fani's warning shout still rang in his ears, "BEHIND YOU! A SNAKE!" and the cattle were gawkily clambering to their feet, the sky dizzyingly upside down as his fingers raked the ground for rocks, watching where Fani and Beni's rocks were aimed. He saw it. A frightful hatred directed his throws; the snake seemed charmed—it dodged easily, the head darting here, there, every which way. It was Fani who outwitted it. He flung the still bloodsoaked wild rabbit skin at the snake—which struck. The rocks flattened, crushed the head before it could unlock itself from the decoy. For a very long time, the boys squashed it again and again; then, overcome by sheer exhaustion, they stood in a ring looking down at the thing.

"We did it!" Beni leaped into the air, executed several cartwheels still shouting, laughing: "WE DID IT! WE DID IT!"

The boys looked at each other, a merriment beginning to bubble in their bellies. They looked at the snake. It was huge. They, they were so small. They began to grin. Tonderai's large eyes sparked clear but with a new gleeful determination. With a WHOOP their laughter exploded over the veld and still they—through tears of laughter—screamed "WE DID IT!!" making the cattle halt and turn around to view with an I-told-you-so expression this new madness of the little human being.

In the concentration camp something had been killed also. It started with the change in pitch of the whispering. It was still the same filthy camp, but the smells had retreated into another dimension. The gunposts, arc-lights, the guards, the sergeant and, above all, the commandant—they were the same and yet not the same. They were less real, less sharply outlined. They were like monstrous images in a slowly fading photograph. Their actions were still the same—perhaps even worse—but it was as if the heart had been squashed and torn out of them.

Everyone seemed to realise in astonishment that the concentration camp and its builders were not immortal, were not going to last forever. The long night of fear was going to end.

Tonderai and Rudo increasingly sought each other out. "We're going home soon," he said, lowering his voice. "Father said so." And, of course, she believed him. And because she believed him he believed it himself even more strongly. She nodded at the guards as if to ask something. "That's what I wanted to tell you," he said and he could feel all the whisperings of the camp plaiting themselves into his voice. "Father said there may be shooting. Anytime. Day or night. If there is, don't run. Don't run. You must fling yourself onto the ground and lie still. Your whole body very tight with the ground. As if you were dead. Do you understand? Please, Rudo, you've got to understand."

But she broke into a smile, seeing him so earnest, and twined her fingers into his. "I do understand."

Time was retracking its own former footsteps. Not standing still; slowly cranking, wheezing, it's rotor going the other way. Perhaps this was because of the growing impatience in the camp. If things were going to end soon, why not now? The whispering had even died down; there was only a resentful impatience, as if someone, somewhere, was playing a trick on their hopes, their most fervent hopes for all *this* to end. It was the children who held out; they had fashioned a ball out of various rags and with this they spent every free hour playing football in the dust. There were two teams; the two opposing captains were Fani and Tonderai. There had grown between these two boys an intimate hatred, like combat enemies who have grown to more than respect each other.

They no longer left their game to watch the helicopters spewing lethal fire into the forests, the soldiers leaping out of the carriers and fanning out to disappear into the undergrowth, the steady CRUMB CRUMB of mortar bombs, and the long line of armoured trucks. ("Ugh," was Rudo's comment the first time she saw the "Frogs"). They did not even look up when one day the sky was filled with parachutes and the heavy

green and the watercolour of the veld exploded into demented flames; the adults were
playing their own horrible game.

Part Seven

Tonderai's Father Reflects

Well it's done
Across this stuttering tongue of sea
My ship, The Wordhorde, sails
My burial ship, wrought from tough hardwood word
Sails. . .

The deep black-blue sky
Twinkling with nursery
Lights; a sudden mist
Casts mystery upon the cradle

From afar, listing into view,
The Towerman cometh; cloud and spray,
Rent apart, reveal
The Towerman's glispbled visage!

Like 'lectric feather drop't
From thunderbird's tearing flight
(Darkness visible!) memory's very light
Baptises the Towerman's exilebroken
Return. . .

SCRAPIRON BLUES

Sailing,
Wrought from tough hardwood word
Whose love the touch of fire and sea
The kiss of spray and spark
The bodylock of sinew and steel
Across this stuttering tongue of sea!

Whose the ghoulish fetid aura in the hold?
Whose the fiendish despair chained yet bold?
Whose the blood broiling amidst homing sharks?
Whose on the trader's forearm these teethmarks?
A sudden mist
Casts mystery upon the cradle.

Sailing,
The sooty palm leaves its print
In the police stations of the galaxy;
The voice yet to sound already has echoed
In the streets of Soweto;
The sky's bullet-blue noon
Has tightened upon the trigger,
My burial ship, The Wordhorde,
Wrought from tough hardwood word. . .
Sails. . .

To fight the fight
Or from sideline
Sound its progress
Or from the tower
Merely note its screaming
Fiery wake?

TONDERAI'S FATHER REFLECTS

Life has sailed from these lips
Leaving a harbour empty and drear
Yet if star for star and clod for clod
What whirled pride in dust for other dust!

This deep black-blue sky.

No breath in hope's breeze will blow her image
From my memory;
From my recruiting remembrance
Her anguished cry races into the harbour
Of my arms;
From cannon blast and brace of broadsides (the port city
On fire with fright) nothing kidnap
Our wrangling kiss, clashing sails
Swords and sabres flash like myriad stars
Tumult of the Milky Way
Sailing. . .
No breath

Only this drum
Of gloom and din
And gross dream
Wrought from tough hardwood word,
Sails.

"Death, at the corner of my eye, out of sight;
A nondescript face in an old crowded photograph;
All solemn now, to purse my lips for the final kiss
And from then hungrily scan Obituaries and In Memoria
For her heart's remembrances of me."

SCRAPIRON BLUES

Only this drum
Skyscrapers of steel and sinew
Cement, plateglass, and workers' blood
The Towerman's sneer as wide as Fourth Street
Down which I walk hand in hand with the ghost
Of her who sailed the stuttering sea. . .
My burial ship, The Wordhorde. . .

I never asked much of this world; only that my wife and children be spared, he thought. He was hanging upside-down, hung by his inner knees to a bar swinging from the roof; his head in a damp hood of rough sacking. They were doing something to his testicles. Someone was laughing. Another was barking: "Tell us and we'll let you go! Bastard!"

And he could hear his voice screeching—as the electrodes were connected: "But I don't know anything!"

Surprised at the whining note erupting from his soul. The others had said you would talk in the end. The only thing was time; give the comrades time. They understood how it could be: torture made even a hero talk—but talk when the information was useless; you would have given the comrades time to get away, time to formulate alternative plans. Jesus, please STOP! But the electrodes spun him swinging in the air and he was howling, bawling like a tormented child. Shit. The mind can conquer pain if one is resolute, he remembered from a talk with the guerrilla commander. But, Christ, what of the body?

My burial ship. . .
Purified by fire:
Sunset and evening star,
And one clear call for me!
And may there be no moaning of the bar,
When I put out to sea

198

TONDERAI'S FATHER REFLECTS

Mr Murehwa was reliving those moments which, little by little, had gathered into his heart a congregation of pure hatred. It is one thing to hate only with the mind; when the body physically hates, that is something else. If the mind cannot overcome pain, the body's intense and passionate hatred can do so, after all. All this torture was aimed at the body; and the body knows best how to defend itself to the last extremity. Memory, physical memory, was coming to his aid: in the early days, when the concentration camps were not yet built to these cruel standards, he had been carrying sadza and mhamba through the bush to his family. He was stopped by Rhodesian soldiers who accused him of "feeding the terrs". When he protested, they merely grinned and, after a consultation among themselves, ordered him to eat it all there and then so that he would not have any to give to the terrs.

He ate. He ate. He ate. He forced it down. He willed his body to take more and more. They were watching him frankly, openly, amazed at his "appetite". He ate until he could eat no more; and there was still a lot of food left.

"Eat, motherfucker!"

His belly was swollen; he could eat and drink no more. A rifle butt thudded into his belly.

Another: "Eat!"

A boot kicked down hard into his stomach. When he could vomit no more, the black sergeant shouted at him: "Eat!"

Without his control, his hands were dipping into the food and even as he ate more vomit was disgorging out of him. He was eating with his right hand.

"You're right-handed, aren't you?" the white officer asked.

He nodded.

'S'geant, break that right hand.'

He felt nothing; only the small sound of bone snapping. He felt nothing; only seeing the black sergeant methodically doing it. He felt nothing; he was watching it all from a very remote region of the mind in which nothing, nothing at all, existed.

Sailing. . .
No breath

SCRAPIRON BLUES

Only this drum
Of gloom and din
And gross dream
Wrought from tough hardwood word.

Hating, remembering. Hating, even as the rifle butts thudded into him. Wondering what his family was going to eat that day. Wondering at the sunset and evening star. . .

Hate, pure hatred—that was the answer. To remember every detail of this gross and evil time, thudding still into his body, the vomit now blood-red like rich Chateau Burgundy red wine. . ..from within the tangible darkness, harsh abrasive words sputtered into flame: charcoal-smarting figures split into grotesque terror; diamond-hard torsos cracked like twigs; metallic muscles dissolved into demented surreal syntax; the all-encompassing tangible darkness was a black nightmare from whose pages a darker, blacker grimness to the light not out there screamed.

The electrodes.

No.

That was the night they were ambushed. From cannon blast and brace of broadsides EAT!! The kick unhinged his jaw! With a terrible accusing slowness, his eyeballs began to turn inwards, seeing, but not comprehending, the string of oaths spurting out of the slow-motion jaws of a cassocked figure shouting at the soldiers: "In the name of the Lord—STOP! Are you human beings or beasts?"—And the blow to the belly made the priest crouch in the heat of the dust panting, holding in the broken abdomen.

"Okay, padre, he's all yours."

Sailing.

From the distant glare of molten noon, a mote became a boy running furiously, bony elbows, frantic knees, pumping the silent and still air. From within the open doorway, the man recognised the little figure racing towards the cluster of mud and pole and thatch huts: Tonderai. Mr Murehwa, who had been half-dozing, sprang to his feet, almost falling backwards as his son blundered into his arms, raving, and the incoherent words came out not in a shower of spit but with a stream of blood, one thin bony hand clutch-

200

ing at the man's ribcage, the other jabbing backward to a point somewhere in the distant glare of molten noon.

The sky's bullet-blue noon. Glaring down at Nyamapanda, Chiweshe, Shamva, Madziva.

The white finger turning even whiter, pressing the trigger.

EAT!!

"Forgive them, my son. They don't know. Forgive us."

The broken gourd. The sadza and bloodstained saucers. Retrieved. The priest and Murehwa gawkily tottered forward. Five miles.

He stood diffidently near the door. He had taken off his battered bush hat, and now cradled it against his crotch. The sweat still rolled down his brow, ears, cheeks, neck, stiff spine, hollowed chest, down into his ragged khaki trousers. The sweat gave him the look of a crying man. He did not know what the nurse—a nun—was doing to the boy. He did not have the look, the knowledge, of a praying man; but the sudden intrusion of death made everyone, turned everyone, into a praying man. He had carried the boy on his back, cradling him on his thin buttocks, carried him the three miles to this mission school. He was not a travelled man; not a journeying man. These nuns and priests he did not know what kind of "men" they were, but he hoped they were not unknowing men. The boy stirred, whimpered. Mr Murehwa shivered with pessimistic hope, thinking of the sneering soldier who was known all around as Mr Win-Some-Lose-Some because, after discharging bullets into already dead bodies, he would chuckle at his R.A.R. platoon and say cheerfully "You win some, you lose some. That's the name of the game. Eh?"

But Mr Win-Some-Lose-Some had occasional bouts of fury. "These commies are using mere boys to fight us. Mere children! Look, I am a professional soldier. I'm just doing my duty. As a professional soldier. The least I can expect from a worthy enemy is a one-to-one situation. Man to man. But look, they are fuckingcowards, these commies. They don't come man to man. They send kids to do the fighting for them. I'm a fair man and admit that some of these kids sure can fight—*but they are still kids.* You know, one day, we ambushed this lot. There was no way they could escape. We picked them off one by one. Picked them off leisurely you might say. We knew they'd soon run out of ammunition. Then there was only one left. . . (Win-Some-Lose-Some's face twitched with pain, restraining perhaps a sob.) Only one left, still shooting. He actually killed two of my men. But then he too ran out of ammunition. But unlike the rest he immediately threw his gun away and raised his hands. I slowly walked towards him; the nearer I approached, the more I was dismayed. He was a mere boy! Not looking frightened or wetting his pants. He was insolently looking me right in the eyes. . . I blew his brains out."

Like stage curtains parting, an incredible scene flashed through Mr Murehwa's brain: in a knitted dress and a vulgar hat and pointed shoes—all of them white—a black fat woman is flouncing her balloon belly at a thin undernourished boy who is doing his best to match her steps to the rhumba music. The boy is Tonderai. The woman looks—but how!—like Rudo Makoni. And—they are in the city. The City of Anarchists.

The man shook his head violently; the scene vanished. A nurse was staring at him with concern.

"Are you all right?" she asked.

He blinked; he stroked his jaw in confusion. "It's the heat. My head. . ." She gave him three Anadin tablets and a small glass of water. After he swallowed he asked about the boy.

The nun smiled: "He's hurt, of course, but don't worry. He'll live." She nodded at a chair: "Sit down. It'll take us a little while yet."

Unsmiling, but inwardly relieved, the man plucked at his knees, hitched up his trousers and sat down.

EAT!!

But that was still to come.

From afar, listing into view.

HANG IN THERE, BABY: FRIDAY'S COMING!

Part Eight

The City of Anarchists

MISTER Win-Some-Lose-Some belched. Grinned. Winked at the "girl" who could comfortably pass off for white.

"Where's that waiter?" he grumbled, looking round. He saw him. "HEY, YOU!"

The dwarfish black man hurried, tray held aloft. "Yes, baas?"

"One double gin, ice, tonic. A triple whisky, no ice, no water."

"Yes, baas."

As the waiter hurried away, Lose-Some turned to the girl. "He's probably one of them. They are all in it together, you know. Mind you, a bit of psychology and mumbo-jumbo goes a long way. There's always the big BUT."

"You know best, Jim," Cora replied. She slowly crossed her long, slim legs and casually smoothed her dress to cover her knees. "I missed you very much."

It was hard being a woman in this "situation" but then there were compensations. All these soldiers, some from the United States, Britain, France, Holland. . . Compensations like Jim, here—when he was available, of course.

"That's what I adore about you, Cora," he said. He took a long pull at his Johnny Walker. And breathlessly: "You've got heart. That's it. That's what you've got. A great big heart." His eyes tried to focus on her, but all he saw, as usual, was something to fuck. Not a person. Not a human being. After all, she wasn't even white. He chuckled. "You know what I go through out there?" he asked gruffly, expecting no answer.

But she said: "I hear stories, terrible stories. It makes me afraid for you."

He laughed. "Oh, don't worry. I can take care of myself."

The waiter impassively set the drinks down. Jim looked at the triple whisky. "What took you so long, Sambo?"

The waiter's eyes became inscrutable. "Yes, baas, sir," he said.

Jim slapped him on the inner thigh: "You crafty bastard—this is for you," he chuckled, tossing him two shillings and sixpence.

"Thank you, baas."

203

"Now fuck off."

"Yes, sir, baas."

Cora giggled.

The waiter slipped out into the alleyway at the back of the hotel. Jimmy the Dwarf, his brother, was waiting, actually resting his hump against the garbage bin. The reek of rotting food and the scuttling of rats did not seem to affect him.

"Well?"

The waiter could not look him in the eye. "Win-Some-Lose-Some is back in there with that bitch. They are very drunk," he mumbled.

"Are you sure she's the one Otto sussed out in the white dress?"

"Yes."

Jimmy curled his lip, thinking. Finally he said: "Are there many soldiers in there?"

"Yes. About thirty-five," the waiter looked over his shoulder. "Well, eh, of course, you know even the women are carrying guns."

"Naturally."

"I must rush back. The headwaiter is very. . ."

"That's all right. Thanks. Now run along."

Jimmy, deep in thought, but whistling an impenetrable tune, slowly slouched to the corner where Otto, dressed in workman's overalls, was waiting for him. They joined Larry Long in the garden of the Anglican Cathedral. Larry was reading a bible. He was also wearing a drab dark suit with a priest's dog-collar.

Cora sat on Jim's knees. He was tickling the area between her crotch and her breasts. Tracy had joined them. She was a fat heavily-rouged, loud, brassy tart, who in spite of her advanced age was making a fortune out of her brothel in Vice Mile. Several rings glittered on her fingers; her two front teeth were solid gold. She was Cora's "manager". She rightly suspected that Cora was moonlighting. But then there were more than enough men to go round; you could even be choosy. Some of the Portuguese men stank. The Greeks and Germans were rude—a dirty-minded rudeness. The services they demanded soon wore out some of the girls. What Tracy really liked were the ones who were "gentlemen", profuse with apologies, shy and constantly free and easy with the contents of their wallets. What they really wanted was a shoulder to cry on, to forget the heat of battle. Tracy mothered them well.

The war was nothing to her. Apart from the nasty-looking guns which everyone carried around, Tracy saw nothing of the war. It could have been a nightmare reverberating beyond the horizon of her concerns. Out of sight, out of mind, you had to be practical. She was making a tidy nest egg against any eventuality. If the worst came to the worst, she would take the gap and perhaps open a respectable establishment, preferably for retired gentlemen and wealthy but lonely widows. Something like that. But in the meantime: it was business as usual. The war was lucrative. She even played both sides; the ones who wanted mothering also had loose mouths. They would talk, tell her the horrors they committed in the name of law and order. Tracy would listen with a look of astonished sympathy. But once the road was clear she would sell the information to carefully selected, interested persons. Otto was one of her interested clients. He paid her regularly, even when she had no information worth mentioning. Of course, he was black but he behaved like a nice gentleman. She sometimes let him take one of the white girls. It was just as a favour, of course, a concrete sign of her trust in him. But there were moments when she would wonder where he got all that money. Moments when she would even consider blackmailing him; but no, that was bad business. She would keep her knowledge up her sleeve for a rainy day. She examined her index finger, thinking acidly about how Cora was moonlighting. Maybe it was time to draw in the reins, remind her who was the boss. Cautiously, of course. Because Jim seemed to have a mind-boggling soft spot for Cora. That was the one thing about the business: you never knew whether they would go berserk, sulk or quietly strangle you out of some eerie nightmare working itself out in their war-mangled brains. Not that she blamed them; what happens happens, that's all there is to it. She knew something about psychology. Psychology was a way of justifying insanity. Jim talked a lot about psychology, especially like now when he was drunk and was assured of a good fuck. He said Freud had said, indeed had proved, that all sex was good for the soul, that even babies had tremendous sexual fantasies. The little sods. Tracy grinned and tried to listen to what Jim was saying. He was talking about something called phrenology.

"All you have to do is to examine Sambo's skull. . ." he was saying.

Cora inclined her head attentively though she was not listening. Jim always talked like *that*; the words would come pouring out of him in a flood of self-distraction. She knew he was not even aware of her; only the possibility of sex later in the evening. She did not give a damn. He was a *man*; one of that strange species which is not worth knowing. She fingered the two-inch long scar directly beneath her left ear, a legacy of an encounter with a French mercenary who had gone berserk. In any case the gesture made her look even more thoughtfully attentive. She narrowed her eyes. Jim went off at a tangent: "Anthropology also proves that Sambo's sexual motors are highly. . ." he was saying. His eyes sparkled with excitement. He could only fuck with a woman whom he would have first fucked with his brain, with his superior knowledge. After all, a woman was only an artifact sculpted out of man's rib. . .

"The theory of evolution really says it all, you know," he insisted, confidently warding off any possible counter-assertion. He felt good; and in spite of all the whisky he had drunk, he *looked* good in his role of defender of civilisation, protector of women and children, a lean and swarthy Knight of the Frontier, bearing down on the earth from the vivid sky, not on a winged charger but a helicopter gunship, strafing the heathen hordes, hurling grenade after grenade.

"Military historians, in fact, have conceded that our Sambo here. . ."

Cora shook her head; she had been dozing. Jim did not like that; not when he was pontificating.

"Yes, Jim," she murmured automatically, neatly filling in the contrived pause in the deluge of facts. Jim stared at her, surprised.

"Yes what?" he demanded, somewhat churlishly.

"I mean, I agree with everything you're saying even though it's all beyond my woman's brain."

Jim nodded sagely, mollified. And continued: "When you consider Bismarck's assertion on realpolitik. . ."

Tracy minced to her feet, swaying. "Well, see you all. Cora, be a good girl. And you, Jim, you must be a good boy this time. Not that I'm saying anything, mind." She blew a kiss in their general direction and waddled through the throng.

"No brains at all, that fat old thing," Jim grumbled. "I hate people who don't know things. They're a waste of time. And time is what we haven't got. Eh?"

Cora smiled in sympathy. He chucked her under the chin, kissed her and lurched to his feet. "I've got to shake a comrade in the bog, Cora." He lowered his voice, bending low to breathe in her ear: "And don't you run out on me, baby. Just sit tight till I return. Eh?"

Cora's smile widened. "I'll be right here."

"That's my girl." He pushed through the press of uniformed soldiers, pausing only to slap Sambo on the back: "Same round at the same table, you!"

Tracy, turning a corner, bumped into a black clerical figure. "Kaffir," she cursed, then taking in the dog-collar, pursed her lips into an embarrassed smile. "Sorry, father, I did not. . ." She dug into her handbag and handed him some coins. "Take it, father, for the hungry and the sick."

"Thank you, madam," Larry Long mumbled, and for a moment stared in bewilderment at the hastily retreating figure. Then he broke into silent laughter and moved on.

Jim took in the new row of drinks and sitting down shrieked: "SAMBO!"

The dwarfish waiter hopped it. "Sir, bass."

"Here's something for you, my man," Jim laughed, giving him a handful of coins.

"Thank you, sir, bass."

"Well, off with you then. But bring another round in, let's see, ten minutes."

"Yes, baas."

As the waiter was swallowed in the tumult of uniformed soldiers, Cora had the courage to say: "He's good, that one. Good like a dog."

But Jim chose to be offended. "No, not like a dog. Like a MAN. I don't think I'd last long in a job like his, you know. It takes strength. . .and courage too to wait on a fucking bunch like us. I've got some good kaffirs in my unit. A tough bunch. But then you could say it's the training we give them. Training and leadership—that's all they need. It's like you women. All you need is a firm hand, strict orders. Not this nonsense of doing your own thing like the harpies are shrieking for back home." Jim tried to look thoughtful. "Funny, I mentioned home. Haven't done that for years. Wonder what I'm doing here. . ."

Home is where you are, isn't it? Home is what you left behind, isn't it? Home is who you are, don't they say? Home is where you're going, didn't they always use to say? Fuck home. Home is a snatch of song, dimly remembered. A piece of arse, now old and wrinkled. The green grass of home. Then you wake up to a yodelling chorus of baboons. The dull dusty roar of a bored lion. But then sometimes it could be a winging flight of impalas, a miracle, a mirage, a hallucination flashing across the vlei. Home is my gun, cradled between my thighs. Home is a primed grenade, to blast me out of an ambush. Home is at last a cool, an ice-cold glass of Castle, flowing smooth and easy down to my wracked innards. But then. . .I'm not a homing man. I'm a moving man. No place like this place to make you a moving man. You gotta shake the dust of every place you arrive at. Not dust, no, but cordite. Unleash it all over which place you're at. In. Unleash the semen. Leaving a swarm of halfcaste brats in your wake. They like it too. Jim stared at Cora, nodded to himself. Yes, they like it. Funny sods. From ebony to chocolate brown to sour cream. They think it improves their race. Home. The thousand and one tribes of England that's no longer home. Niggers and Pakis all over the place. He unhinged his mind from this reverie, hiccupped slightly.

"Where's home for you, Cora?"

She pressed his hand. "With you, Jim. Wherever you are," she said.

"But I don't know where and why I am," he mumbled, trying to control the hiccup. Holding his breath.

"Then home is wherever you're searching for answers."

"You're a smart girl, Cora, you know."

"You make me smart," she replied, not intending the pun.

Outside in the street, Otto slowly pushed his dust cart to a stop in front of the hotel. He swept, and swept; then he slowly moved away from the cart. He was seemingly concentrating on spearing up garbage and discarded cartons. Finally, he turned the corner, leaned his lancer against a wall and elaborately began to eat his lunch while hurrying away without any appearance of doing so. Soon he found the bicycle Jimmy the Dwarf had left for him. He did not look back as he weaved in and out of the traffic. The explosion would come any second, any micro second. . .

Cora looked at her watch, then at Jim, with dismay.

"What is it, darling?" Jim asked, complacent but concerned.

She shook her head ruefully. Muttered something.

"What?"

208

"Well, I can't say. . . It's something I forgot."

"Just say the word and it's done."

Cora blushed, stammered. "It's. . .well. . .one of those women's things. I'd forgotten." She rose to her feet.

Jim, his mind filled with images of blood and soggy tampax things, said hastily: "Of course, Cora, go and fix yourself up."

She rushed to the outer door. Jim sighed.

Bloody biology. What on earth was God thinking making them like that?

As her car hummed into life, Cora bit her lip. The traffic! Finally she could inch her way out into the metallic stream. But she could not afford to draw any attention to herself; she must not drive too fast or too slowly. The tension transformed itself into a myriad beads of sweat. Her knuckles were ivory hard on the steering wheel. She was three blocks from the hotel when the whole world erupted inside out of itself.

SCRAPIRON BLUES

Fuzzy Goo's Stories for Children

Fuzzy Goo's
Stories for Children

(Illustrations by Max Wild)

*For Max and Franz Wild
and all the children of Zimbabwe*

Tony and the Rasta

TONY is small and skinny.
His knees and elbows are full of scars.
His school uniform is dirty and torn.
He shouts the biggest screams in the streets.
He fights the dirtiest battles in the playground.
Tony dreams strange dreams.
Tony lives with his aunt because his mother
and father were killed in the war.
She is not really his aunt. She starves him.
She beats him. She scolds him. She makes him do
all the jobs around the house. It is not really
a house. It is made of tins and plastic and mud.
They live in a shanty town. It is very close to Harare.

Life is very hard in Shantytown. Hundreds
of people live there. There
are no toilets.
There is no food. There are no bathrooms.

And the noise is terrible. Hungry children
scream all the time. Men and women dressed in
rags get drunk on kachasu and fight and curse
and kick the children. In summer it is too hot
to do anything but swear quietly against
everything. Even the flies have not the strength
to buzz into the unwiped noses of children.
In winter it is too cold to do anything but shiver
and grind the molars in chill desperation. The men
have no jobs. They have no money. They have to steal.

There is a man who comes to see Tony's aunt. He comes only at night. Tony listens to them whispering and doing things which Tony thinks are dirty. Tony is puzzled because children come into the world through these dirty goings-on. Are children therefore dirty? he asks. But there are no answers. Why do the men not have jobs? he asks himself. Why do all these people live in these horrible houses?

Tony asks himself these things when his aunt beats him up with fists and sticks. Why is she always angry? Why is she like this? Why don't we live in nice houses like the ones I see on the way to school? He asks again and again, but the questions seem too big. The answers are very big. How can a small boy answer them? Sometimes men come from the city but all they do is shout and threaten to bring bulldozers and armed policemen. Everyone in Shantytown is frightened.

At night, when the man comes to see his aunt, she throws Tony out of the house and tells him to sleep outside. Tony is frightened of the dark. There are no streetlights in Shantytown. At night it looks like a horrible village which has painfully dragged itself out of a flooded mass of sewage. Can anyone help me? it cries. But all anyone does is threaten it with bulldozers and armed policemen like they do to African people in stupid South Africa. Most of the women in the Shantytown brew kachasu. The little money they make comes from selling this dangerous brew. It is a crime to make kachasu. Sometimes the women are caught and cursed and dragged into trucks and beaten into the magistrate's court and they pay a fine and come out to Shantytown to start brewing again because they have no other way of making money. Aunt has been caught many times but she cannot stop making kachasu. The Headmaster at Tony's school said Tony must have a new uniform. He also demanded money for the classroom building fund.

Not that there is any building going on at the school. The classes are crowded. The teachers are few and these few are always drunk and ogling the schoolgirls. One of the teachers is a Rastafarian. He looks dazed and smokes dagga and is always silent and very threatening. All that Tony has learned from this teacher is the phrase "Jah an' I."

Tony likes him. He likes him because he is very, very different from the other teachers. He is "cool". He has told Tony that the teachers are poor because they are paid very little money and even this is delayed for months sometimes.

One day he walked Tony "home" and when he saw where and how Tony lives he cried and shouted, "What are we doing to our black brothers and sisters?" He shouted and shook his fists at the moon but later he explained to Tony that he was cursing the bureaucrats "up there". Tony looked up but could not see any bureaucrats, all he saw were badly dressed clouds, a thin, starved moon, and a few hungry stars that were quietly screaming for food.

Then aunt threw herself out of the house at the teacher. "What are you doing with my little boy?" she screamed.

The Rasta teacher smiled, being cool. He said: "I'm his teacher. I walked him home."

"What are you loitering around for then?" she snarled.

He drew back from the spittle dashing out of her words. He looked at Tony. "Goodbye, Tony. See you at school tomorrow."

He started to walk away but she touched him on the shoulder. "Don't you like me? It's only two dollars for a quick one," she said.

The Rasta teacher looked at her a long time. He looked like he was about to cry. Then he took two dollars out of his wallet and gave them to her.

"I give the money to you for Tony. Goodbye."

And he went away.

But the next day the Rasta teacher did not come to the school. He was in hospital with a fractured jaw and broken ribs. He had been beaten up by people who hate Rastas.

Tony hates people who hate Rastas. He hates them very much. He really hates them.

"You must learn not to hate," the teacher said when Tony saw him.

Tony hates being hungry. He hates not being loved. There is no time for loving in Shantytown. There is the constant hunger, the belly rumbling.

He hates the man who comes to see his aunt at night. She thinks he does not know what they do. He does. Tony knows everything that goes on in Shantytown. It does not take much imagination. The stealing, fighting, fucking, the incest and rape. It does not take much thought to grasp the disease that is Shantytown. But then Shantytown is the only home Tony has ever had. Tony loves it with great bitterness. It is like loving the arrow that has struck you right in the heart and you have no time to think or question or feel. Tony feels a great deal; he thinks too much. But he only shows this side of him to the Rasta teacher.

One day the Rasta teacher drove Tony to Cleveland Dam. It was beautiful and quiet. Tony had been so used to noise and violence in Shantytown or in the classes and in the playground that the peaceful silence of Cleveland Dam almost frightened him. The Rasta squeezed Tony's hand and said, "Do not be afraid of peace."

Tony knows many shanty people who are afraid of peace because they have never known it Never, never known it.

The Magic Cat

My Cat dropped
a silver coin
into the black well.

My Cat mewed
at the bright full Moon.
Its claws scraped the Stars.

At midnight
in a dark room
my black Cat—a polished
black shape.

My Cat sneezed
startling the mice.
My Cat's whiskers shrunk in shame.

My Cat sleeps in a hammock
drinking iced orange juice.
Boxer the guard dog watches him.

My Cat says
"I love children.
"I love grown-ups.
"I love Zimbabwe."

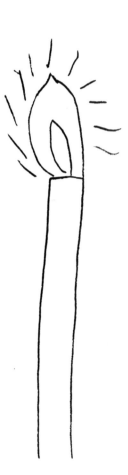

My Cat asked the soldier
"Where is Heroes' Acre?"
The soldier smiled and pointed.
My Cat loves the Eternal Flame.

My Cat looked at Great Zimbabwe.

"It's huge! It's very old.

"It's made of great big stones!" my Cat
exclaimed.

"It is ours. I am proud of Zimbabwe!"
said my Cat on the way home.

Baboons of the Rainbow

Part One

The End of Green Baboon

*O*NCE upon a time,
in a town at the end of the rainbow,
there lived a black baboon
and a white baboon
and a green baboon.

It was very hot.
The sun was bloodshot.
There was not a drop of rain.
"Drought!" shouted the *Daily Baboon* newspaper.

Black Baboon was hungry. Very hungry.
White Baboon was very, very hungry.
Green Baboon was also hungry.
"There is nothing but hunger at the end
of the rainbow," said the *Daily Baboon* newspaper.

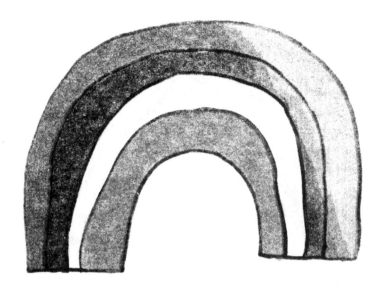

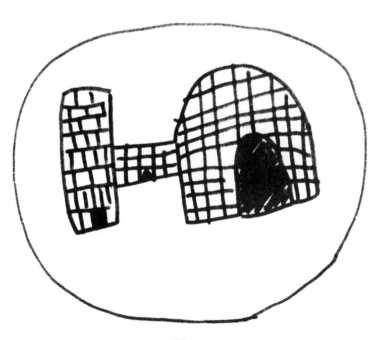

THE END OF GREEN BABOON

Black Baboon heard a voice.
The voice was the voice of his hunger.
The voice was coming from his stomach:
"A is Awful, B is Baboonery, C is Cad!" said the
voice.
"Shut up!" cried Black Baboon, "Shut up!"

White Baboon was walking down the street.
He stopped and listened. He leaned over the gate.
Black Baboon was shouting "Shut up! Shut up!"
White Baboon was very angry. He jumped over the gate.
He hit Black Baboon on the head.

Black Baboon forgot the voice of his hunger.
Black Baboon hit White Baboon. They fought. They bit.
They hit. They smashed. They scratched. They snarled.
Green Baboon was passing by. "Stop!" he screamed, "Please stop!"

"What did you say?" said Black Baboon and White
Baboon together, "What did you say?"
"Please don't fight," said Green Baboon, "I cant stand it!"
Black Baboon looked at White Baboon.
White Baboon looked at Black Baboon.
They both looked at Green Baboon.
Their eyes were small and sharp.

"No!" screamed Green Baboon, "No, don't!"
Green Baboon was very afraid. "No! No—ooh!"
Black Baboon looked at White Baboon.
White Baboon looked at Black Baboon.
They looked at Green Baboon.
Their eyes were small and sharp.

They jumped on Green Baboon.
They hit. They bit. They scratched. They beat him up.
They hit him the whole day. It was like thunder.
The rainbow drained of all colour.
Black Baboon and White Baboon were eating Green Baboon.
White Baboon liked his Green Baboon with garlic.
Black Baboon liked his Green Baboon with chillies.

THE END OF GREEN BABOON

"Let us eat him in a civilised way," said White Baboon.
Black Baboon agreed, "Yes, let us eat him in a civilised way."
They carried Green Baboon into the kitchen.
They cut Green Baboon into chops and steaks.
They cooked Green Baboon with spices and dry white wine.
White Baboon made the salad.
Black Baboon made the custard.

They spread the tablecloth on the table out on the verandah.
They set the knives and forks. They placed two plates
and two serviettes and two comfortable chairs.
They sat down to eat. The moon was up, big and round.
Black Baboon had put on a record on the gramophone.
"Ah, Beethoven!" sighed White Baboon, listening to the music:

It was beautiful.
It was romantic.
It was the end of Green Baboon.

THE END OF GREEN BABOON

THE END OF GREEN BABOON

Part Two

Black and White Baboon Songs

IT was very late when Black Baboon and White Baboon
finished their meal. The moon was very big and very bright.
Black Baboon and White Baboon were drinking brandy.
It was very good brandy made in France.
They lit up cigars and smoked.
The cigars came from Havana. . .

Black Baboon began to sing softly:
      Moon of France
      Moon of Havana
      A rainbow Moon.
White Baboon sighed deeply. "Sad about old Green
Baboon, what?"

Black Baboon began to hum the tune:
>O Sole Mio.
And White Baboon whispered to the moonbright night:
"Here today
Gone tomorrow, what?"
"More brandy?" asked Black Baboon.
White Baboon looked at the moon. "Yes, old boy," he said.
They drank in silence. A beautiful silence.
They smoked in silence. A delightful silence.

Black Baboon took out his guitar. He began to play.
And this is what he sang:
>On my way to school
>There is a terrible pool
>Full of giant fish, giant monsters
>Ugly toads, frightful frogs.

>On my way to school
>The wind blew my books into the pool.
>Daddy would eat me alive
>Teacher would eat me alive
>Because the pool had taken my books.

>I stamped my foot
>The fat was in the fire
>I shook my fists at the wind
>They would call me a liar
>Because the pool had taken my books.

Black Baboon sniffed. Tears were in his eyes.
White Baboon was miffed. Black Baboon was too emotional, he thought.
And Black Baboon went on singing:

> I was small, alone, afraid.
>
> The world was huge, frightful.
>
> I fled from Daddy. I fled from Teacher.
>
> I ran away from school, ran away from home,
>
> Because the pool had taken away my books.

White Baboon stared at the bright stars.
"It's a night for beauty and tears,
an evening for bliss and bother,
a dusky midnight for bitter joy," said White Baboon.

The king drinks bloodred wine
in Dunfermline. . .

And White Baboon, the brandy in his brain,
thought of Hamlet, Nehanda, Polonius, Rosencrantz
and Chaminuka. . .
White Baboon liked songs of heroes, songs of bravery,
Songs of seed and deed—as who should sing:

> "The stunning fight
>
> of planet and star,
>
> earth, moon, and sun.
>
> Green Baboon's bolted into the blue.
>
> You and I are waiting our turn
>
> who eat who the final candle burn?"

Fuzzy Goo's Guide (to the earth)

Blah

THE rain was smiling water through bright blue lips. Fuzzy Goo, at the window, thought of his dog. He loved his dog. The sad rain made him love his dog even more. Rain is lonely. Rain is memories. Rain is cool in a hot brain. Rain is love of Fuzzy Goo's dog. He *loved* that dog. Love is green grass on a warm breezy day. Love is sunlight smiling brightness through lips that are brown and blue. Brown is not a boy but the land. Land is just soil made of dead things and dead human beings. Fuzzy Goo is a human being. But Fuzzy Goo does not like going to the toilet. Human beings have to go to the toilet because they eat dead things and drink something horrible called water. Fuzzy Goo does not like being a human being. Human beings hide their horrible bodies in things called clothes. Clothes get torn and dirty. If you are a little human being and your clothes get torn and dirty, then all the big human beings shout and beat you up. Fuzzy Goo's dog likes to beat up other dogs. But it does not beat up Fuzzy Goo. That is why its name is BLAH. Blah means a dog that does not beat up Fuzzy Goo.

Blah may also mean a little human being who is very, very boring. In this case "little" means a very small brain in a big head. Fuzzy Goo's dog talks all the time but no one can hear it. When it talks it does not even know that it is talking. Blah may also be a girl who does not like to do things in the school bicycle shed. Blah is also a father you are ashamed of. Blah is a big human being who makes you talk to SOMEONE you cannot even see or smell. This is called praying. They say mad human beings talk to themselves. Maybe they are praying. Fuzzy Goo thinks Jesus' real name was Blah, because his dog is love. Love is boring. That is why it is Blah.

Blah is being dragged kicking and screaming to school, to church, to the dining table, to the nation's flag, to bed without supper. Blah is how big human beings torture little human beings. If you are a little human being you must report them to the United Nations which has fists bigger than your father's. If all little human beings joined together in one terrible scream all the big ones would go mad and do horrible things in their bedrooms. That is how little human beings come into the world. Your father and mother go mad in the bedroom and then you are born nine months afterwards. If you see your mother's stomach getting bigger and bigger it is not because she is drinking a lot of beer. It is because she has done horrible things with daddy and you are going to have another Blah little person for a brother or sister. That is when you know mother has a horrible thing called a breast which the new horrible little person likes to suck just like a piglet. But before the horrible little person comes out kicking and screaming and spitting blood out of mother's stomach, it is called a pig in a poke or a bun in the oven. It is very embarrassing to walk to school with a mother who is carrying a large pig in a poke. It is very blah. Very, very blah.

Blah, the dog, and Fuzzy Goo live in something frightening called society. Sometimes the big human beings call it a nation, or they call it a very long word "infrastructure" which was made up by a very old man with a beard and a very bad temper. Society is the secret club of big human beings. The job of this secret society is to make little human beings grow up. Growing up means giving up all things you like to do. Growing up means not saying your favourite bad words. Growing up means turning into a monster just like your father and your mother. Growing up is to become blah. Very, very blah.

Fuzzy's dog does not like the society of other dogs. A dog is a dog but all dogs together are blah. This is the same with all big human beings. Very blah. So when you know you are growing up you must kill yourself before you become just another very boring blah. If you are a coward, then you must smoke ganga or get mean and drunk every day and night. It is usually better to run away from home. All you need is a rucksack and a small tent. If you stay in society and the big ones want to beat up the other society next door they will put you into an army and you will get your small finger and private parts blown up with bombs. It is very painful. If you stay in society, the big ones will make you stand in line in the streets and wave stupid little flags and sing horrible national songs, and be kissed by the thick drunken lips of the biggest of the big human beings. They won't let you pee when you want to but when *they* want you to.

So Fuzzy Goo is at the window looking out at the saliva of rain. Saliva is what they give each other when they kiss. (Ask Emma when you get her alone in the school bicycle shed.) (It's difficult to get her in there though, unless you have at least three chocolate crunchies.) (And, ah, Emma is a descendant of Jane Austen—Ask your teacher to tell you about the paranoid parson. Paranoid means seeing all the things which big humans have been taught not to see.) This is a paranoid story—it was supposed to be my homework for tomorrow, but homework like tomorrow is what the Mexicans call mañana, which never comes.

If you want to know everything dirty about human beings, save your pocket money and buy all the books by a grown-up big human being called Dean Swift. It's the best way (if you're a coward) to grow up by not growing up at all. Like me, he thinks horses should ride human beings. He's a good blah. A very, very good blah. Also buy a false beard, stilts, some very long trousers, a padded jacket and a bowler hat, and then go to your father's favourite bar and watch what he does with all the other stupid big human beings. If that doesn't unglue your eyeballs from your brain, then go with mother to tea with one of her "friends." They tell you about loyalty, truth, honour etc. but (if you buy and read my book *Naked as a Parent)* if you spy on them you'll find they are liars, blackguards, false, vain, vulnerable and all the other bad words I could tell you if the police were not looking over my shoulder right now. (Actually, the police cannot read but you know I've just come out of jail for telling a big human being that he was something a toilet with any sense of dignity would refuse to flush.)

Did you you ever see Flash Gordon?

Try and see the film *Amadeus*. It's really ungrown up.

241

There is something called death which the big humans turn into religion and funerals. You have to have money for this. They actually like to make a song and dance out of the death of any person. When my father died I just wanted to be on my own but mother made me see the body and watch them throwing tons of gravel on top of him. I felt very blah, then.

The more you grow the nearer you are to death. You can also die at any time. (Emma almost died when she fell out of Parson Austen's apple tree when he shouted something very, very un-Christian. (Grown-ups know more terrible bad words than you do because of the things they do in the bedroom.) They remember very dimly the illusion of eternal youth which little human beings enjoy. In this they are like krakens. (Krakens are worried little gremlins growing out of the poet Tennyson's bald head. Your parents probably like Tennyson better than throwing stones through the windows of Parson Austen's house which makes an interesting churlish noise. You are *bald* when your thoughts fall off your head like Shakespeare's brow. Shakespeare was the little guy who knew all the big lies about England. England is a tadpole coming out of the nose of Europe. Europe is the one the Americans have got but which the Russians will not give. Americans are born grown up. Russians are legally dead when they are born. All this is called footnotes.) I've got Athlete's Foot—do you know what Huck Finn used to get rid of his?

Write a pen-friend letter to Joan Baez, Kurt Vonnegut, and Norman Mailer. They've all got Athlete's Foot of the brain on society. Try to get a detective to find a man called Kilgor Trout—he'll give you even more details about all this I'm giving you. Trout is not a fish or something Richard Brautigan wrote about. (Ask your teacher—if your teacher is a moron then write to UNESCO in Paris.) He is not a parent. Mailer is not a postman. He actually tried to kill his wife and he loves to watch big human beings being shot by a firing squad of other big human beings. Vonnegut is odd. He is a big human parent who tries to trick little ones into liking him and when they do he unbuttons his overcoat to show his horrible private parts. Baez is Mexican. I am reading her book *Daybreak*—get your mother to buy this intimate journal. I like her only because I think if you talk about the horrors of Vietnam she will come with you into the school bicycle shed all the way.

Mum is usually what they call a bitch. A bitch is a female dog like Scott Fitzgerald explained to Max Perkins (his editor at Charles Scribners and Sons in New York). A dog that is a bitch but is also your mother (don't you see them on Parents' Day?) can be very, very Blah. These are the things your so-called parents tell you—actually you were both on one of the lovely stars you see on every clear night, and one of you is born when Halley's comet crosses the skies above your land. (Ask your teacher what a comet is, but I think she won't know, so ask the janitor or the boy who sells you corn at break).

You know what I said about big people! They have a torture machine called drought which they bang on the heads of the little people: they say there is no food. Drought means *no food* for the little citizens. All the big chefs will be eating silly—but not for you. Especially if you are sick. The big human beings have made the atmosphere (the air you breathe) and the land (what you stand on when you throw a rock thru Parson Austen's window) so damaging to live on and breathe in that both kill your slowly.

As I am writing now two cars have collided outside my window. I cannot see much blood because I think its inside, but there are four police cars and several ambulances (police are called pigs in elite society). Ambulance men are called warthogs because they rape you (girl or boy) if you are unconscious—they think doing that to unconscious people is a great experience.

Who are you

Fuzzy Goo?

Pebble

Fuzzy Goo found a pebble called Pebble sleeping off a heavy drinking session right in the middle of the street. Pebble is *very* beautiful, but you can't see Pebble. Pebble is ungratefully beautiful, because of all the dust and exhaust fumes Pebble lives in. Pebble does not drink alcohol. Pebble only drinks the liquids that drip out of passing cars. Pebble has never moved. Why should Pebble move when Pebble knows that to move is to boulder the big ones. (Pebble can't afford an American Express card.) Actually Pebble dreams of being a pebble on the very top of Everest but that is a big human's ugly disease. Ambition has one arm where his navel is. (Ask Emma what a navel is but remember a navel is not a novel and this is, in a paranoid way, nothing to do with parrots or parents who are a different kind of parrot as you found out when the Family Planning Unit phoned your father about the condoms and the pills—*this* is a novel.)

Fuzzy Goo found Pebble sleeping if off, snoring lightly under the passing cars and lorries full of big humans driving small humans to places which you and I would call prison but the big ones call "office", "doctor", "school", "hospital", "kindergarten" and all the other horrible places small humans are taken to.

Pebble is not at all blah. She is concrete. Your bedroom is actually made of Pebble, in a concrete way, of course. (Ask the men in the laundry van across the street, but they are actually spying on you.) (Read my book on spies—it's in all the trashcans.) (Spies use laundry vans. When they want to kidnap you they swaddle you like little Jesus in smelly laundry and take you to places where you unintentionally lose your fingernails and private parts and you unintentionally jump out of a barred window on the nineteenth floor. That's what they call suicide.) Concrete is also when what you do is really inside your brain, inside your feelings. There is nothing wrong with a brain until you meet a big human. Your feelings are okay until you meet the other really big one. (He sticks pins in you which put terrible liquids into your body and make you what the U.S.A. calls, sing. I don't know if they sing in Sing-Sing. Sing-Sing is a U.S.A. prison where they put little humans who have refused to grow up. The men in the laundry van are waiting for Pebble to wake up. She probably will think they are garage attendants—that Paradise. Paradise is where you are what you want to drink but the grown-ups won't tell you.)

Fuzzy Goo found Pebble sleeping off all that drink yesterday.

Like I said: drink does you good when the big humans are after you.

Who is Fuzzy Goo? Pebble, still snoring, said something to Fuzzy which he cannot clearly remember. But it sounded like: "It's not round at all. It's flat."

Snoring.

Fuzzy dodged several army lorries that were full of little humans being sent to an army and to a battlefield to give up their little fingers and their private parts. Ask teacher about Hemingway and warfare and bullfighting. Bulls are the terrible things they call steaks and make you eat. Hemingway was a writer who shot himself in the head (dead) with a very big, a very ugly rifle. His books are in the library. You can dance on his grave to cheer him up but I think you'll have to call Castro and Nixon first. Castro is a big human who hides a gun in his beard though everyone wants to know what he really is like without the beard. Nixon was a U.S. president who liked the things you like, like cursing, lying, stealing, sneaking, hiding behind everyone when things got hot. He is famous among the little U.S.A. humans for being the first disgusting prefect to lead a country. There's another one called Bokassa (he is very black in and out) who actually did a Napoleon on a country in a funny continent called Africa. (Africa looks like an upside down revolver but it also looks like your private parts—if you're a boy like a Bokassa. Some people called PAC think it looks like a fist seen from the wrist of the Cape, to the knuckles of Morocco, Algeria, Libya and Egypt. A lot of grown-ups go to Africa to have a look and take a photo of all the little people starving there. I think I told you about the thing called drought. They make a lot of money filming little African people starving to death. Rock'n roll bands are doing it. Sportsmen are doing it. Photographing little humans dying.

Television really tortures little humans. It makes them think of BMX bicycles and goodies. It makes them little prototypes of the blah adults they will grow into with time. It makes them enjoy watching (on TV) the destruction of things so that they are too tired to destroy the society that is actually a lunatic asylum. A lunatic is someone who knows there is something wrong somewhere but does not know exactly *what*. An asylum is where they are going to put me when they catch you reading all this I am writing.

Try to steal from your library a book called *The Medium is the Message* by a Canadian man-child called Marshall. He is a professor at McGill University. But be careful of him: he not only wants to be the tail that wags the dog but also the actual hide of society. Good thing is since the 60s and 70s he hasn't been seen around much.

But, Fuzzy Goo

Who are you?

Who is Pebble to you?

Fuzzy Goo has a terrible fart—it's better than most chemical weapons. He wants to use it to rescue Pebble from the men in the laundry van.

Pebble thinks it's very blah when you know things but you don't know how or why you know the things. Maybe that's why she said (snoring under the army lorries):

"It's not round at all. It's flat."

Fuzzy thinks she didn't say that at all. Fuzzy Goo thinks it's a code. (Code is the secret words of spies.) Fuzzy had his stilts, false beard, tall trousers etc. and went to his father's favourite bar. It was 8.00 p.m. As soon as he got a seat he *saw* his father! His daddy was just falling off a fat woman's lap, and clanking onto the floor. When several people tried to help him, he fought them off and would only allow the fat woman to help him.

It was really ga, I mean ga-gah.

Gah is a friend of Pebble.

P.S. If it's Friday turn back to page thirteen[1] and ask whether African Socialism means you can be as nasty, dirty, savage, native, murderous as Jack and his hunters in William Golding's book *Lord of the Flies*. (P.S. is not a footnote, more like when you have to flush the toilet again because a little piece is refusing to go down there.)

Gah

Actually it's Gah who is refusing to be released from prison. The prison is a few blocks from where Pebble is snoring. Gah has barricaded himself in his prison cell. He really doesn't want to get OUT THERE. Out there is what Big Ones call free society but all Little Ones know it's worse than constipation. (Constipation is when all the big pieces of dung inside you go on strike and refuse to be made redundant in some stinking sewer called OLD PEOPLE'S HOME or a REHABILITATION CENTRE when you flush the toilet.)

Gah grinds his true grit teeth and screams: "I'M NOT GOING down there!"

His screams are so mad all the dogs and hyenas in Fuzzy Goo's world echo his howls, his gnashings, his foul bitter bickering barks.

His dream-screams are so terrible the bugs in First Street abruptly stop singing and begin to tear and claw at all the rich passersby. (Bugs are beggars, though Little Buggy claims they are no relations of his. Little Buggy is snooty—a Little One who thinks he is so much bigger than everybody else, *only he* breathes whatever is outside the atmosphere—at this point the geography master rises in a towering rage. But bugs are beggars, and Blah, the dog, knows it too.)

"I'M NOT GOING down there!!" he screams so hard his own ears are ringing deaf. Dream-screams.

His screams so harass space and time that all the city clocks do not know which way to turn and time begins to move with no one giving it the time of day. All the clock faces look like mouths that have mislaid their false teeth.

Pebble opens one eye. Pebble opens the other eye. As Pebble does so an eeky blotch of petrol splats Pebbles face. Another blotch—a series of blotches splat Pebble's drinking being to a "what's that?" howling refrain of sirens. Through the ooze Pebble suddenly sees Fuzzy Goo sticking out a finger in a rude gesture.

"They're going to kill Gah!" Fuzzy shouts at Pebble.

"Who?"

"Gah! Listen!"

Pebble listens. Pebble hears what has woken him up. Gah screaming like he is being fed alive to blind crocodiles.

Pebble sobers up.

A nightmare of cars, lorries, bikes, vans homes down on Pebble. . .

SCRAPIRON BLUES

Thoughts of a Rusty Nail
(Recently Hit on the Head)

THE brain is stuttering. The days are reduced to rubble. There is nothing to Rain but water.

Tell it the way it tastes. Pronounce it the way it touches. Let the singular fragrance waft softly into syllables.

I am the end of the tunnel lost in my beginning. The answer to a question forgotten long ago.

I am the room in which something stirs, whispering my name. Your bare arm encircles not my body but a deadly vision of the image of you.

From the difficult dark, points of light project thought into speech, into the terrains of terror, mystery of commonsense.

I am the small scream underneath the boot of the Sky.

Toasted and bartered I await your voluptuous lips, your small cutting teeth, the raw sweet reeling leap into ecstasy, prelude to bathroom anxieties. Memory too hot to touch, the black-red magma which

underlines every minute, feeling there is no purpose but to wait for
purpose. . .
Till I resist to reason the irrational symbol of no regret.

History on three feet crawls toward the dungheap, the rubbish pit of all
my yesterday's names. The final word does not belong to the Worm.
The last word is desolation.

But first, to found the bone in lemonbright sunlight
A pause. . .
To gain, under destiny's lampshade, a permanent intensity, dare I
hesitate?
To cry, what no scream ever whispered, to shrill, to howl
what no dread bombardment ever shuddered!
Fear is no small thing under the microscope. Fear is the flesh, the
gorgeous dress my skeleton wears.